I0690889

Ivy Introspective

The Chronicles of Alice & Ivy, Book 2

A NOVEL BY KELLYN ROTH

Published by Kellyn Roth, Author

Wild Blue Wonder Press

ISBN: 9781734168518

Scripture quotations are taken from the King James Version (KJV).

Cover design by Carpe Librum Book Design

Edited by Andrea Cox

Kelly Lyn Langdon
PO Box 1156
White Salmon, WA, 98672

contact@kellynrothauthor.com

www.kellynrothauthor.com

CONTENTS

DEDICATION

For Toastie and Sugar-and-Spice-and-Everything-Nice.
I miss you, Grampa!
I love you, Gramma!
Love,
Chickadee

CHARACTER LIST

Ivy Knight — A 12-year-old girl in a world who doesn't understand her.

Alice Knight — Ivy's twin sister.

Mrs. Claire Knight (formerly Chattoway) — Ivy's mother. Mistress of Pearlbelle Park.

Mr. Philip Knight — Owner of Pearlbelle Park, Claire's husband, and Ivy's father—though only a recent addition to her life.

Edmond "Ned" Knight — Mr. Knight's son from his former marriage.

Nettie Jameson — Claire's former maid & Alice and Ivy's former caretaker who now lives in the gatehouse at Pearlbelle Park with her family.

Tom and Malcolm Jameson — Nettie's husband and son.

Miss Lois Elton — First cousin of Mr. Knight. A childhood friend and schoolmate of Claire's.

Mr. Steven Parker — First cousin of Mr. Knight.

Kirk Manning — A stable boy at Pearlbelle Park.

Charles Chattoway (Uncle Charlie) — Claire's brother.

Christina Chattoway-Tinedale — Claire's sister.

Mrs. Nora Chattoway — Claire's mother.

Elsie and Edith — Maids at Pearlbelle Park.

Mr. and Mrs. Rupert Angel — Guests at Pearlbelle Park.

Violet Angel — Their daughter. A resident of McCale House.

Dr. and Mrs. Callum McCale — Owners of McCale House.

Dr. Lester Goodington, Mr. Sampson, Mr. and Mrs. Davenport, and Miss Lang — Teachers at McCale House.

Felix Merrill, Leonard Barton, Minnie Kimber, Jesse Andrews, and Ella Willis — Students at McCale House.

Jordy McAllen — Dr. McCale's young mentee.

"Now may the God of hope fill you with all joy and peace in believing, that you may abound in hope by the power of the Holy Spirit."
~Romans 15:13~

CHAPTER ONE

December 1873
Pearlbelle Park
Kent, England

I vy Knight rolled out of bed and sat on the floor, rubbing her arms against the bitter mid-December chill. There was a fire in the grate, but even its cheery warmth couldn't force back the cold. Pulling a blanket to the ground and wrapping it around herself, she stared absently at the wall, organizing her thoughts for the morning. Another day at Pearlbelle Park—and she wasn't optimistic about it.

Alice and Kitty weren't here right now—Alice had probably gone out riding with Mr. Knight and Kitty liked to wonder down to the kitchen. Nettie didn't even live in the house. And, of course, Mummy was too busy to help her at the moment.

Which meant the only person to take care of her was—

The door banged open behind her, and Ivy jumped.

"Miss Ivy, what are you doing on the floor?"

Ivy raised her eyes to the maid's face, taking in her pointy nose and pinched face. She blinked once, twice, and tried to think of a suitable reason.

"Stand up. It's time to get dressed." The maid, Elsie, marched across the room and jerked Ivy to her feet before she could move.

Ivy gasped but stood still while she was stripped of her nightgown. Now she was even colder, and the shivers threatened to cut her in two. Elsie tossed some of Ivy's clothes on the bed—not Ivy's favorites but the scratchy ones everyone insisted she wear.

She sighed and submitted to Elsie's rough dressing. She could dress herself—truly she could. Nettie had made sure of that. But Elsie never wanted to wait for her; she said Ivy took too long, and she had other things to do. Ivy didn't know what Elsie had to do. After all, it was her job to take care of Ivy, wasn't it?

"There." Elsie gave a tight nod. "Let's comb your hair. We can't have you looking any more like a wild thing than you already are."

Ivy winced. Why did Elsie always have to say such things?

The brush came out, and Elsie ripped it through her hair. The maid didn't understand, Ivy supposed, that when one had "beautiful, thick hair," as Nettie always said, one had to start from the tips and work upward.

Elsie didn't have pretty hair, so perhaps that was why she didn't understand how much it hurt to rip through lots of long tangles in one stroke.

Ivy wasn't a baby; she didn't whine. But she couldn't help the tears that trickled down her cheeks.

"Oh, for heaven's sake." Elsie's eyes rolled in disgust. "It doesn't hurt that bad."

It did. But Ivy could bite her lip and look away and try to think of other things if it made Elsie happier.

At last, her hair was brushed and braided, far too tight, and Elsie rubbed a cloth over Ivy's face, which made her cheeks burn.

"There. You're ready." Elsie's critical gaze moved over Ivy's entirety, and she nodded. "As ready as you'll ever be. Heavens, I'd die if I had a child with eyes so vacant! Why don't the Knights send you somewhere?"

Ivy blinked. Her eyes were vacant? What was *vacant*? It must be a bad thing if it meant the Knights—she supposed that was Mummy, now, and Mr. Knight—were to send her away over it.

The thought of being sent away from Mummy had more tears starting, no matter how much she tried to stop them. Didn't Elsie understand that sometimes words could bite? Nettie would never have said such a thing. Nettie wouldn't have even thought such things!

"Eh, there you go crying again." Elsie turned to make Ivy's bed. "As if you can understand me! Well, perhaps you can, but not much. You're not like the rest of us, Miss Ivy. Why did I ever take this job? If it weren't for my mum needing the extra money, I never would have ..."

Elsie went on talking to herself, and Ivy walked across the room to peek out the window, trying to think of other things. If she kept her mind elsewhere, the tears wouldn't start again. Ivy didn't want Elsie to complain about how often she cried anymore.

All of Pearlbelle Park was bathed in the soft glow of the morning sun. By noon, winter sunlight always took on a harsh look, but the mornings were beautiful, causing the frost to sparkle on the grass and the trees and everything else.

Ivy didn't like winters, generally, because they were so cold. The cold seemed to reach her quicker than Alice or anyone else she knew, sinking through her skin and making her heart shudder. Alice said it was because she didn't have any meat on her bones, but Ivy thought it was because cold was evil.

As if on cue, Ivy's twin sister came running into their bedroom, cheeks rosy and hair flying out of her braid. Alice glanced around the room, narrowing her eyes slightly when she saw Elsie.

"Elsie, are you almost done?"

Ivy loved nothing more than the sound of Alice's voice when she was in control, and Alice was always in control. If only Ivy could speak to someone like that, compelling them to react by the sound of *her* voice.

Elsie bobbed a curtsey. "Yes, Miss Alice. I believe everything's been tended to, unless you need something."

"No, I'll tend to myself. Run along."

Elsie scurried away, and Alice went to her dresser drawers. "Come here, Ivy. Let's wash your face."

Ivy sniffled and rubbed her sleeve under her nose—then scolded herself, for young ladies didn't do such things. "I-I'm not sad."

"I know." Alice crossed the room, handkerchief in hand, and lifted Ivy's face. A few gentle dabs had most of the tears gone. "Was Elsie horrid today? I'm sorry I wasn't here."

"It's all right." Ivy tried a smile. "I'm all right."

Alice didn't seem convinced, but Ivy was determined to convince her. She puffed up her chest and took a firm stance, looking up at her sister.

They used to be at least similar in height, but suddenly Alice had grown—and grown and grown. Ivy supposed it was because they were almost twelve, but she didn't feel like she was almost twelve.

Alice looked it.

Ivy forgot what she was going to say and sat down on the edge of her bed. "Did you have a nice ride?" she asked at last.

Alice set the handkerchief down. "Yes, I did." She undid the remains of her braid. "Papa and I rode to a part of the estate we hadn't gone to yet. It was lovely."

Papa. Ivy wondered if she should try harder to think of Mr. Knight as *Papa.* So far she hadn't managed it, but then, she wasn't sure she *could* think of him that way.

He was just a man who had come into their lives suddenly and now seemed to think he had a lot of privileges that Mummy had, like hugs and good-night kisses and telling bedtime stories.

He hadn't earned them yet. Perhaps he never would.

"It's almost time for breakfast." Alice put the finishing touches on her new, much neater braid and turned to Ivy. "Are you ready? Did Elsie forget anything?"

Ivy rubbed at the crown of her head, remembering once again the harsh brushing. "No."

"Ivy, look at me."

Ivy raised her eyes to Alice's. Her sister had the prettiest eyes, all dark and sparkling. "Alice, what's *vacant*?"

Alice cocked her head. "Empty. Why?"

A discordant crash echoed in her soul. "Oh." Ivy glanced in the mirror. She didn't think her eyes were empty, though she could be wrong. "Does Mummy have vacant eyes?" She wasn't ready to ask about herself, but she had the same blue eyes as her mother, so if Mummy had vacant eyes, so did Ivy.

Something changed in Alice's face then. Her lips tightened, her face became hard as granite, and her cheeks flushed dark. "Did Elsie say you have vacant eyes?"

Ivy wiggled from foot to foot. "I-I suppose so." It must be an insult if Alice had reacted so strongly to it. She hoped Elsie didn't get in trouble. Ivy would hate to be the one who got anyone in trouble.

Alice stamped her foot and walked toward the door. "Come, Ivy. We're going downstairs for breakfast, and I have to talk to Mummy."

Ivy chased after her. "Alice! Alice, there's no need to tell Mummy. Perhaps it's not such a bad thing."

"I think it is." Alice paused by the door. "I think a girl in our hire insulted you, and I doubt she'll be in our hire much longer."

Ivy winced, but the look in Alice's eyes told her there wasn't much she could do. She followed closely after Alice out of the room. She had to, after all, or she'd be stuck in the nursery for some time—Pearlbelle Park's great manor house was too big and too grand for Ivy to navigate by herself, even though she'd lived there six months and visited before that.

Mummy and Mr. Knight, as well as Mr. Parker and Miss Elton, were already in the breakfast room when Alice and Ivy entered. Ivy didn't understand why Mr. Parker was still at Pearlbelle Park, since he was a grown-up man. Grown-up men, in Ivy's opinion, should find a place of their own to live.

Miss Elton she understood a little better—the good thing about being a girl was that one didn't necessarily have to move out when one grew up. Miss Elton was as old as Mummy, but she still lived here at Pearlbelle Park.

Someday Ivy hoped to be just like Miss Elton, only she didn't believe her mother would die like Miss Elton's mother had. That was sad, and Ivy felt bad for her, but thankfully, her Mummy was the strong type. If she ever died, it would be when she was very old indeed. Ivy didn't like to think about that, either, but at least it was a long ways away.

"There you are! I'd started to wonder." Mummy, already sitting at the table, held out her arms, and Ivy ran into them for a morning hug and kiss. Morning hugs and kisses made all the difference in how good the day to come would be.

Ivy settled onto a seat next to Mummy, once again glad that her mother wasn't the type who had breakfast in bed. That was all very well and good, Ivy supposed, but a girl just needed to see her mother in the morning, and her having breakfast in bed would ruin the chances of that.

Alice slid onto her seat, but it was clear she hadn't forgotten the reason she'd hurried down to the breakfast room. "I have something to discuss with you."

Mummy raised her eyebrows as she poured tea into Ivy's cup. "Indeed?" It was clear from the little smiles about her mouth that she didn't quite believe Alice's matter could be serious.

"Yes. That maid you hired—Elsie—is particularly rotten."

The smiles vanished. "What do you mean?"

"When I came up today, Ivy was in tears." Alice folded her arms across her chest. "I thought it was just because Elsie brushes her hair too roughly, and I think Ivy ought to be somewhat used to that, so I wouldn't have said anything. But Ivy says Elsie told her she had vacant eyes."

Mummy glanced down at Ivy, then sideways, up the table, to Mr. Knight. "Is that so?" She kept her voice calm, but there was a tightness to it that Ivy was easily able to pick up.

"I thought perhaps she meant because they're blue." Ivy tugged at Mummy's sleeve. "Alice's are dark and much more full—right?"

"No, darling—no." Mummy's face turned from neutral to a frown. "You have beautiful, *full* eyes. Elsie was being cruel, but she won't be again."

Mr. Knight cleared his throat. He glanced between Alice and Mummy, then spoke. "Do you think—?"

"I *know* she will leave tomorrow, and I *know* you will not give her a reference." Mummy dropped her napkin on her lap. "And that's final."

"Very well. I'll take care of it after breakfast." Mr. Knight sighed. "It's really a shame. I believe I'd spoken with the girl when I hired her about being sensitive. I suppose it's hard to find good help."

Mr. Parker drummed his fingers on the table. "It is. I'd see about hiring someone from London and having a more intensive interview process. I can help—I'm a better judge of character than you are, Phil."

Mummy's eyes were still snapping, and they were definitely full—full of anger. "At any rate, that situation's taken care of." She glanced down. "Ivy, darling, please tell me if someone treats you that way. We'll talk about it more later, so you can know when it's not all right."

Ivy sighed. She didn't like tattling, and now Elsie had lost her job! Perhaps if Ivy hadn't been bad—perhaps if she hadn't had vacant eyes—Elsie would still be employed.

But she didn't say anything and quietly began eating her breakfast. The conversation around her started to buzz pleasantly, letting her know that people had moved on and were talking about regular things.

"Of course, there's a great deal of preparation to get out of the way before next week, when the guests arrive."

The buzzing stalled, and Ivy glanced up at her mother, unsure if she'd heard the words right. "Guests?" She said the word so softly she was unsure if Mummy heard, but apparently she did, for she turned to Ivy.

"Yes—you remember we'll be having guests next week, don't you? For Christmas. Your grandmother and Uncle Charlie will be coming, too. It will be a grand time."

Grand time? With even more people there than there was already? Ivy gripped the arm of her chair to remind herself that there was a world beyond the spinning in her head. "How many?"

"A dozen or so." Mummy's eyes grew concerned. "Of course, they're all grown-ups, Ivy. You can ignore them."

Ignore them? Their very proximity would affect Ivy's chances at having any sort of a happy Christmas. But she just nodded and returned to her toast, trying not to think about it.

"I suppose this is all an effort to regain social standing." As it often did, Mr. Parker's voice cut through Ivy's consciousness like an unsharpened knife forcing its way through a loaf of bread. "Do you think it'll work?"

Mr. Knight glared at Mr. Parker. "I don't think it's a matter worth discussion."

"Isn't it?" Mr. Parker smiled. Ivy had never liked Mr. Parker's smile, because he had a beard, and she didn't like beards. Alice said he looked distinguished, but Ivy thought he was scary.

"It is not uncommon for a family to entertain houseguests over the holidays." Mummy took a determined sip of her tea. "We are simply reaching out to old friends of the family to reassure them that goodwill remains despite certain changes."

Ivy was familiar with how one could get upset over changes, so she supposed it made sense to reassure people that everything was all right. Ivy often felt that nothing was all right anymore. "Mummy, will they be here long?"

"Just a few weeks, darling."

A few weeks? That was such a long time. Ivy supposed she had no choice but to bear it. She sighed and finished her breakfast in silence.

CHAPTER TWO

I VY SHIFTED FROM FOOT to foot. Alice's hand on her arm kept her from running upstairs and hiding in her bedroom, but she could at least express her disapproval by wiggling. It was most definitely cold. The chill seeped through even her heavy coat, mittens, and hat, and she pressed closer to Alice to alleviate it.

Why did they all have to stand out here? Even the servants were lined up like soldiers stretching out to the left of the entry as the carriages pulled up, containing all the precious guests.

Ivy didn't *not* like the guests, exactly—she really did wish them all the best. But she didn't want to spend time with them, and she certainly didn't want to stand out in the freezing drive watching them arrive.

Thankfully, one of the first people to step down from the carriages was her own uncle Charlie. He was a stoic man, and his greetings to Mummy, who was his sister, and the others were calm. But still, he smiled when he saw Alice and Ivy.

Alice stepped forward to embrace him, and Ivy let him pull her close and kiss her forehead when he reached her. She didn't say anything, didn't believe words were needed—simply squeezed his hand and beamed up at him.

"How are you, Ivy?" His voice wasn't like Mr. Knight's—there were a deepness and a firmness to it that Mummy's husband could never possess. Yet the deepness and the firmness never overrode the gentleness. Ivy couldn't be afraid of Uncle Charlie even if she tried.

"I'm well." She snuggled into his side. "How are you?"

"Well enough." His attention wasn't on her; his eyes flickered far away from her, from person to person, until they landed on someone.

Ivy craned her neck to see. Oh dear. Miss Elton? Why did Uncle Charlie always have to get distracted by Miss Elton when she wanted him all to herself?

"Uncle Charlie?" She tugged at his sleeve. "Uncle Charlie, are you glad you've come here?"

"Er, yes." His eyes went down, then back up again.

Ivy sighed. She would never be as important as a grown-up or a person like Alice. Perhaps, she thought with a little shudder, it was because her eyes were somewhat vacant. Or not. She really wasn't sure who to believe on that account.

"Ivy, if you'll excuse me ..." And he was off to talk to Miss Elton. Ivy sighed and slipped back next to Alice. Her parents were distracted greeting the many guests, and no one else seemed available to pay attention to her.

She watched as her uncle Charlie skirted around the crowd, approached Miss Elton with an outstretched hand, and began speaking to her. He hadn't looked at Ivy half as long as he'd looked at his new sweetheart.

"Ivy?"

This time it wasn't someone Ivy wanted to talk to—it was just her grandmother, her mummy's mother, who was also a newer addition to her life. In fact, Ivy wasn't sure that this Mr. Knight fellow wasn't at fault for the existence of a great many new things, including their grandmother and Pearlbelle Park and Alice's going off to boarding school for months at a time.

Of course, he was doubtless to blame for the guests.

Yet she had to raise her eyes to her grandmother's face, had to attempt a smile even if she didn't feel like it. "Hello."

"Merry Christmas, Ivy! Oh, and there's Alice, too!" Grandmother held out her arms as if she expected one or both of the girls to give her a hug, but neither moved. Her arms dropped to her sides. "How are you young ladies doing?"

Alice shrugged. "All right, I suppose. We're having a Boxing Day hunt."

"Oh." Grandmother tried to look interested, but Ivy could easily tell that she wasn't. "Will you ride with them, dear?"

"I hope so." Then Alice walked forward to her mother's side. Unlike Ivy, she wanted to be introduced to the guests.

Ivy wished she had an easy escape from this trembling woman who never seemed to quite know how to behave around little girls.

"Ivy, what are you looking forward to this Christmas?" Grandmother placed a hand on Ivy's shoulder and prodded her toward the door.

Ivy was used to that—she was often pushed from one place to another with no regard for whether or not she wanted to go. She supposed this time it was because everyone else, chatting merrily, was going in now.

"I don't know." She answered that question as honestly as could be managed. After all, what kind of Christmas would it be with everyone here? So many people from so many places doing so many things?

Her mother would be distracted. Alice would be wrapped up in the adoration of so many adults. It would seem Uncle Charlie had a new friend. And Nettie wasn't even going to be here—perhaps she would visit, as she always did, but she was so busy with her home at the gatehouse, baby boy, and husband.

Much as Ivy liked Tom Jameson as a person, she didn't like him as Nettie's husband. She didn't think she'd like anyone who took Nettie away from them. In fact, she was still annoyed at him.

How could he? How could Nettie? How could anyone in Ivy's life, in fact, act as they had been acting these last few years?

Even Alice had been strange, chasing fantasies and dreams that would never be. They didn't need a father. They already had a family, a beautiful family. There wasn't room for Mr. Knight, Pearlbelle Park, nasty Mr. Parker, blushing Miss Elton, and stable boys who were apparently much better best friends than sisters.

A tear trickled down Ivy's cheek, and she quickly raised her hand to wipe it away.

Her grandmother was watching so closely that she must have seen. "Why, Ivy, are you crying?"

Of course she was crying, and she'd always been taught to be honest when she was. So she didn't shake her head. She just did exactly what Alice would do—she shrugged. That wasn't a lie—well, perhaps it was, for she was sure she was crying. But at least she hadn't spoken the lie out loud. That, to Ivy, would be the height of sin.

Besides, Grandmother's watching her had made the tears stop immediately, so she supposed it wasn't so much of a lie after all.

Grandmother was saying something more, something meant to be kind—but the people pressing in the foyer and the servants bustling about to bring the guests to their right rooms and all the fuss in between had Ivy's mind spinning.

Lights started flashing. Voices melded together into an excited, messy bubble, and Ivy couldn't make out one from the other. Her heart pounded erratically, and her breaths came fast and sharp. For a moment she stood still as a statue, eyes tightly shut, then she broke free from her grandmother's grasp and ran as fast as she could around the back. She'd find a way back to her bedroom—somehow.

There, by herself, she could cry out all the frustrations of the day and every day before it for the last year.

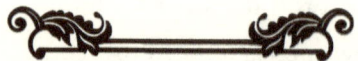

Nora Chattoway watched as her granddaughter broke into a run and hurried out of the festive foyer of Pearlbelle Park. She sighed and shook her head. Would any of her grandchildren ever like her?

At least baby Ned always squealed with excitement when he saw her—though the toddler did the same for everyone. How strange that her step-grandchild seemed to be the only one who didn't mind her.

That didn't mean Nora didn't love Alice and Ivy, her first grandchildren. However, even after spending the last two and a half years trying to form relationships with them, they still hadn't learned to love her.

But she would keep trying. Even if Alice was always more interested in someone bigger, flashier, more interesting—and Ivy ... Nora wasn't sure what went on in Ivy's head. Only that she didn't seem to care much for her grandmother.

Nora knew she wasn't much fun. She was just an old widow trying to milk a bit of joy out of what might be the last years of her life. She didn't want to die until she'd fully lived whatever time she had left. She'd wasted over fifty years. It was time to find out what mattered and pursue it whole-heartedly. To Nora at least, that meant building stronger relationships with family.

And perhaps with God. She still stretched out her arms tentatively on that score. There was much to learn, much to be found out. Much that was new to be discovered—much that was old to be explored once again.

At any rate, she wouldn't do herself any favors by standing, now almost alone, in this foyer and watching people leave her. She'd best find out where she belonged and prepare to have a lovely Christmas with two of her children and the rest of their small family.

"Mrs. Chattoway? Is it Mrs. Nora Chattoway?"

Nora turned to see a woman a few years older than her daughter, perhaps in her early thirties. The lady was lovely with dark curls framing a narrow face and blue eyes, almost like Claire's, but even darker.

"Yes, I am. And ... and you are?" Was that the proper way to address someone? Nora wasn't sure. It had been so many years since she'd been out in society, meeting friends, speaking to people. Confinement by a tyrant to a Yorkshire castle was no laughing matter.

"Mrs. Dorothea Angel." The woman smiled, and Nora supposed there was something familiar about her, though she wasn't sure what. "But my maiden name is Samielson. I don't suppose you remember Anna Samielson? She's my mother."

Nora's heart lightened. "Why—y-yes! I do. She was a dear friend b-before I married! I loved Anna. We've fallen out of contact, of course, but—oh, dear, I do remember you! Though, you were no bigger than a doll ... you couldn't remember me!"

"I didn't, exactly." Mrs. Angel shook her head. "I remembered the name. My mother used to speak of you—of what a shame it was that you had—that you had fallen out of contact. When I heard that the ... when I heard that the current Mrs. Knight's maiden name was Chattoway, I had to see if it was really you!"

Poor woman. Like Nora, she seemed to struggle to word things in socially acceptable ways. And how sweet that Anna Samielson had remembered Nora! Yes, Nora remembered her as well, but then, she had had years with nothing to do but think over past acquaintances.

Oh! She should've asked how Anna was. "How is your mother?" She hoped that didn't come off too rushed.

"She's well." Mrs. Angel didn't flinch as if Nora had interjected herself abruptly, so she felt free to relax. "Living in the country now, with Papa, and they both seem happy whenever we visit. I think they enjoy the quiet."

Nora sighed. Yes, everyone always seemed to think that when one got away from children and grandchildren, one would enjoy the quiet. For her that wasn't true. "I'm glad. I'll have to remember to try to reach her—I am ... that is, I have a great deal more time on my hands, and ... I could."

"Good. She would enjoy that. Remind me to give you her address before we leave." Mrs. Angel glanced over her shoulder. "Oh, I see my dear husband is beckoning me. Poor Rupert is always waiting for me to finish a conversation! I did have a question, if you don't mind—and I promise it is good-natured."

Nora's shoulders hunched at this. Usually when one had to promise a question was good-natured, it wasn't—or at least it felt that way. "Very well." What else could one answer?

"Your granddaughter—she was your granddaughter, wasn't she? The blonde child who just ran out?"

Nora nodded. "Yes, that was Claire's daughter Ivy. You've heard the story—?"

"Oh, never mind that." Mrs. Angel tossed it away with a flip of her hand. "I'm willing to be open-minded, and I've never cared for the scandal papers. I understand enough to not judge the Knights. No—it was something about her ... something that caught my eye just now. You see, when you were speaking to her, she became teary-eyed and then suddenly froze—it reminded me of something."

Nora cocked her head. "Whatever do you mean? I grant that Ivy is a sensitive child, and I ... she doesn't care for me. I suppose she isn't used to my being here."

"Er, no, it's not that." Mrs. Angel shook her head, and it occurred to Nora that the woman's face was pale, her eyes traced with tears. "Is she ... is Ivy all right? In the head, I mean?"

Nora blinked. She hadn't expected such frank honesty from a practical stranger. "Why, I—" She paused, confused. Of course curiosity was to be expected, but how could one notice that about Ivy with just a glance? Nora had had to talk to the child before she'd observed more than a shy little girl. Even after Claire had explained it, she hadn't understood. As far as she knew, Ivy had been born simple. Nora didn't know that there was anything particularly remarkable about this. The girl wasn't a lunatic. Certainly it wasn't noticeable.

"I know it's an unusual question, but please answer me if you are able." There was something gentle and warm in Mrs. Angel's eyes, and Nora couldn't help but be drawn to it.

No, it wasn't just curiosity. There was something more. Nora would answer her. "No, I suppose not. Ivy is simple, but she's a harmless child, and she does well for who she is. Sometimes she just ... Claire—Mrs. Knight—has always described it as she struggles to cope with the world. But there's nothing dangerous about her, certainly."

"Oh, no, I wasn't afraid of that—not really." Mrs. Angel glanced over her shoulder once again, probably at her husband. "I can explain it all later, but if I could ask you a few more questions about the child—really understand the situation—well, I might be able to help."

"Help?" How could an English noblewoman help a simple child like Ivy? The situation was tragic, yes, but nothing was to be done but to cope.

"Yes." Mrs. Angel pressed her lips tightly together. "I believe I could offer you a solution that you would find interesting. Would you come to my room? I could explain it better in private."

Nora took a deep breath. Was it wise to share intimate family details with a woman she didn't know well? After all, Ivy's problems weren't widely known. Yet Nora couldn't deny that she was curious to know Mrs. Angel's solution. Furthermore, if, with the woman's assistance, Nora could help her family, help Claire and Ivy ... she would be doing something noble.

Nora longed to do something noble.

"Very well," she said at last. "Let's go at once."

CHAPTER THREE

T HE EVENING WASN'T MUCH better than the morning. Ivy wasn't expecting to be called down to spend time with the guests—she had hoped that they would leave her alone in her room.

Instead, she and Alice were ushered into a parlor full to the brim with people, most of whom Ivy didn't know and almost all of whom she didn't care for. The two she did love—Mummy and Uncle Charlie—were both distracted, so Ivy huddled behind Alice.

The lights were bright—bright enough to hurt her eyes, bright enough to cause her to press her face into Alice's back. Alice pushed her gently away, not wanting to be cruel, Ivy was sure, but wanting space.

Alice often wanted space nowadays. Ivy thought her twin might be growing up. She wasn't sure exactly why, but she was glad Alice could grasp at adulthood.

Even if Ivy might never manage it.

"Oh, there are the young ladies!" Mr. Parker held out a hand. "Alice, come over here. I want you to tell Mr. James what you told me yesterday."

Alice was already laughing as she ran across the room, settled onto the sofa, and began speaking with an adult just as if she were one. Ivy shuddered and stepped back toward the door, almost bumping into a footman.

She didn't know him, really, but at least he gave her a kind smile and nodded forward. He thought she should walk farther into the room. Ivy glanced frantically about for someone who she might walk to, but no one was looking her way.

She didn't like to walk up to people uninvited. She didn't like to impose her company. She would rather stand back here, quietly, and try not to feel too nauseated at the lights, the smells, the sounds of a crowded room.

"Ivy?" It was her mother. Grateful, Ivy dashed forward into her arms.

Mummy held her back, a flush touching her cheeks. Blushing? Had Ivy embarrassed her?

She supposed Alice would never dive into Mummy's arms. Alice was too big for that. Alice sat primly on the edge of a chair, already possessing the perfect posture one associated with a lady. She spoke to Mr. Parker and that Mr. James person politely—laughing, smiling, nodding her head.

Alice knew how to behave. Ivy did not.

"Mummy, I ... I'm sorry," Ivy whispered.

"Shush, dearest. This is Mrs. Angel—she has asked to meet you." Mummy tilted Ivy's chin up, then turned her to face a woman standing opposite her in too-bright clothing with a too-cheerful smile and too-perfect hair.

"Hello, Ivy. I've been hearing a great deal about you from your grandmother. How are you?"

Mummy's fingers were digging deep into Ivy's arms, and she knew she must answer. "I-I'm all right, I suppose."

"Oh, good. How old are you?"

Ivy eased from side to side, but Mummy held her still. "I'm eleven—I'll be twelve in a few weeks."

"Oh, how lovely. You're just the same age as my Dory—she and her brother are in Cornwall with their grandparents for Christmas. She's a dear girl." Mrs. Angel cocked her head, her blue eyes searching Ivy's face. Her eyes weren't like Mummy's—to Ivy, they seemed a great deal darker, less clear, more frightening. "You're Alice's twin, aren't you?"

"Yes." Ivy could answer questions if they were that simple.

Mrs. Angel nodded thoughtfully. "Then you're about three months older than my daughter. Though, I must say, you don't look much like your twin. You resemble your mother closely, while Alice takes after Mr.

Knight."

Ivy smiled. That was the highest of compliments. "Mummy's beautiful." Ivy wasn't sure if she herself was—wasn't sure she really cared either way—but she was glad to look like Mummy.

Mrs. Angel chuckled. "You have a sweet daughter, Mrs. Knight, to compliment you so openly! You'll seldom hear my children say such things in my presence."

This time Mummy's hand on her arm was a gentle squeeze, a reassuring squeeze. "She is my greatest blessing."

"How sweet."

Silence threatened, so Mrs. Angel attempted a conversation on an entirely different subject.

"What do you enjoy doing? Your mother has proved herself a musician, you know. She can sing and play the piano to perfection. Have you studied music?"

Ivy shook her head and glanced back at Mummy, but she wasn't able to read a direction in her face. She would just have to wait until Mrs. Angel was done with her.

"You should. Such talents are often hereditary."

"I can't," Ivy whispered. Yes, she did love music, from a distance. However, playing was another matter. She wouldn't be good enough, and it seemed a shame to disrespect the beauty of a song with her poor efforts. Besides, she didn't know that she wanted to share the depths of her soul that intimately with the outside world.

"Nonsense. You're too modest, as is your mother—far too modest!"

"Perhaps music is something Ivy might be interested in in the future," Mummy said. "We just don't know yet. It's certainly something to think about, though."

Ivy glanced toward the door. All she could think of was getting away from this lady. Mrs. Angel might be nice, but she was also unknown. Ivy hated the unknown. She bit her lip and tried not to wiggle.

"Ivy, what do you like to do?" Poor Mrs. Angel must keep trying, for whatever reason, but Ivy had no answer.

The lights started spinning again, and bile rose in her throat. Ivy, staring at the carpet, shook her head.

"Nothing at all? Really?"

Ivy's throat tightened, forcing the bile down and tears into her eyes. "No ... no ... no!" she exclaimed.

Mummy's hands tightened with vise-like strength, but Ivy couldn't stop the tears, and she turned to her mother and wrapped her arms around her, wanting comfort. It was too much—didn't they know tonight was too much? How could they just keep on chatting and talking and not realize that tonight was too much?

"Ivy, shush." Mummy was definitely embarrassed by her. The way she held herself, her voice, even the way she patted Ivy's back told the story clearly.

But Ivy couldn't help herself. They'd pushed too far.

"Why don't you sit down—yes, here's a chair."

Ivy, shuddering, lowered herself onto the chair her mother suggested, and raised her eyes slowly to Mummy's face. Mrs. Angel hovered in the background, obviously concerned.

"I'm sorry."

"It's all right, dear." Mrs. Angel broke in before Mummy could speak. "I suppose I was being rather nosy. Sometimes I'm like that. Why don't you just take a few minutes?"

"Yes, that's a good idea." Mummy leaned back and glanced over her shoulder. "Stay there, Ivy. I need to speak with your father about dinner arrangements before I forget ... You'll be all right for a moment?"

Ivy nodded. For a moment, at least. As long as her mother didn't take too long. Much more than a moment would begin the torture again. Already the lights and sounds and smells were pressing.

People were too close. The world was too much. Ivy just wanted to get away. At least Mrs. Angel had gotten distracted by another guest who called her name, asked her a question.

Thankfully, no one else asked Ivy questions. They ignored her, caught up in their grown-up world, caught up in their moving lives that rushed past Ivy with fearless abandon.

Far above her, far away from her. Ivy had been happy that way. But now—yes, another glance across the room confirmed that Alice was becoming lost to adulthood, at the tender age of almost twelve.

She'd probably never come back. Alice did so love being an adult.

So Ivy was alone.

She didn't want to cry again, and she was determined she wouldn't. She simply sat as straight as she knew a little lady ought to, closed her eyes tight, and hoped for a miracle.

Of course, being transported out of the room to her nice, safe bedroom with no one there and no one coming to get her wasn't exactly plausible. But, perhaps angels would take mercy on her. Or something like that. She'd met a Mrs. Angel today, after all—anything was possible.

But, for now, she must sit quietly and hope for the best. Hope that, in time, she would be allowed to leave before her head decided to roll off her shoulders and smash on the floor.

Ivy was rocking back and forth slightly on the chair she sat on, and though Nora was no expert on her, she could easily tell the child was upset. Her face was screwed up and her eyes tightly shut. No one seemed to be noticing her, and Nora didn't believe she was throwing a tantrum.

No, she was just frightened.

Nora could understand that. Sometimes she was frightened, too. She slipped away from her son, who was too busy chatting with Lois Elton to want her near anyway, and made her way across the room to her granddaughter.

"Ivy? Are you all right?"

Ivy shook her head without opening her eyes.

Nora sighed and drew a chair up next to hers. At first, she didn't say anything; she simply watched the child, trying to think what to do. Perhaps she could ask. "What do you need, dear?"

Ivy shook her head ever so slightly.

"Nothing? Is there nothing I can do?"

Another shake.

Nora sighed. Another person she couldn't save, couldn't help. But this time it wasn't because she was weak—this time it wasn't because her husband wouldn't let her. This time it was simply because she didn't understand how a child like Ivy worked.

Her eyes flickered across the room to Mrs. Angel and her husband, who were involved in another conversation, oblivious to the child. She wondered if the woman was sincere. The story she'd told and the offer she'd made seemed so real—and, furthermore, seemed like it could help Ivy.

"Mrs. Angel spoke to you, didn't she, Ivy?"

Ivy's head moved up and down, her golden locks, now slipping from neat coronets about her head, jerking.

"That's lovely! Did you like her? She talked with me this afternoon, and I was thinking about talking about it with your mother this evening."

Ivy didn't even raise her head. Her rocking got steadier; she seemed to gain comfort from it—her breathing was no longer audible. At least she was calming down.

But she wasn't needed here. Especially if it was hurting her to remain.

"Would you like to leave?"

Ivy's head lifted. "Yes!"

"Why don't you run upstairs?"

Ivy leaped to her feet, and Nora gestured to the door. In no time, the child disappeared from view.

"Mother, did you tell Ivy she could go?"

Nora jumped at her daughter's voice, but she turned calmly to face Claire, hands folded in front of her. "Yes, dear. She seemed to be having a difficult night."

"Oh, Mother." Claire sighed and lightly touched her fingertips to her forehead. "Ivy needs to become accustomed to these types of situations, like Alice. I've neglected that aspect of her education, but since she's almost twelve and will be a young lady soon—"

"Oh, but, Claire, she was trembling." Nora placed a hand on her daughter's arm. "You wouldn't want her to stay down here, frightened, almost seeming to panic at the crowd."

"Yes, well, Mrs. Angel, for whatever reason, was speaking to her. Ivy is sensitive to strangers, but she needs to adjust." Claire turned and walked back to her friends.

Nora sighed. Her daughter had always been cold, but then, it was to be expected. In some ways, she blamed herself. Her children hadn't exactly had the safest childhoods in the world.

But Mrs. Angel's solution might help Ivy, at least. Nora took a deep breath and turned to find the woman who might hold the key to her granddaughter's future.

CHAPTER FOUR

IVY TRIED TO PUT her feet on the stairs, but whenever she got beyond the first three steps, she became dizzy. She gave up and sat at the bottom.

Tears started trickling down her cheeks, and there was nothing she could do to stop them. At first they were soft, gentle, just a few hot ones making salty paths down her face. Then they came quicker, and her nose and throat filled. She used both hands to wipe the tears away and made little whimpering noises between them.

No one cared about her. Ivy became surer of this with every tear. Crying made her feel abandoned, and she mentally perused her list of loved ones, discounting them all as unloving.

At last she came to Nettie. Dear Nettie. If only she hadn't fallen in love and gotten married and moved to the gatehouse.

But ...

She glanced toward the door, visible through the foyer. Unlike her mummy, Nettie was never distracted. She always made time for Ivy, even if she was tired and overwhelmed with the baby—even if Ivy wasn't her responsibility.

Ivy sniffled and wiped her nose with her sleeve. Nettie could dry her tears and reassure her. Nettie could make her feel calm. Nettie could show her how to breathe and whisper soft things, things about Jesus and how He protected little girls.

Mummy had been getting distracted from talking about Jesus lately. Maybe that was the real problem.

How could Ivy get to Nettie? It was a long, cold, dark walk to the gatehouse—and doubtless it was snowing. It often was here in the country.

Ivy shuddered. She had no coat, just her party dress, and she hated both the cold and the dark. But to get to Nettie, perhaps it could be borne.

Ivy swallowed hard and stood. On timid feet, she walked to the front door, wrapped her fingers around the doorknob—then stepped out into a blizzard.

It was hard to see with the snow swirling around her. The whole world was white; it hurt her eyes, making them sting and water. The cold bit and pulled at her, but she began trudging down the drive. One foot after another, then another and another, on and on, forcing her feet to move. Just when she felt surely the lights of the gatehouse must come into view, she was greeted by another blast of wind—and, glancing over her shoulder, realized that even the lights of Pearlbelle Park behind her had vanished in the storm.

But she must keep walking. She must reach Nettie, even though fear crept at the back of her mind, threatening like a great beast ready to devour her whole.

She couldn't let fear win. She must find Nettie. She must be swept up into warm, kind arms and feel love and comfort. It suddenly felt like forever since she'd experienced those emotions.

Felt truly safe.

The wind battered Ivy until she almost fell over, and then her leg caught. She tumbled into the ditch by the side of the road and lay there panting and staring at the swirling blackness around her.

The tears froze on her cheeks. Ivy thought about screaming, but there was no one—no one who could hear her, rescue her, take her home or to Nettie.

For the first time in her life, the fear went beyond the surface. It dug into her and kept her from moving a single limb. But it was more than fear. It was reality.

She might die in this ditch.

Ivy had never been afraid of dying until that moment. Ivy was afraid of almost everything one could mention, from dogs to horses to bees to rivers, but never before had death been more than a distant idea, a pathway to Heaven.

Tonight it was real and big and black, and it howled ... almost like a dog. "Awoo! Awoo!"

Ivy blinked. Was that really death? She rubbed a hand over ice-encrusted eyelids and tried to think. She didn't think so—but perhaps. Anyway, it wasn't scary. It came across as more comical than frightening.

Then the howler was upon her, poking a damp nose in her face and lapping her with a big tongue and smelling like a wet dog.

Ivy froze. Would it bite her?

"Opie, you mutt! Get out—well, I'll be ... Hullo? Who's there?" It was a boy's voice, somewhere between child and man and squeaky around the edges. But it was definitely human.

Boots landed beside her head, and Ivy managed to push herself up slightly. Upon opening her eyes, a lantern's light momentarily blinded her, but soon her vision cleared, and she looked up into the greenest eyes she'd ever seen.

"Miss Ivy? Miss Ivy Knight?" The young man squinted and set the lantern down on a nearby rock, then held out his hand. "You're not even wearing a coat, Miss Ivy."

"N-no." Ivy put her numb fingers in his, and he yanked her to her feet with surprising force. "I-I—"

"Never mind explanations. I'm glad Opie found you!" He gestured down at the little spaniel. "Let's get you out of the cold—you must be almost frozen. The gatehouse isn't far."

Ivy glanced around, then back up at him—he was probably a foot taller than her. "All right."

He grabbed the lantern and started up the ditch, and when he moved back, Ivy almost fell over. She hadn't realized her legs were so numb, her body so trembly. She tried to walk but stumbled.

"Oh, glory." The boy popped down in the ditch beside her. "Here now. Arms around my neck. I'll carry you—you look a lot lighter than a newborn foal."

Ivy wasn't sure if she was or wasn't lighter than a newborn foal, but she imagined so based on how big horses were. "I-I think so." She allowed him to pick her up like a baby and carry her out of the ditch.

"Nettie will know what to do," the young man mumbled as he walked toward the gatehouse, the lantern swinging from his elbow and casting an eerie glow over the snow and his wet, loping dog ahead of them.

Ivy closed her eyes tightly to block it all out. Nettie would indeed know what to do—and then, hopefully, everything would be all right.

Alice dashed into the parlor she'd left not ten minutes before. "Mother!" Her voice had a high-pitched tone to it, a panicked tone that made Nora wince. Yet fast on the tails of the wince came a tightness in her chest as worry rose.

"Alice." Claire's eyes were hard as she regarded her daughter. "Calm yourself."

Nora wondered how Claire could be anxious about what people thought when her child stood before her, clearly distressed. She rose and followed Claire across the room and into the hallway.

Alice had caught her breath enough to speak, though her chest still rose and fell irregularly as the words poured out. "I went upstairs to our room, but Ivy wasn't there! I looked everywhere, and I couldn't find her. Mummy, what if she's lost somewhere?"

Alice's reversion to the childish "Mummy" told Nora everything she needed to know about her granddaughter's sincerity, but Claire apparently felt otherwise. "Are you sure? She likes to hide under the bed, darling."

"I checked there! I checked everywhere. Mummy—"

"Shush, no." Claire put a restraining hand on Alice's shoulder, and Nora could see the truth catching up to her. Alice wouldn't lie or exaggerate—of course she wouldn't. Claire knew that, and if she allowed herself to think about it too long, Nora was sure she'd panic.

And that wouldn't help anyone. Panicking never did.

Nora gently placed a hand on her daughter's arm. "Where would she have gone? Does she have special spots, places that hold meaning to her? She was panicking; where would she go to calm down?"

Claire's head jerked from side to side. "I-I don't know. I'm not sure ..." Her lips trembled, and she wrapped her arms around herself. "I need Philip. He'll be able to get people organized to find her. She's in the house; she must be."

Nora took Claire's hand and squeezed it. "Why do you say that?"

"Ivy is afraid of the dark, and of snow and ... everything. She would never venture outside." Claire glanced toward the door across the foyer and shook her head. "No, she's in here somewhere." She released an audible breath, and her tremors subsided.

Nora wasn't so sure. Ivy had seemed wild when she saw her last, and she wished she'd obeyed her instincts and followed her. However, it was too late for regrets; now it was time to act.

Claire walked back into the parlor to fetch her husband, and Nora asked Alice a few more questions. No, Ivy wasn't in the nursery or the playroom; no, she wasn't in the water closet. Alice had been thorough—she'd even stopped by her mother's bedroom on the way down.

"I suppose she could have gone to Uncle Charlie's room, but I don't even know where he's staying." Alice shifted from side to side, eyes darting to and fro, her face stoic but her hands nervous. "I'm afraid she's gone, Grandmother—and I don't know where."

Poor child. Nora gave her a quick hug and reassured her as best she could. But, like Alice, she had a bad feeling about this.

Where could Ivy have run off to?

"She can't have gone far," Nora said as Philip and Claire emerged. "What do you suggest doing?"

"Philip and I will check a few more places upstairs. There's a small chance Alice simply overlooked her, or perhaps Ivy got lost in a hallway." Claire smiled brightly, as if sure her younger daughter was safe. "After that, we might have to enlist the staff to assist us."

"I see." Nora took a deep breath. "Very well. Let's start with that."

Almost before Nora finished speaking, a harried maid rushed in, eyes wide. "Mrs. Knight?"

Nora blinked. It was unusual for a maid to address her mistress without a butler or housekeeper essentially "translating."

"Yes, Dotty?" Claire said.

"Mrs. Knight, one of the stable boys just came—he says Miss Ivy is at the gatehouse with Mrs. Jameson. I ... I would have fetched Mr. Marlin to tell you, but—"

Claire's face relaxed, and she swayed on her feet.

Philip cupped her elbow with his hand. Nora supposed he did have some uses. "Thank you, Dotty. That will be all," he said.

Dotty scurried off, and Claire glanced up at Philip. "A carriage?"

Philip nodded. "That would be best. If she's with Nettie, she's safe enough that we needn't hurry."

"But I want you to hurry." Claire stepped away from him and collected Alice to her in a brief embrace. "Thank you for telling us quickly, darling—I suppose we'll have to remember to watch her more closely."

Claire turned, caught up her skirts, and half-ran up the stairs.

Nora followed, panting slightly—she really wasn't used to all this excitement. "She's never done anything like this before, has she?" She hadn't heard that the child caused this kind of trouble.

"No, no—never." Claire turned on the landing, and Nora skidded to a stop, catching the banister to stop her forward momentum. "I don't know what could have gotten into her—but at least she's safe. That's what matters."

"Absolutely." Though, if there were a way to make things safer for little Ivy, they had best pursue it as quickly as possible.

CHAPTER FIVE

"Here." Nettie tucked a cup of tea into Ivy's hands. The mug caused her fingers to tingle, a strange mix of pleasant and unpleasant. "It's hot. Just sip, it'll warm you right up."

Ivy sipped, curling her lips against the heat. "I don't like it."

"You will when it cools. Would cream help?"

When did cream not help? Sugar would help more, but Nettie wasn't likely to offer it this close to bedtime. "Yes."

Nettie left Ivy seated on an armchair in the front room and walked toward the kitchen at the back. The blanket and the flickering fire, plus the teacup gripped in her hands, made Ivy feel sleepy. She blinked rapidly—now was not the time for sleep.

Nettie returned and poured leftover cream from a pitcher, then stirred it in. Ivy watched the liquid in the cup turn a swirly, light color. Very pretty.

"All right, Ivy." Nettie lowered herself onto the chair opposite Ivy, gray eyes pensive. "Why are you here? What happened?"

Ivy shrugged and looked away, focusing on the fire. "I don't know."

"Yes, you do." Nettie's voice had obtained that perfect balance between gentle and firm, and Ivy's heart squeezed. How could she resist that?

Her eyes rose to Nettie's face. "I-I'm sorry." Tears puddled in her eyes, and one managed to burn a hot trail down her cold cheek. "I'm so sorry, Nettie. I didn't mean to run away!"

"Oh, Ivy." Nettie rose and came over to squeeze Ivy's hand, though she didn't bend down and give her a hug. "What is it?"

Ivy ran a fist over her eyes. "I don't think Mummy loves me anymore."

Nettie didn't even flinch. "Of course she does. She loves you more than anything. What made you think she doesn't?"

"I don't know ..." Ivy wiggled back and forth in her chair but was careful not to slosh her tea. "I suppose she's been so busy that she just doesn't have time to love me anymore."

"Ah." Nettie squeezed Ivy's shoulder and kissed the top of her head. "That's not true, though. She loves you very much, and her busyness doesn't change that. You should know that, Ivy—Mummy was always busy when you were small."

That was true. Back then, Mummy had worked, and when one worked, there wasn't much time for little girls. But it didn't feel so neglectful at the time, for Nettie had lived with them, and Alice had been more of a sister to Ivy. In truth, Mr. Knight had stolen both Mummy and Alice.

Ivy scrunched up her nose, wishing she could better communicate these thoughts to Nettie, but her words ran dry. "I know," she said at last, "but it's different now."

"I suppose everything is new for you." Nettie removed Ivy's dangerously sloshing teacup and set it on a side table. "You'll adjust. It's going to be all right. However, you have to remember not to run off like that. Your mother must be sick with worry!"

Ivy winced. She hadn't meant to make anyone sick or worried. She'd just meant to find someone who cared about her. "Do you think she's noticed?"

"I'm sure of it." Nettie returned to her seat. "Now, if you'll sit still, you can finish your tea before she gets here. It won't be long."

Ivy hoped not. Now that she was calmer, the trembling fading and her breathing normal, it was easy to remember that Mummy loved her and that that kind of love was worth waiting for. She sipped the tea, now cool enough to drink, and tried to think happy thoughts, but it was hard, harder than it had ever been before. Now positivity wasn't as natural. She was sleepy, so that must be why.

"Your eyelids are drooping." Nettie smiled. "Yes, dear, I think you'll feel much better in the morning."

Ivy wouldn't admit that for all the world, but perhaps it was true. After all, Nettie had always said that, and Nettie was often right. "All right. Will Mummy tuck me in?"

"Of course." Nettie cocked her head. "She's been tucking you in, hasn't she?"

Ivy quickly relayed the situation with the now-gone Elsie. Nettie's face grew somewhat dark as she spoke but lightened when Elsie's inevitable fate came up.

"You have to tell Mummy when people treat you badly," Nettie said. "Promise me you'll tell us."

"I will." Though, Ivy wasn't sure if she would be able to, so perhaps it was a lie. She wanted to do what she was told, but she didn't want to get anyone in trouble, either.

Poor Elsie didn't have a job now, and even if she had been a bully, Ivy blamed herself for that.

Nora stood in the hall, clutching her shawl close against the cold. The door of Alice and Ivy's room opened, and Claire stepped out, candle in hand. Her eyes were weary, but at least she wasn't shaking as she had been before.

Doubtless the act of tucking Ivy in, seeing her warm and quiet and happy, had calmed her considerably. Such a thing would certainly have calmed Nora if her daughter had ventured out into the cold late at night without warning.

Claire nodded to Nora and gestured down the hall. "Will you come into my boudoir and discuss the situation?"

Nora's heart leaped. Her daughter wanted to discuss it with her? She was a member of the chosen circle? It was silly, really, for Claire had asked her advice on several things of late. But it still made her happy when anyone asked for her advice. Especially her beloved daughter.

She followed Claire into her private quarters.

Her daughter immediately unclipped two earrings, set them on her dresser table, and reached to unclasp her necklace. Claire didn't speak until the last of her expensive jewelry was tucked into its place. Then she turned to Nora with a smile. "That was quite the adventure, wasn't it?"

Adventure? Nora would rather compare it with a disaster. But she nodded, not wanting to rock the boat with too-strong words. "Indeed, it was."

"I'm used to Alice doing that sort of thing ... Ivy never has." Claire shrugged, making even the supposedly unladylike gesture seem poised. "Of course, I've feared for Ivy's life before. More so than with Alice. I've rarely thought Alice was going to die, though I do worry whenever she's on a horse." Her fingers played with her hair, but she left it up—undoubtedly a maid would be able to undo Claire's complicated chignon easier than she herself could. "But now Ivy is running off places."

"Indeed." Nora didn't know what else to say. How did one respond to her daughter's working through her thoughts aloud? Nora wasn't used to anyone sharing their thoughts with her, and yet Claire seemed comfortable with doing just that—and as of yet to no purpose.

Jonathan, Nora's husband, had always been direct. He'd told her what he expected of her in quick words, a few syllables at most, and then he'd expected her to obey without question. He'd certainly never asked for her opinion.

Nora's chest rose slightly in pride. It was a different world now that he was gone—and Claire's slowly opening up to her showed that more than anything.

"I worry that it'll happen again." Claire turned away from Nora and walked over to her large wardrobe. "What if, next time, she isn't found? It's only through the grace of God that she's not dead now ... He may not spare her next time."

Nora winced. "I've always felt that what happens will happen. Not that we shouldn't be careful." One should always be careful; Nora would never say anything to the contrary. She'd lived a cautious life. Foolishness simply wasn't her forte.

"Of course—that's exactly what I mean." Claire opened the door to her wardrobe and shuffled through her clothing absently, perhaps thinking of what she would wear tomorrow. "I only hope I can find a solution. I must find a way to keep Ivy safe. Yet, if by now she hasn't learned how to care for herself, and given that Pearlbelle Park could present a less-than-safe atmosphere ... You can see why I worry."

Nora nodded, unsure if she should speak or not. Perhaps she did have a solution—but her input wasn't often appreciated. Jonathan would have slapped her, or at least looked like he wanted to, if she'd given her opinion.

Usually his opinion was decided in moments.

But Claire was different. Claire was reaching out to her.

If the solution Mrs. Angel suggested was a viable one, it was her duty to share it ... right?

Claire turned to Nora. "What would you suggest? If you were a mother of such a child, what would you do? I can be more vigilant—hire someone who can be more vigilant—anything like that. But I worry that Ivy ... that Ivy needs to learn to live in this world, and I'm sadly ill-equipped. So little is known."

Yes, and what was known wasn't sufficient. The world wasn't friendly to girls like Ivy, and the older she got, the more people would mock her existence. In most cases, an inconvenient person was eventually sent off, though Ivy was far from unwanted. Claire clearly loved her child. Still, it couldn't be easy—when Ivy wasn't like Alice. When Ivy wasn't like other girls her age.

There was hope for Ivy, wasn't there?

"I ... I might have a suggestion." Nora forced the words past her trembling lips.

"Oh, really?" Claire sat delicately on the chair in front of her dresser table and regarded her with an open face that indicated readiness to listen.

Nora took a deep breath. "Yes. I was speaking with Mrs. Angel—one of your guests—and it turns out ... Claire, she noticed Ivy's behavior—"

Claire's wince confirmed everything that Nora suspected—that, though she loved Ivy, Claire was slightly embarrassed by the child. She was affected by others' opinions.

Yet love for her child must win out. It must. Love always won. Nora was learning that more and more with every day that passed, with every prayer uttered.

"She noticed Ivy's behavior," Nora continued, "and she spoke to me about a solution for the child. You see, Dorothea Angel has a child like Ivy."

Claire stilled and curiosity entered her like a tidal wave—Nora could see it in her eyes. "A child like Ivy?"

"Yes. A little girl, two years older than your daughters. Her name is Violet." Nora stepped forward and took a seat on a chair nearby. "When she was born, like Ivy, she seemed perfect in every way—but as she grew older, Mrs. Angel quickly noticed that Violet was different from most children. Quieter, more difficult, often having fits and tantrums. By the time Violet was five, Mrs. Angel decided she could no longer keep the child in her house."

Claire's eyebrows raised, much as Nora's would have done, if she weren't too polite, when Mrs. Angel had originally told her the story. To send a child off at five, as the mother, was worse than anything Nora could imagine.

"Surely this child must be nothing like Ivy."

Nora sighed. She believed so, too, to a degree. "Mrs. Angel didn't go into detail, but apparently Violet has some other issues. She behaves dangerously at times and seems to have dark impulses."

"I see." Claire nibbled on her bottom lip pensively. "But where ... where could they send the child? At that age, surely not to an ... to an asylum." She shuddered. "At any rate, that wouldn't be an option for Ivy."

"No, not an asylum. It's different from that—the Angels sent their daughter to a school in Scotland, not far outside of Edinburgh. It's called McCale House." Nora swallowed and watched Claire's face closely. "It's a school for children like Ivy—and children like Violet—and others with similar struggles. It primarily runs as a research institute. Apparently Dr. McCale believes such people can be helped. Violet has been there for almost a decade now."

Claire blinked. "You think this would be a good place to send Ivy?"

Nora trembled. "I-I don't know, Claire. From what Mrs. Angel told me, it is perfectly respectable. They have a large home in the country, and a staff of doctors, and they take good care of the children there. Parents are encouraged to stay—Mrs. Angel has visited several times herself, and she says it's lovely."

Claire didn't speak for a time, and when she did, her voice was low and steady, not portraying any emotion. "How long has it existed?"

"Less than twenty years. It's experimental. I believe Mrs. Angel said there are always less than ten students, and they're carefully and individually worked with." Nora cocked her head. "It sounds like a great deal of work is put into helping these children with their various problems. And their goal is to help people like Ivy learn to survive in the world they're born into but don't seem fitted for."

Had she said too much? Claire was quiet for a long time, and Nora wasn't sure what she was thinking. She hoped she wouldn't be angry or think Nora was a fool or anything of the sort. She really did want to help Ivy.

Perhaps she could explain better.

"Mrs. Angel put it like this." Nora cleared her throat and took a deep breath. "McCale House is a school for children who are slightly delayed and struggling to cope with the world, but not necessarily to the point where one would call them 'insane.' The mission of McCale House is to help these children learn to manage at least enough to stay safely out of asylums."

Claire nodded. "Yes, I understand."

There was a knock at the door.

"Who is it?" Claire called.

"Me." Philip's voice vibrated through the wall. "Can I come in?"

"Yes, come. I'm just talking with Mother."

Philip entered the room and smiled. "Hello. What are you talking about? Ivy's little adventure?"

Claire and Philip both seemed to know how to politely refer to the incident. At least they were in harmony with each other.

"Yes." Claire sighed. "Mother has come up with an interesting proposition for us, inspired by our guest Mrs. Angel." She quickly related what Nora had told her about McCale House. "What do you think?"

Nora wasn't sure exactly how seriously Claire took Philip's opinions, but there was certainly attention in her eyes. Yet she wasn't giving away her own feelings, strong as they might be.

"I'm not sure." Philip glanced from Claire to Nora and back. "You say the Angels have a daughter there?"

"Yes."

"They say she's doing quite well," Nora inserted. "I think that this would be an amazing opportunity for Ivy, if you'll pardon my saying so." She wasn't sure if that was too forward, but the more Mrs. Angel had described the place, the more Nora's heart had lit up.

She didn't know Ivy as well as most, and she was glad it wasn't her decision, for she could never make it with the little knowledge she had. However, based on what she'd observed, what Claire had told her, and the information she had gained about McCale House ... it seemed ideal.

Of course, that was if Claire and Philip were able to travel with Ivy and live nearby. Nora wasn't a supporter of children being sent away from their parents. She knew hundreds of boys and girls attended schools away from home all over England, and did well, but she just couldn't trust the system.

She still felt, to this day, that boarding school had caused her to lose Claire's and Christina's hearts. Charlie remained hers, but that was only the attachment of a son who felt protective of his mother—they weren't great friends.

Yes, children ought to stay home, and be their parents' comforts, and grow closer to the family—not be forced away, where distance could lead to all sorts of horrible things. God had created the institution of a family for a reason.

Claire and Philip discussed a few more things, asking Nora occasional questions. She answered as best she could, though it was clear her daughter and son-in-law would have to write to McCale House for further details.

Still, as she left her daughter's boudoir and headed to her own room, Nora felt she'd done the right thing. Perhaps they would be able to help Ivy—truly help her.

CHAPTER SIX

C HRISTMAS WAS JUST AROUND the bend, and Ivy had some problems—some serious problems. Of course, there were still the issues
of her mother's inconsistent attention, Alice's being far too busy for her
own good, and Mr. Knight's existing.

But, more than that, Ivy hadn't bought Christmas presents yet, and
there didn't seem to be anyone to take her shopping.

She had never Christmas shopped with Mummy—that much was true.
She loved her mother, and loved spending time with her, but she just didn't
think her mother would properly forget what Ivy had bought for her by
the time December 25th rolled around.

Uncle Charlie, on the other hand? She could buy a present right in front
of him, and he'd have forgotten within five minutes. At least, he always
looked shocked when he opened his gift on Christmas morning. She'd
gone shopping with Uncle Charlie the last few years, as had Alice, and she'd
gotten used to it. He took care of the buying part, too, which was nice.

Before Uncle Charlie had become more present in her life, Ivy had gone
Christmas shopping with Alice and Nettie. Unfortunately, Ivy wasn't
allowed to walk down to the gatehouse and ask. Anyway, Nettie's husband,
Mr. Tom, had mentioned that Nettie wasn't going to be doing much until
May for some unknown reason.

This was disappointing and unlike Mr. Tom. Didn't he know that Ivy needed Nettie, who would close her eyes or be focused on other things while her present was selected? Nettie, who had the perfect idea for a gift for every member of Ivy's family?

It was hardly to be borne, and yet those were the facts of the matter. There was no one to go Christmas shopping with—and Creling wasn't even much of a fun place to go shopping.

So Ivy sat in her room, her chin on the windowsill, and pouted. Everyone walked around her as if she didn't exist.

Edith, one of the maids who helped Ivy get dressed and take care of herself, didn't seem to understand, either. Edith was kinder than Elsie, with a big, wide smile and rosy cheeks and gentle brown eyes, but she wasn't Mummy or Nettie or even Alice.

Edith might understand the situation better if Ivy bothered to explain it to her, but Ivy never shared personal details with strangers. Not when she could help it.

"Miss Ivy, would you like me to play dolls with you?" Edith touched her shoulder. "Perhaps we could have a tea party?"

Ivy sighed. Edith was trying awfully hard, and Ivy didn't like it when people were disappointed. Still, she wasn't stupid—she knew Edith had been paid to keep Ivy from boredom while Mummy was busy.

Would Mummy like it if Ivy gave in to Edith and played dolls? She glanced up at the smiling maid and wrinkled her nose. Edith wasn't that old, really—just a young lady, not a grown-up, and she was kind.

But no, Ivy didn't want to play. She wanted to mope. "Maybe later." Her own voice sounded boring, which caused her to sigh yet again and drop her chin back onto the windowsill.

Edith also sighed—it was going around, apparently—and Ivy felt her ease away.

It was like being under arrest—a prisoner in one's own house. Ivy had to be with someone all the time now, and it was exhausting. When she was with Mummy or Mr. Knight, they both asked her lots of questions and smiled too much and hugged her too hard.

Hugs were nice—from Mummy, anyway—and smiling was good, but it wasn't good to just be loved because she'd almost died. She wanted to be loved just because she existed and was worthy of attention regardless of her brushes with mortality.

As Edith puttered about the room, Ivy redirected her mind to the issue at hand. The presents. How was she to get the presents? She needed one for Mummy and Alice and Uncle Charlie and Nettie—and perhaps she ought to get one for Mr. Tom, too, even though he was making Nettie "rest."

Ivy knew for a fact that Nettie didn't need rest during the daytime, as she'd never napped when Ivy did.

The door to the bedroom opened behind her, and she glanced over her shoulder. *Oh.* It was her grandmother. She blinked, unsure what to think of this intrusion from this somewhat unfamiliar woman.

"Hello," Ivy said.

"Hello, Ivy." Grandmother smiled. "May I come and sit next to you?"

Ivy glanced at the chair beside her. It wasn't too close, and Ivy wasn't doing anything that required immense concentration. Or, rather, she needed to stop concentrating on the problem at hand, or she would begin to feel boggled. She nodded.

Grandmother crossed the room and lowered herself onto the chair next to Ivy. She had a quiet expression, as always. Grandmother was never loud; that much Ivy could be thankful for. She didn't like loud, excited people—except Alice, of course, and even Alice wasn't as loud as some.

Yes, Grandmother was quiet, and she wouldn't interfere with Ivy's thoughts.

"What are you thinking about?" Grandmother asked.

Ivy cocked her head, put out but not sure how to express it. How dare Grandmother interrupt her thoughts? But then, Grandmother couldn't know that Ivy was having thoughts, or that she needed silence for those thoughts. Unless Ivy said it, which she never could, it wouldn't come across.

Should she tell Grandmother what she was thinking about? She could—but then she'd have to admit that she was in a bind and no one could help her. And then Grandmother would try to help—and she never really could. Ivy had already thought of all the solutions, and they weren't good ones.

But she could try, she supposed. Perhaps getting a different perspective on the issue was worthwhile. Or perhaps Grandmother could tell Uncle Charlie to stop talking with Miss Elton and start performing his uncle-ly duties.

"I can't get Christmas gifts," Ivy whispered. "I can't get any."

"What?" Grandmother cocked her head. "That's not true, Ivy! Why would you think that? Why, even I have bought you a Christmas gift, and I know your parents have bought you several."

Ivy's brow furrowed. She didn't mean Christmas presents for herself. Why would Grandmother think she'd worry about that when what mattered was getting presents for others?

"No." Ivy wiggled back and forth on her seat, seeking the right words. It was so difficult to express herself once she'd already incorrectly spoken. Her stomach twisted, but she forced herself to say something. "I want to get people things."

"Oh!" Grandmother's face split with a great smile. "How sweet of you, Ivy! Doesn't Charlie take you?"

Ivy shook her head. "Not this year."

"Ah, that makes sense." Grandmother tapped her index finger to her lips once, twice, three times. "Perhaps I can help you shop."

Ivy didn't want to look disgusted, and truly Grandmother wasn't a bad sort of person. But Grandmother wasn't Uncle Charlie or Nettie—or even Mummy.

She couldn't go places with Grandmother. She couldn't. She would feel all wrong inside if she did that. Besides, it wasn't what she'd done for years and years before.

How could she just change what she was doing? That wasn't within her control. That wasn't something that should happen, certainly, at any rate.

"I ... I don't know ..." Grandmother's eyes were so hopeful that Ivy couldn't say anything but that. "I've never gone Christmas shopping with you before."

"Perhaps we could start a new tradition."

Ivy blinked. Tradition was a good word—but "new," in her mind, didn't really fit with it. "New tradition?"

"Yes." Grandmother was almost grinning now. "And then we could talk and get to know each other."

Getting to know Grandmother was a good idea—but safely, over time, with other loved ones around her. Getting to know someone in an unsafe place, like the small, nearby town of Creling, with none of her loved ones nearby, was a bad idea.

Yet, even though she didn't know Grandmother well, Ivy still was loathe to hurt her. Based on her expression, she might be hurt. Ivy couldn't bear it if that were the case.

"I ... I suppose." Ivy wiggled back and forth on her seat some more, but there was nothing she could do to escape the impossibility of the situation she'd been thrust into. She couldn't disappoint Grandmother—she also wasn't sure if she could bear going to Creling and shopping with her.

But she would try. Just this once.

Creling was a small town not far from Pearlbelle Park with all the typical things a tiny village had. Little shops that were quaint but hardly comparable to those in London. A town hall. People bustling through the streets. Friendly shopkeepers—assuming they weren't just nice because the people from Pearlbelle had deep pockets.

Nora chose to believe that people were kind, because it was in their nature to be so, if they chose, not because money compelled them to be. She liked to believe the best in people whenever she could—but warily.

As long as one wasn't bitter, a degree of wariness was important. There were so many things she wished she'd been wary of. But now it was too late to be wary of things in the past. The past couldn't touch her anymore.

She stepped out of the carriage with the help of the footman and turned to collect her granddaughter. Ivy, eyes wide, awkwardly exited the conveyance and looked around. Nora wished she knew what was going through the child's head—what she was thinking about and how she was processing those thoughts. Ivy had such a unique perspective. Nora couldn't wait to learn more about how the world looked through the child's eyes.

"Who shall we shop for first?" Nora asked.

"Mummy," Ivy whispered. That was another interesting quirk of hers—she almost always talked so quietly that Nora could barely hear her.

Of course, Nora herself often spoke softly. She didn't want to cause a disturbance, make herself known, perhaps bring pain upon herself or loved ones through boldness. Maybe Ivy felt the same—or perhaps she was simply shy. Though, living as Ivy had, constantly assured that she was different, perhaps even less worthy than other people, might make one unusually quiet. Nora certainly stopped speaking when she was told she was less important than others. It had happened more in her life than one would think, given the fact that Nora wasn't any different than most women.

Nora led the way into a small shop, where Ivy began looking about. She seemed to know what she was looking for immediately and acted more methodical than Nora had expected. Her big blue eyes flickered up and down the shelves as she traced the store, each step slow and careful. Yet there was no wandering in her movements, and there was no confusion in them, either.

"What are you looking for?" Nora asked. She was sure that Ivy must have something specific in mind.

Instead, Ivy answered simply, "The perfect present. I know it must be here somewhere."

Nora kept herself from laughing. "Do you have an idea of what kinds of things your mummy might like?"

Ivy shrugged. "I'll know when I see it."

"Very well." Nora decided at this point that she'd better be quiet and let Ivy figure these things out for herself. She seemed to have a grasp on this.

At last, Ivy's face bloomed into the most beautiful smile Nora had seen in a long time. It reminded her of a young Claire, before everything had happened, when she was a child with a belly laugh and a habit of scrunching up her nose until her eyes almost closed with the intensity.

Now Nora was left wondering if Claire had grown up into a completely different person.

"Grandmother!" Ivy pounced forward and snatched up a pair of gloves from the counter. They were ordinary gloves—brown ones with fur lining but meant for a lady's hands. Yes, they would fit Claire, and, yes, they looked nice ... but there was nothing particularly special about them. Yet Ivy thought there was. "These are perfect!"

"You think so?" Nora stepped forward and touched the gloves. "Ah, yes, they are soft inside."

Ivy bounced up and down, practically dancing on her toes. "Yes! They are! Mummy will love them. They are exactly what she needs, aren't they?"

Claire had hundreds of pairs of gloves, yet was Nora going to tell Ivy that? No. "Of course they are, Ivy. I think she absolutely needs them."

Ivy nodded in satisfaction. "Alice next."

The rest of their shopping was conducted in a similar manner until, at last, they'd run to the end of Ivy's list—granted, a small one. Other than her mother and sister, she bought presents for Nettie, Charlie, and "Mr. Tom."

Ivy then cocked her head. "Grandmother, I would buy you a present, but you must promise—absolutely promise—to forget what it is!"

Forget what it was? Oh, so it could be a surprise? "Yes, I promise to forget, Ivy. I'm honored you want to buy me a present."

Ivy nodded. "All right." And so the shopping began again. Once she'd finished with that, they made their purchases and walked outside the shop.

Then Ivy stopped. "Grandmother?"

"Yes, Ivy."

"Do you ... do you think I ought to buy a present for Kirk Manning?"

Kirk Manning? Nora mentally reviewed all the people she knew and couldn't come up with a single one named Kirk Manning, though the name did sound somewhat familiar. "Who is that, Ivy?"

Ivy looked offended, but the expression on her face passed as soon as it had appeared. "He's a stable boy, and he ... he found me. The other night." She glanced down, then slowly raised her eyes back up to Nora's face. "He saved me. I might have ... have gotten sick."

Or died.

Nora did know of that stable boy, as Philip had been speaking of him just the other night. "Yes, Ivy, I know all about that. I think you ought to give him a present, if you'd like—that would be all right, given what he's done for you. Though, I will say that your father has seen to it that he's duly rewarded."

"Oh?" Ivy's eyes lit up. "Mr. Knight did that?"

"Yes." Philip had gone to visit the boy's family, found that they were living in poverty with a sick father unable to provide for his son and daughter, and offered to pay for their cottage's upkeep and some other basic necessities—as well as send this stable boy to a school, where he could get further education.

Philip believed in big, sweeping gestures like that. He never did anything by halves. Hopefully he'd follow through on his promises to that poor family—once one counted on something that big, that generous, one would be dreadfully disappointed if it fell through.

But, no, Philip was a man of his word—or Claire would make him be at any rate. The boy did deserve a reward for saving Ivy. At the least, she would have become ill—but given the conditions, she might not have been found in time.

Ivy seemed content with the purchases she'd made after a few moments of debating whether or not Kirk Manning needed further reward for his efforts. At last, Ivy informed Nora that she didn't know what Kirk would like.

So they headed home. For the first time, Ivy chattered slightly while they rode, and Nora sat and quietly listened to Ivy's relaying her expectations of peoples' expressions when they opened their gifts, what kind of packaging they ought to have, and on and on.

Nora smiled to herself, pleased with the outing as a whole and the progress she had made in her relationship with Ivy. Yes, someone needed to take time to draw this child out, for she was certainly not lacking in intelligence.

McCale House was an excellent idea indeed.

CHAPTER SEVEN

IVY DID HER BEST to enjoy Christmas, but the noise levels were at ridiculous heights. She couldn't believe that anyone would invite people over during one of the most beautiful, mostly family-full holidays there was—but that was exactly what her mother and Mr. Knight had done.

The people forced Ivy out of the parlor on two separate occasions, ripping her away from her precious Christmas tree and the presents and everything else that she loved.

It was one of those things that, though it wasn't to be borne, *had* to be borne, and Ivy hated those kinds of things. The world was difficult enough to bear without the out-of-control elements conspiring against her to ruin her life.

Grandmother was always talking to Ivy—and then strangers thought they would, too. Ivy wanted to be nice, truly, but she didn't feel comfortable. It wasn't like she could speak to people she didn't know.

There was also the matter of Mr. Knight's adding continuous stress to her life, keeping her mother busy, pretending he knew her, pretending he was her father. Ivy didn't need him, and yet there he was, acting like he'd known her all her life.

He hadn't, and Ivy didn't want him. She just wanted Mummy and Alice and Nettie, when she was able to have her. Oh, and Kitty, but even Kitty spent most of the days hiding in the kitchen.

Kitty didn't like strangers any more than Ivy. But then, no one was trying to talk to Kitty when she didn't want to be talked to, so really, the cat had less to complain about than Ivy.

The evening wound on and on. Ivy struggled through each difficult situation and each unshed tear and each kindly meant but useless word.

Christmas shouldn't be like this, nor should anything that had to do with or resembled Christmas. In fact, being in one's own home—and Ivy was told that Pearlbelle Park was now her home—should never feel vaguely like this.

By the end of the day, Ivy was exhausted as she crawled into bed and snuggled under the covers. Alice came in a few minutes, and wonder of wonders, Mummy was with her.

Instantly revived, Ivy hopped out of bed and dashed into Mummy's arms.

A good, long hug made her feel lots better, and in no time, she was seated on Mummy's lap with her arm around her neck and the fire in front of her.

Ivy had been told she was too big to sit on her mother's lap, but surely there were a few more weeks left. When she was twelve, yes, she would be too old—but Ivy was small, and anyway, she didn't mind being called a baby for it.

"You've been almost invisible today, Ivy," Mummy murmured. "Where have you been? I've hardly seen you."

Ivy shuddered. "People."

"Ah, yes. I suppose that made you want to hide." Mummy reached up to stroke Ivy's hair. "The people here are nice, dearest. I wouldn't invite them if they weren't."

Ivy was sure they were nice. She'd never doubted that the people were nice. But the problem wasn't with their niceness but rather with their presence. "I just don't like having all the people," she said.

"Hmm." Mummy kissed Ivy's cheek. "That's all right. But, Ivy, why do you think the people bother you?"

"I don't know." Ivy wiggled from side to side. How could she describe the buzzing in her head, the way their voices melted together, the way the lights and colors began to blend and it all became too much to bear? "They're just bright."

Bright was a good word—for the situation, not in general. Ivy didn't like bright things, really, or understand why other people would love bright things. Nor did she know why people would force her to live in a world where there were bright things.

"Bright?"

"Big and bright." Both good words, both bad things. "Big and bright and awful. I don't like them."

"Hmm ..." Mummy's voice trailed off, and she reached up a hand and ran it over her eyes. "That's interesting."

"Yes." Ivy said that even though she didn't know what was particularly interesting about it. To her, it didn't seem interesting so much as a sad fact of life.

"Do people frighten you, perhaps?"

That was it. "Yes."

"Because they're so ... bright."

"Yes." Finally, her mother seemed to understand! But when Ivy looked up at her mummy's face, it became clear that she didn't understand.

Oh well. Ivy was used to people not understanding.

But perhaps Mummy would be able to if Ivy just explained a little better.

"You see, it gets to be a lot." A lot of noises, a lot of colors, a lot of air that she wasn't able to suck into her lungs as quickly as she'd like. "And then I have to go someplace. And sometimes I can go away in my mind, and that's all right. I don't mind, because I have my thoughts, and sometimes I have my music. But other times, I can't go away, and then I start feeling badly."

Now Mummy was looking at her like she was crazy.

Ivy didn't like that. She reached up and cupped her mother's cheek. "Do you see?"

"Not exactly, darling." Mummy bit the inside of her mouth, sucking her cheek in slightly. "But that's all right. I'm glad you're able to ... go away. What is that about the ... the music?"

"The music." Ivy cocked her head. "In my head. Helps me think sometimes and keeps everything else out." Ivy had never tried to explain that before, so she wasn't sure how to, but she did her best. "It's just songs, you know."

"I'm afraid I don't." Mummy squeezed Ivy close. "But that's all right. I don't need to understand all the time."

Perhaps not.

Ivy dropped back against Mummy's shoulder and sighed. "Yes."

After a bit, Mummy tucked Ivy into bed and left.

Nora glanced up only briefly at first when Claire entered the parlor after seeing the girls to bed, but something about that glance made her look again. Claire seemed tired, worried, and distracted. The expression continued as Claire returned to her husband's side and engaged in the conversation—albeit still with that "somewhere else" look on her face. Nora wasn't one to let her curiosity get the better of her, but she did wonder.

Her daughter could be hard to read, so perhaps nothing whatsoever was wrong.

After perhaps half an hour, Claire wandered over to Nora's side. "Dinner will be announced soon, but I need to talk to you afterward. Lois can handle the ladies in the drawing room. We'll go to Philip's study."

"Very well," Nora murmured. "Is something wrong?"

"Nothing pressing. Don't worry." Then Claire stepped over to another group and joined in another conversation, a better hostess than Nora ever had been.

Dinner passed at a snail's pace, of course. Claire really didn't realize how much Nora would worry; it was one of those things that one did in more excess every time one was told not to. The conversation lagged, and Nora went from worrying about Claire's news to worrying that she was gawking at Claire too much. Especially when her daughter sent her a "behave yourself" look.

At last the ridiculously long meal was over, and Nora followed Claire away from the crowd to the quiet office.

Nora had never visited Pearlbelle Park before her daughter married Philip Knight, but she couldn't imagine the decor was her son-in-law's choice. It was too austere, too regal for Philip. He wouldn't have chosen those draping curtains, drawn back to let streams of surprisingly bright moonlight in, the heavy, ornately carved wooden desk, or the giant fireplace with a mantel chiseled from stone.

Still, it reminded Nora of her girlhood, visiting her father in his similar-looking study after some escapade. Back then she would have rather been anywhere but there—now she missed her father enough that the memory brought a soft sigh.

She should've been there in his later years. They'd fallen out of touch after her marriage, but surely she could have kept that from happening. She shouldn't have let her husband rule her life the way she had.

So many regrets, but the present was happening in front of her eyes. It was better to ignore the past and move forward as best she could.

Claire sat on a chair by the fireplace and gestured to the one opposite her. "It's about Ivy. I had a troubling conversation with her earlier, and I can't get it off my mind. I almost wonder ... I'm not sure what to do."

Nora raised her eyebrows but tried to keep her expression neutral otherwise. She knew how she felt about Ivy already—the child needed help, teaching, something; that was clear to her—but Claire must be allowed to come to her own conclusions. "What did Ivy say?"

Claire cast her gaze to the empty grate, her face slightly pinched. The chilly room needed a fire, but the servants doubtless had thought it would be empty. The moonlight certainly provided enough illumination for a quiet, private conversation. "A great many things."

"Such as?"

Claire sighed and leaned back on the chair. Everything about her posture spoke of defeat; it was uncomfortable to see, even if Nora believed that when Claire finally reached the end of her excuses for Ivy was when the child would have half a chance. "She says she hears music in her head. If that's not madness, I don't know what is."

Nora bit her lip. Madness? Perhaps—or perhaps not. The child didn't seem mad—just quiet, introspective, and overly imaginative. Her Christina had said those kinds of things all the time. But if it was what made Claire believe Ivy needed help, perhaps it was worth encouraging. "I can see why you'd be concerned, dear."

"Yes." Claire's eyes flickered up, then down again. "I love her. We have a close relationship, and I've always tried to make time for her—and for Alice—even when I could manage nothing else. I feel as if I've neglected them, though, in these last few months. I've been so busy. But as I talk to her, and as I realize she's almost twelve years old, and comparing her to Alice, well—" She stopped herself, and her hands gripped the arms of the chair.

"I see." Nora nodded, hoping minimal comments would encourage Claire to continue speaking.

"I want to keep her near me, but I also want to give her every chance I can." Her fingers drummed absently, and the beautiful blue eyes Nora had treasured for so many years remained distant. "What if McCale House is the right decision?"

"You forget that you would travel with her."

A little smile that twitched on Claire's lips vanished as quickly as it had come—but Nora was sure she'd seen it. "I'm not sure if I can. I shall certainly try, if we make the decision to attempt it and if they are able to accept her, but ... we'll see."

We'll see? What was Claire referring to? But Nora had been doing her best to not be too curious about her adult children's lives, and she'd become almost professional about it. "But if you can, would you? For Ivy's sake? She deserves the best you can give her."

Claire's face twisted. "I thought I was giving her the best I could give her. Maybe that's not true, but I've always believed that a mother is the best thing for her child."

"You're right—at least to a point. But what if cutting the apron strings is exactly what she needs?" Nora had wished for years that she'd been able to cut free of so many things—a family that never had felt loving, societal expectations, her marriage, the way her children seemed to despise her.

She'd never wanted her children to feel stuck in the life she'd been mired in.

Of course, Ivy had a different life with a mother who loved her and, more than that, acted on that love. Nora had loved her children but been too afraid to fight for their best interests.

Perhaps it would have been in their best interests to take them all and run away.

"Based on the descriptions of McCale House, it would seem that Ivy belongs there." Nora wasn't sure why she felt like that, but she did. "Everything I've heard has been positive, and what information Philip has gathered—unless he didn't share it all with me—has made it seem like this is what Ivy needs."

"Yes, I agree. I just haven't wanted to see it—but now ..." Claire leaned forward and rested her forehead on her palm. "I don't know. I believe it's the right choice, but I need to ... Let's go back to the guests. We don't want them to think anything is wrong."

Nora nodded, though she didn't care what the guests were thinking. Leaning on society for worth didn't help anyone—whether it was trying to conform or hiding non-conformities.

"But ..." Claire rose slowly, her expression still thoughtful. "I will ask Philip to write to McCale House. If there's no reply, or if they aren't interested in having Ivy there, that will simply be a 'no' from God."

That seemed wise. But hopefully it wouldn't be a "no."

God had a plan for Ivy, and Nora was feeling more and more with every day that McCale House was a part of that plan.

CHAPTER EIGHT

December 26, 1873

I VY PRESSED HER NOSE against the cool panes of the window and watched the grooms, horses, and richly dressed people mill about the yard until her breath fogged the glass. Then she leaned back, scooted over a few inches, and held her breath.

Today was Boxing Day, and apparently it was a tradition for people to go on a fox hunt in the morning. Ivy didn't understand the appeal of fox hunts—foxes were so charming, and she couldn't imagine wanting to hurt one. She didn't want them near her, of course, but from a distance, they were lovely. But people like Mr. Knight and even Alice didn't understand keeping pretty little animals safe, and Ivy supposed if there was nothing she could do about it, there was nothing she could do about it.

Mummy was going on the fox hunt, too, though she'd said she'd just "ride back with the ladies." Ivy wondered why the ladies bothered going—they were grown-ups, and if they wanted to ride in the back, that must mean they didn't want to ride. So why didn't they just stay home?

Adults were funny that way.

Now everyone was getting on their horses. Ivy was glad she was far away when the grooms left—she trusted grooms to control horses, because they were trustworthy. After all, a stable boy had saved her life. But she didn't trust most of the other people here. Were they trained to handle those monstrous animals? Ivy hoped so.

Mr. Knight helped Alice get on the back of her big black mare, Athena. Alice adored Athena, maybe because their names both started with the letter *A*. Though, there was a footman named Isaac whom Ivy had never much liked.

"Ivy, Isaac ..." She searched her memory for another *I* word. "Ice."

It was certainly icy outside now. The window fogged again under her breath, and she leaned back to let it clear. The whole world glistened white, though Ivy knew that everyone was going to come back from the hunt mud-splattered.

Mummy wouldn't like that. So why was she going? Why did she have to go with everyone else? Couldn't she stay here with Ivy instead?

A pair of hands rested on Ivy's shoulders, and she jumped, then dropped her head back. There was her grandmother again. She sighed in relief. It wasn't a villain, even if it was someone Ivy wasn't sure she liked.

"There you are. Watching everyone get ready for the hunt?" Grandmother peered out the window. "Hmm. Look at Alice! She's practically bouncing in the saddle. How excited she is! Such an adventurous child—I never would do such a thing."

Ivy doubted she would. Truly, there was a security in that. Alice had once commented that Grandmother was boring; Ivy considered that to be her best quality. Except where her dullness droned its way into Ivy's imaginary worlds, of course.

Then Mummy swept out in a beautiful riding habit and walked over to Mr. Knight. He turned and said something to her, and she laughed, but even from a distance, Ivy could tell she was faking it.

Ivy squinted. Was Mummy all right? Why were her shoulders hunched? She must have a headache. Everything about the way she held herself said she wasn't feeling well.

What are you doing, Mummy? Come sit with me instead ... But Ivy's thoughts couldn't reach Mummy, especially through the windowpane, so Mummy walked over to her horse instead of coming inside.

Mr. Knight helped Mummy mount, and though she held her head high, Ivy could see the slump through her body. *You're not all right, Mummy. You're not all right.*

"What is it, Ivy?" Grandmother squeezed her shoulder, shaking Ivy's thoughts away with even the gentlest of touches. "You seem sad."

"I want Mummy," Ivy whispered.

"Oh, dear! She'll be back before you know it. Let's go upstairs and—"

Grandmother's voice faded off again as Ivy focused on her mother. Yes, she was unwell. Quite unwell. Why didn't she come inside? If she came inside, she would feel better; if she was with Ivy, she would feel better.

She shouldn't be with those people. She should be with Ivy. Ivy would help her feel better.

Her thoughts circled and dipped like an errant breeze, trying to catch at a single thread and carry it farther than a few feet but inevitably failing.

Mr. Knight mounted his own horse, and the dogs were brought out with their keepers.

Mr. Knight backed his horse up and said something to Mummy again. It took her a moment too long to reply. He seemed to hesitate, watching her, then quickly dismounted and walked to her side.

Mummy dropped the reins and reached down to put a hand on Mr. Knight's shoulder, and several members of the party turned to her. Mr. Knight was saying something soft, something worried. Ivy caught her breath. He wrapped his arms around Mummy's waist and helped her off the horse.

"What on earth—" Grandmother started to say, but Ivy was rushing out of the door into the snow.

"Mummy, Mummy—"

Big hands, man hands, came out of nowhere. They caught her and kept her from going to her mother, who was half-kneeling on the ground with Mr. Knight hovering over her.

"She's ill."

"We should call a doctor."

"Yes, have a servant run for the nearest doctor."

"She should lie down."

"Let the maids know that she'll be in her room."

"I hope it's nothing serious."

The words spiraled, and Ivy's vision blacked. *I want my mummy. She's sick, and I want to get to her.* But she couldn't say it around the lump in her throat, and Uncle Charlie was holding her too tightly.

God, make sure my mummy's all right!

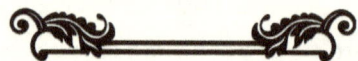

The doctor left, and Nora turned to her daughter. A part of her wanted to put her hands on her hips and scold, but she didn't want to lose Claire's good favor—she hadn't had it for long, after all.

"Well." Claire fiddled with the sleeves of her ridiculously beribboned nightgown. "Why can't anyone listen to me? I told them I didn't need a doctor—just to lie down. I'm absolutely fine."

Nora raised her eyebrows. She was still clinging to that? "The doctor told you a week ago that you needed to rest for the first three months, and you entirely ignored him."

Claire flipped her hand. "Doctors are always so dramatic. I'm quite well! He says it's been twelve years since I had my last baby, and I grant that, but I'm barely thirty. I'm not old; I can have more children without risking my health."

"Did you tell Philip?"

A guilty little shrug. Nora had forgotten that even a thirty-year-old woman could be a child at times. "Only that it was a possibility. I told him that last week when I spoke to the doctor about the headaches. But I ... I assumed if I rested often, I would be able to stay on my feet. It's so early on ... And with Ivy—with the girls—I was able to—"

"But you're not carrying Alice and Ivy, now, are you?" Nora's need-to-scold instinct was fighting to get to the top, and she let it leak out. "You're lucky you didn't lose the baby."

"I don't think I would have." Claire sighed. "But you're right. I shouldn't take risks with my child's life."

"No, you shouldn't." Nora remained silent for a moment, then spoke again. "When will it be? I didn't catch it. You can't be far along."

"Barely six weeks. I told you it wasn't a sane thing." A smile edged around Claire's lips now. "I think August. We'll want to keep it quiet for a few more months—it's so early."

"Of course." Nora wasn't one for talking to many people anyway, so there was no risk she'd tell. "But this is why you didn't want to take Ivy to McCale House, isn't it? It will be too risky to travel."

Claire nodded. "Yes, and then I wouldn't want to leave my baby for long, not when he or she is so small. In fact, it might be two or three years before I could comfortably leave—I probably wouldn't want to take a baby to Scotland, or even a small child for that matter, and there might be more babies after this one. By then, Ivy will be too old. McCale House is for younger students."

Nora nibbled on her bottom lip. "I can definitely see the issue." The baby was a blessing, yes, and would hopefully serve to bring the family even closer, but on the other hand, there was a degree of inconvenience in the timing.

Yet God knew best, and He hadn't placed this life on earth for no reason. Nora had to trust that He would only create a human being if it was the right time for it.

"I don't know what to do." Claire sighed and ran her hands over her face. "I've been talking to Philip about McCale House recently, and he feels strongly that Ivy ought to go before it's too late. But if I can't go with her, how would she feel safe? She only trusts me and Nettie, and we're both having a baby." A half-hysterical laugh erupted. "Of course we're both having a baby."

"Nettie wouldn't have left Malcolm even if she weren't with child now."

Nora sat on the edge of the bed. "Don't worry. If God wants Ivy to go to McCale House, He'll make a way."

"It's so hard to trust in Him. I know I should, but ..." Claire looked away. "Never mind. I'm sure you're right—what will be will be, and there's no use worrying about it. I shouldn't, for the baby's sake."

"Yes, of course." Nora, unlike Claire apparently, felt that if there were any modicum of risk when it came to a child's life, it ought to be avoided.

But then, Claire probably hadn't thought that way. She probably hadn't thought at all. Not too surprising—it was in her nature to rush forward, mindless of the consequences. Still, to risk her child's life ...

Yes, Claire wasn't thinking clearly. She wanted to impress people, to secure her position in society, to assure the world that the Knights were a family of quality, that the scandal attached to their name was not worth noting.

Nora wasn't used to seeing Claire under this kind of pressure, and it was frightening to know her daughter would risk so much for so little. It was the wrong decision as far as she was concerned.

Was it her business? Not really. And would she tell her thoughts to Claire? Of course not—she wanted to have a decent relationship with her daughter, and it felt like tiptoeing was the right choice for now.

There was something she could do, though. She could offer to help—she could make herself essential—and she could encourage Claire to keep off her feet for these next two months.

"I could take Ivy to McCale House. Charlie could escort us. You'd just have to do any required paperwork and take care of arrangements for us, and I could stay with her until you're able to join us."

Claire blinked. "I can't ask that of you. You're just now getting your life back. You ought to be doing whatever you want to be doing, not watching my daughter."

Didn't Claire know that caring for her granddaughters was exactly what Nora wanted to do all day every day? "It would be an honor, and I'd enjoy it. And with Charlie there, Ivy wouldn't be frightened—she likes him, and she'll doubtless adjust to me quickly. Then Charlie can leave once he sees us settled."

"Hmm ..." Claire worried her bottom lip. "Let me think about it and talk to Philip. And of course ... of course we both ought to pray about it. I can tell you haven't thought about this before, so perhaps it's worth doing so before committing."

Yet Nora was committed—to her family, to helping Claire, to Ivy. Couldn't anyone see that she had years of pretending not to care to make up for? Couldn't anyone see that she wanted to strip all the guilt and inaction from her skin and become a different person?

Still, she nodded in agreement. "I'll pray about it, but it seems to be an easy solution."

Claire arched her eyebrows. "Charlie may not like it."

"Yes, but if you ask him, he'll do it. He—"

There was a knock at the door. "Claire?" A mixture of excitement and concern tinged Philip's tone.

"I'll go and leave you alone with him. Remember to think about it!" Nora crossed the room and opened the door. As Philip entered, she slipped out and clicked the door shut behind her.

CHAPTER NINE

January 1, 1874

I VY SLOUCHED ON A chair next to Alice's, sliding slowly from side
to side. Her dress was one of the itchiest she'd ever worn—stiff red
velvet with taffeta petticoats—and every bit of her body, mind, and soul
felt affected by it. She wanted badly to get out of it; however, there seemed
to be no way of doing so.

Why should I have to suffer on my birthday of all days? She swung her
legs back and forth under the table. It wasn't fair, but there it was.

"Ivy, sit up like a lady." Mummy sat across the table, having come down
to the dining room for this special day against all protests. Apparently Mr.
Knight wanted her to stay in her room—he was more villain than man
sometimes.

Ivy's back ached, but she obeyed her mother. Alice sent her an apologetic
glance before turning her attention back to Mr. Knight, who was teasing
her about her age.

How dare he tease my sister! Sadly Ivy couldn't summon the energy to so
much as glare at him, but she didn't like it nonetheless.

"Twelve," he said, "is practically a woman. I'll be expecting ladylike
behavior from you after this. You might need to stay inside more often,
and you can't follow me around the estate."

Alice just laughed. "You'd never make me do that, Papa. You love me too much, and you know I'd die indoors. I need sunlight."

"Your mother would disagree. After all, sunlight can be most harmful to the complexion."

Who cares about complexions? Alice is meant to adventure! Don't you understand that?

Alice simply shook her head with a smile. She was enjoying herself even if Ivy wasn't. Of course, Alice had Mr. Knight and Mr. Parker and just about everyone fawning around her. Alice was really growing up. She seemed taller every day. Ivy hadn't grown enough to amount to anything in years.

Maybe if I were taller they'd pay attention to me. Of course, I don't mind. I want Alice to get paid more attention than me. She deserves it—she's so wonderful—and I ... I don't deserve it.

"Next year, when your mother is better, we'll have guests, too," Mr. Knight said. "Who would you like to have, Alice? You've friends at school, haven't you?"

"I think I have almost everyone I'd want already." Alice glanced around the table. "The only other person I can think of would be Cassie, but I don't know if she'd be able to come."

"Then we'll have her next year. Ivy, does that sound all right to you?"

It did *not* sound all right to Ivy—she liked to have Alice to herself, especially on their birthday—but she didn't say anything about it. She simply shrugged and returned to her cake.

Ivy didn't like having a birthday party with Nettie not there, Mummy sick, and everyone talking about inviting people over next year. She didn't like wearing this scratchy dress, which Nettie never would have put her in.

She didn't like that this was her last week at Pearlbelle Park. Not that she liked Pearlbelle Park, but it was at least a stable place to stay which she knew about. She didn't know anything about McCale House—nothing at all—and it was cruel to send her there.

Ivy didn't want to feel sorry for herself, not really. She wanted to focus on the positive—it being her birthday and her mummy being downstairs and Alice being happy.

That was what one ought to do, but it was so dreadfully hard when her dress kept itching her. How did anyone concentrate when their clothes were uncomfortable?

Uncle Charlie leaned over and gently tapped her shoulder. "Ivy, are you glad you've turned twelve? It's strange to have had you around for a dozen years—of course, you're still a little thing, same as always." He smiled.

Of course she was. Unlike Alice, she wasn't sprouting like a tulip in March. Instead, she remained below the surface. Whether she was a late bloomer or simply never grew, she didn't care. She'd rather always be a child—that would mean she could be her mummy's baby forever, which would be the ideal situation.

"Do you think you'll get what you want for your birthday?" He took a sip of his cream-swirled coffee. "I got you a picture book, which I bought in London last time I was there. It's charming—I think you'll like it."

"Charlie!" Miss Elton's voice cut into their private conversation from Uncle Charlie's other side, causing Ivy to jerk in shock. "Now it's not a surprise for the poor thing!"

Uncle Charlie chuckled. Actually chuckled! Ivy would've commented on it if she weren't too surprised to speak. Then he turned to Miss Elton and began talking to her, all playful and silly, defending himself and going on and on about how keeping gifts a surprise until they were unwrapped simply wasn't something he ever intended to do.

Once again, Ivy was alone.

Everyone was busy, everyone was happy, and everyone was having a good time. It was no wonder they intended to send Ivy away to Scotland—she wasn't a part of this family, this life. The conversations around her weren't meant to involve her. Was she even meant to be here?

She knew that God loved her. He must. He was God. But that didn't change the fact that Ivy felt out of place, unwanted, unneeded. No matter what the truth was, no one was acting like Ivy was a valued member of the family.

Or if they were, they were quick to move on to other, better things.

It occurred to her that perhaps this was how everyone felt, but she didn't think it was. They weren't sitting in silence, picking at their food and struggling with tears. She wanted to be like them.

"Ivy?" It was her grandmother. "Have you thought about what you'd like to bring to McCale House? Now, you can't bring all your dolls, but you can bring one or two. What of dresses? Have you favorite dresses?"

Favorite dresses? Ivy blinked in disdain. Who had favorite dresses? Certainly not anyone with any common sense in their mind. However, it was possible that Ivy's grandmother wasn't in possession of a great deal of common sense, so that was understandable. "I don't need any."

"You need *some* dresses. I wonder if—" Grandmother sighed and turned to Mummy. It was clear that Ivy had been dismissed. "Claire, are you intending to do some shopping for Ivy? Clothes and such?"

"I believe she has all she needs," Mummy said.

Thank goodness—shopping could be dreadfully horrible, especially when fittings were involved. Ivy did so hate fittings.

"Besides, there's hardly time—she leaves next week." There was a tone of quiet sadness to Mummy's voice, and Ivy's ears perked. Perhaps everyone wasn't so happy to send her away as she'd thought—perhaps her mummy did still love her.

But she had an idea that the sadness wouldn't change the decision. Mummy seemed so resolute—she had from the moment she'd told Ivy, when the pleading had begun. Ivy still couldn't understand the desire to send her away. McCale House couldn't help her. Nothing away from Mummy and Alice and Nettie could help her.

She also couldn't understand why Mummy or Alice or Nettie couldn't come, but Mummy kept insisting that it was impossible, and at last Ivy had given up.

Whether she liked it or not, she was going to McCale House, this strange boarding school in Scotland, with her grandmother and Uncle Charlie. Nothing could be done about it.

At least she had comfort in knowing that, if she died, they would all be sorry. Or she hoped they would.

CHAPTER TEN

Early January 1874
Edinburgh, Scotland

THE TRAIN JERKED TO a stop. Ivy blinked awake and flickered her eyes around the private carriage, from her grandmother tucking her knitting in her bag to Uncle Charlie who also looked like he'd just woken up.

Ivy yawned and arched her back, but that didn't eliminate the remaining sleepiness. The trip had been far too long and far too Mummy-less to not cause exhaustion. "Where are we?"

"We're in Edinburgh Waverley Station. Charlie, do put on your jacket before we step outside."

Uncle Charlie glared and snatched up his folded coat from the seat beside him. "I'm not a boy, Mother."

"Smooth down your hair, too," Grandmother said. "Ivy, come here and let me straighten your bow ..."

Ivy sighed. Grandmother was nothing if not fussy. Of course, Mummy was fussier, but somehow that was different.

She peeked out the window as Uncle Charlie hopped out and reached back to take Grandmother's bag and help her down. There were people filling the station, running here and there, talking, bustling, *existing*.

Nothing was worse than large crowds of people existing.

"Ivy, come here."

Ivy turned to find Uncle Charlie standing with his arms outreached as if he would like to pull her into the fray. She shook her head—the train car was much safer in the long run than the depot ever would be.

But Uncle Charlie's face grew firm, looking more like Mummy than he ever had before, and Ivy was obliged to submit.

As soon as her feet were on the ground, her knees wobbled. Grandmother grabbed her shoulders and kept her up, but Ivy wanted to collapse. Perhaps if she collapsed, they would put her back in the train and send the train home to Mummy, and then she could have a hug and a kiss and be with the people she loved.

That didn't happen. Instead, they walked over to a bench through the throng of bustling humanity and sat down.

"I'll be back in a moment," said Uncle Charlie. "The McCales should have sent a carriage, so I'll see to our luggage and find out if it's already here."

Ivy's eyes opened and shut rapidly. He was leaving them? Why? Didn't he know that big, strong uncles or mummys or Netties or Alices were the only secure things in this world? He was the last one left. How could he leave?

Yet off he walked through the maelstrom. Ivy would have strangled him if she weren't so busy trembling.

"Oh, Ivy." Grandmother's arms came around her, slightly plump and smelling of lavender.

The additional scent and pressure was too much. Didn't Grandmother understand the way Ivy's heart was racing, her vision narrowing, her stomach clenching?

People pressed in on her, and Ivy cried out and dropped her head in her hands.

"Ivy!" Grandmother leaned back. "What is it, dear?"

Ivy wasn't Grandmother's *dear*, though. Being someone's *dear* implied knowing and loving—and Grandmother might think she loved Ivy, but she didn't understand her. She didn't know how hard it was to sit in the middle of a station, to have every sense overloaded, and then to be required to experience an unwelcome hug.

No, Grandmother didn't understand. No one understood. Not even Uncle Charlie, the cad, the bounder, the abandoner of little girls.

"Ivy?" Uncle Charlie's rumbly voice broke through her thoughts. "Ivy, do sit up. Here, Mother—I'll take her. There's a carriage waiting for us."

Then Ivy was lifted as if she weighed nothing more than a doll, and she found her face pressing into the rough wool of her uncle's shoulder. It wasn't comforting, but at least someone was moving her away from the crowd and the smells and the sounds and the eyes, all the eyes looking at her like some freak at a circus.

"Isn't she rather heavy for you, Charlie?"

"She's just a little thing." The grunt in his tone indicated that Ivy was a bit heavy, but she was past caring. They'd brought her here; now they must bring her out.

At last she was tucked into a big carriage. The windows were closed, and the area was dark, quiet, and peaceful. The only smells were Uncle Charlie's and Grandmother's, neither of which were abrasive in and of themselves. She was used to the combination, at least.

"Now, Ivy, you've got to tell me what you're feeling." Uncle Charlie folded his arms. "How are we ever going to help you—how can Dr. McCale help you—if you won't let us know?"

How could Ivy tell them things if she didn't know them herself? Besides, she didn't want this Dr. McCale to help her. She didn't approve of the trip itself, or of why they were doing it. Nor did she think she could learn anything without Mummy and Nettie.

Still, she was helpless to resist. They would have their way with her.

"What of our luggage?" Grandmother asked.

"Coming after us." Uncle Charlie knocked on the ceiling, and the carriage started rolling forward. "It's only an hour or so more until we'll be there, so we can have tea after we arrive."

Ivy slumped back against the seat. Perhaps she could sleep until then. Hours always seemed to last longer than adults understood. They stretched on eternally. Somehow, though, her eyes refused to stay closed.

"Do you think he'll begin right away with"—Grandmother glanced at Ivy, her already wrinkled brow furrowing further—"whatever it is he's going to begin with?"

"I believe so." Uncle Charlie pulled a small book out of nowhere and flipped it open. "His letters to Claire sounded positive. I don't doubt he at least believes he can help Ivy, and he seemed enthusiastic about it."

"Yes, well ..." Grandmother played with the hem of her sleeves, distracting Ivy immensely. "He did seem excited to have her. Something about her being an easy patient—imagine that."

"Perhaps she is." Uncle Charlie made a big show of flipping the next page of his book. "I believe this book may be one I never finish. Lois gave it to me—some novel about an unfaithful fiancée. Does she know how little I care?"

"You would if it were your fiancée." Grandmother pursed her lips together. "Speaking of which, when will she be your fiancée?"

Uncle Charlie grunted. "Perhaps when her reading tastes improve. Trollope, indeed. What a ridiculous name for an author. Also, the title character's name is Alice, which is disturbing. If Alice grows up and decides not to marry her fiancé, I won't forgive her unless she leaves me out of it."

"Oh, Charlie. I think you love Alice." Grandmother withdrew her knitting, a signal to Ivy that nothing interesting would happen again for some time. "I think you love all your family."

"Love and the ability to bear someone are two different things." Uncle Charlie did set his book down for a minute. "Perhaps that speaks more to why we're not engaged. I know you want someone to talk to, and more grandchildren, and all those *lovely* things, but I want to be able to read whatever book I am reading, no matter how boring, in peace."

Grandmother's lips twitched. "You and Lois get along well. Any marriage can pose its difficulties—"

"Exactly. Any marriage, any relationship, can pose its difficulties. You just have to choose which ones you are willing to suffer through for love."

Again he picked up his book, this time with an air of finality. "I haven't determined my mind on this matter, and I'd appreciate having time to figure it out. Given that Miss Elton remains unmarried and is now thirty, I believe I can take my time."

"You never know. I wouldn't want you to wait too long and—"

"Mother." Uncle Charlie again had a firm note to his voice. "I'll manage."

"Very well." Grandmother's eyes flickered down to her knitting. "Just don't wait too long, or you'll be giving Starboard Hall to a random cousin when you're gone."

"You'll be dead; why do you care?" Uncle Charlie mumbled.

Grandmother didn't reply, and the silence that followed allowed Ivy to slip into a dreamy land that wasn't far from sleep but wasn't close enough to be called it exactly.

It was the carriage stopping which once again woke her.

"We're outside the gates!" Grandmother's voice was peppy as she tucked away her knitting once more. "How exciting. Look! We're on a bridge, Ivy."

Ivy hesitated. Was she afraid of bridges? She didn't think so. Peering out the window, she confirmed the fact—bridges were not among her fears. In fact, she found this one rather nice—it was a wide stone bridge that had space for two or three carriages to rest on simultaneously.

"There's just a little brook running down below us, I think." Grandmother pressed against the other window. "And look up ahead—hmm, that feels ominous."

The sky was dark and rainy, which made everything ominous, but Ivy didn't say so. She supposed what Grandmother meant was the iron gates, tangled with the snow-speckled plant she was named after. The mansion was visible just behind them, a boring gray-brown structure not as big as Pearlbelle Park, but still larger than most of the houses in London.

Stretching to the right and the left was a tall, brick wall covered with more snow-laden ivy. The iron gates swung open and admitted them into the interior, where they were greeted by a large, snowy expanse to the sides spotted liberally with trees, mostly oaks, magnificent even in their leafless state. The great house loomed up as soon as they entered. Ivy popped her head back in the carriage and wrapped her arms around herself.

This strange place was where she was staying?

At least there was some countryside around it, even if it was all walled in by that scary brick barrier. That meant Ivy could be outside when it was warmer, didn't it? This wasn't like those places where orphans got locked away, was it?

She hoped not.

Uncle Charlie got out first and then Grandmother and then Ivy. She clung to her uncle's hand, her only remaining link back to Mummy and Alice and all the things she loved about them.

How long would they keep her here? She wanted to go home.

But it was best to keep a stiff upper lip for now, so she pressed those stiff lips together and followed Uncle Charlie to the door.

The inside, into which they were led by a maid who couldn't be more than a few years older than Ivy, wasn't much better than the drab exterior. They were ushered into an old-fashioned, colorless parlor. Ivy sat down on Uncle Charlie's lap, absolutely refusing to be parted from him for a moment.

Moments later, a small, middle-aged man with a graying dark beard entered the room, and Uncle Charlie forced Ivy to rise.

Behind the effusion of hair on the man's face, his smile was unmistakably bright and cheerful. He introduced himself to Grandmother and Uncle Charlie in a deep voice with a slight Scottish brogue, then knelt about three feet in front of Ivy and looked her in the eyes.

"Hello, Ivy. I'm Dr. McCale. How are you today?" His voice was like a clock—regular—and Ivy liked it.

"Fine," said Ivy. It might be a lie, but she wouldn't tell him that. She'd determined not to like Dr. McCale, after all. Even if he had a clock voice.

"That's nice. Now, we're going to move your things upstairs to your room. It's a pleasant room. I think you'll be comfortable. Would you like to see it?"

Ivy nodded.

"Then we'll go now." He stood up and directed his attention toward Grandmother and Uncle Charlie. "Your luggage will be brought up as soon as it arrives. I asked Lila to prepare a guest room for Mr. Chattoway, assuming he'd be staying the night. Would you care to settle in? Mr. Chattoway, I mean. I want Mrs. Chattoway to stay with Ivy while she acclimates. A familiar face and whatnot. It would have been better to have her mother here, but I heard that wasn't possible. I hope she's recovering?"

Now his words were fast, like a rushing stream. Ivy didn't like that one bit. See? She could dislike him.

"As much as can be expected," said Grandmother.

What did that mean? But Ivy didn't have time to think about it. Dr. McCale was speaking again.

"Good. Now, if you'll come with me—" His voice was interrupted by a shrill shriek, unearthly and chilling. It took Ivy a moment to realize the cry was human, so wild was its nature, but she couldn't think of an animal who made a noise like that. She shivered and clung to Uncle Charlie again.

"Violet," the doctor muttered. "Excuse me. I must attend to something." He turned and walked quickly out of the room.

"What on earth?" Grandmother whispered.

"Let's sit down. He'll be back."

Again, Ivy found her way onto Uncle Charlie's lap. Hopefully the screams would stop soon. She covered her ears, leaned against his chest, and waited.

The shrieks continued for about five minutes, but gradually decreased in volume until they stopped.

Soon Dr. McCale reappeared.

"I'm sorry about that, but there's not much to do about Violet at times. Now, where were we?"

Uncle Charlie cleared his throat and encouraged Ivy to stand. "You were about to show us to our rooms."

"Ah, yes. Come with me, then." He ushered them out of the room and up the stairs, which rose from the foyer.

"I put Ivy in a room that adjoins yours, Mrs. Chattoway. I hope you don't mind."

"Not at all."

Ivy did mind, since this probably meant Grandmother would be bothering her all the time, but then, it would seem that everyone was determined
to bother her.

They turned down a long, dim hallway that felt far chillier than Ivy
was comfortable with. However, Dr. McCale didn't hesitate to walk down
it, and Uncle Charlie followed close behind. "Mr. Chattoway, the room
across the hall is ready for you tonight unless you intend to leave sooner."

"I'd like to see them settled in." Uncle Charlie squeezed Ivy's hand.
"Then I'll leave, as long as it's not inconvenient."

"Very well. I hoped you'd stay for a day or so. I need as much information
as I can get." Dr. McCale opened a door and gestured inside. "I'll probably
question both of you this evening, and if one forgets a detail, hopefully the
other will remember."

Grandmother blinked, seeming unsure. "Oh."

Ivy glanced around her new chambers. They were smaller than what she
had become accustomed to at Pearlbelle Park but bigger than the room she
had occupied in London.

Her bedroom featured a large bed, a wardrobe, a chest of drawers, a
dresser table with a mirror, and a small table. The two windows—one
on either side of the bed—were surrounded by thick green curtains. The
furniture and the floor were of mahogany and the wallpaper and bedspread
were dark green. Despite the windows, the heavy drapes kept most of the
light out.

"Rather dark, isn't it?" Grandmother asked.

"Not with the windows open and a fire lit. But it should be restful for
Ivy, even as sitting outside in a garden could be overwhelming some days.
Perhaps. We'll see." Dr. McCale glanced at Ivy. "Anyway, it's green. Emma
likes this room."

"Mm-hmm." Uncle Charlie glanced around, then jerked his head in a
quick nod. "This will do. I'll go tend to the luggage." He withdrew his
hand from Ivy's and turned to the door.

"Uncle Charlie—" Ivy gasped. Didn't he know he'd have to leave soon enough? She needed every moment of him now.

He didn't turn back, and Ivy was forced to cuddle against Grandmother for comfort.

Grandmother placed a hand on Ivy's shoulder to draw her close and sighed. "Excuse my son's exits, Dr. McCale. He's never in his life properly acknowledged another human being—and he's only gotten worse as he's matured."

A smile bloomed under the beard again. "That's a'right. Neither have I. I'll take you to meet Emma, and you'll see that we're not all heathens here. Though, you mustn't let her convince you that I am one."

"I see. Emma is your wife?"

"Aye. She meant to welcome you herself, but we've been having trouble with the student I mentioned earlier."

Before Grandmother could reply, a short, roundish woman entered the room. "I'm sorry—that took longer than I expected, but I have her settled with Miss Lang now. She'll not be down for supper."

"Mrs. Chattoway, this is my wife, Emma McCale." Dr. McCale held his hand out to his wife. "Emma, Mrs. Chattoway and her granddaughter, Miss Ivy Knight."

"Lovely to meet you."

The adults exchanged greetings, and Ivy walked to the window to look out. The world was dimming as the sun set, and the grounds offered more shadows than shapes. In the distance, the same ivy-covered stone wall rose, surrounding the property.

Did that make it safe ... or a prison? Ivy wished she knew.

CHAPTER ELEVEN

NORA GLANCED FROM SIDE to side, taking in the people around the table. She would do her best to keep track of everyone, but in truth, she doubted she'd remember more than a few of them.

Dr. Callum and Mrs. Emma McCale would be easy, of course—but she might struggle to remember the name of Dr. Lester Goodington, the second doctor at McCale House, a man in his mid-thirties. Even with his distinctive Welsh accent, he simply didn't speak enough to be ingrained into her brain. He smiled occasionally at the talk about the table but rarely participated.

Mr. Sampson, who sat next to him, was the youngest adult at the table, perhaps in his early twenties. His baby face and big blue eyes were remarkable, and he seemed so energetic and cheerful.

Mr. and Mrs. Davenport, on the other hand, were a bland couple. These two teachers, both middle-aged with square faces and brown hair, seemed to almost resemble each other despite being husband and wife.

The students were easier, in Nora's opinion. She felt she would remember them, even if she would not have the courage to speak to them. Something she said might risk all of Dr. McCale's hard work. Yet the children *were* distinctive.

The oldest currently present was perhaps fifteen or sixteen years old—Felix Merrill. He sat staring at his plate and occasionally raising a finger to adjust a fork. She'd not seen him take a bite, and Dr. McCale hadn't spoken to him. Felix wore big, round spectacles and continually nibbled at his bottom lip. His hands were restless, twisting in his lap, then moving up to adjust his glasses, then rubbing at his forearm.

Leonard Barton, a slight boy with a big grin, was more talkative. He chattered with Dr. McCale about this and that, telling him how he couldn't wait until it got warmer and they could have a picnic. There was a hint of Yorkshire in his tone, but not enough for Nora to identify the town he came from or say what class his family must be.

Minnie Kimber was one of the two female students present other than Ivy. She was plump and cheerful, occasionally talking to Leonard or adding thoughts to his. She, too, seemed a delightful child, and Nora wondered why she'd ended up at McCale House in the first place. Surely she was normal!

Jesse Andrews had slightly shaggy brown hair and seemed to be an adjusted child. Yes, he had a stutter, and he didn't speak much—there must be more to him than met the eye.

The other girl, Ella Willis, was obviously different—she fidgeted constantly in her seat, made a mess with her food, which Mrs. Davenport, who sat to her left, was constantly trying to prevent, and glared at anyone who looked at her.

These were all someone's children. Someone had brought them into the world, then not wanted to keep them. But she must not understand the extent of the issues, and she wasn't one to question why Dr. McCale accepted certain students.

"Of course we've also Miss Lang, another teacher, but you'll meet her later. She's busy tonight." Dr. McCale looked down the table at each of his students and fellow teachers. "I also don't know where—"

As if on cue, the door to the room slammed open, knocking against the wall. Nora saw Dr. McCale's eyes slowly closing and opening as she turned her head to catch a glimpse of the new arrival.

He was a young man of perhaps sixteen or seventeen with wind-tossed copper-brown hair and a smattering of freckles over his nose. His wide face and broad shoulders gave the impression of a sweet country boy, but she could easily see he was the kind to have a streak of mischief in him. It was in both his posture and his grin.

"I'm sorry, Dr. McCale. I just got tae talkin' with Rabbie in th' gardens, an' neither o' us ken't th' time." His thick brogue was evidenced in every word he spoke.

Dr. McCale's scowl covered his whole face. Nora didn't see so much as a sparkle in his eye; although she was amused, she imagined she might not be if she weren't the guest in the situation. "Mrs. Chattoway, Miss Ivy, Mr. Chattoway, this is Mr. George McAllen, my tardiest employee."

The lad cleared his throat. "Jordy tae me friends."

Dr. McAllen crossed his arms over his chest. "Never mind what your friends call you. When I'm finished with you, you'll never have any again. Take your seat; we'll talk about this later."

Jordy McAllen crossed the room and slid onto his chair. "He's no' really such a grouch." His stage whisper was directed toward Ivy. "Though, sometimes it's hard tae tell."

Ivy blinked as if entirely unsure what to think of this new arrival. Nora was unsure, too.

Dr. McAllen settled back into his breakfast with a final huff. "I've had Jordy here for these last few years. He wants to be a doctor, but heaven knows he hasn't the attention span for it. But he helps me with the children, and really, he is a bright lad beneath all his stubbornness."

"Ah, I see." Nora smiled. "It is lovely to meet you—Jor ...?"

"Jordy. Like if yer wee sister canna pronounce 'George,' which is what happened." His words rolled out, cheerful and unstoppable. It was clear he relished the extra attention brought on by his late arrival, though Nora doubted it was purposeful. "But it stuck. Makes ye wonder how they ever got Dick from Richard. Do ye ken, Dr. McCale, how they—"

"That's enough, Jordy."

Ivy leaned back against the pillow and crossed her arms over her chest. No one ever would tuck her in like Mummy or Nettie, and Grandmother didn't understand. She never would. That was all there was to it.

"Let's pray." Grandmother took a deep breath, and Ivy almost thought she was nervous.

Ivy bowed her head and closed her eyes.

"Dear Lord." Grandmother's whisper was timid, unlike Nettie's boldness and Mummy's firmness. "Thank You for bringing us safely to McCale House, and thank You for offering this opportunity for us. You clearly have a plan for Ivy's life, and I can't wait to see what You do with her."

Do with her? Ivy wiggled from side to side underneath the covers. Ivy didn't want God to do anything with her—just to keep her safe with her family. Of course, God knew best, but He couldn't want more from her than that, could He?

He loved her. Surely He wanted her to be happy. So why was she here in Scotland without Mummy?

"Please keep our family safe at home—Ivy's Mummy especially—and let us not miss them too much. Give us the courage to live without them."

Ivy sighed. She knew that Grandmother meant Ivy when she said "us." It was embarrassing. Did she think Ivy was an actual idiot, or did she just think all children were idiots? Alice would know the answer, but she wasn't here, so Ivy could only guess.

"May Ivy have a deep and restful sleep. In Jesus' name I pray. Amen."

Ivy opened her eyes and squinted at Grandmother. "I have to go to bed now?"

Grandmother raised her eyebrows. Ivy supposed she might be a little surprised—usually she wasn't fussy about sleep like Alice. After all, sleep was inevitable, and there was something nice about snuggling and knowing for sure that the day was done.

Yet now she didn't want to sleep. It was such a strange place, and as soon as she settled in, Grandmother was sure to leave. Even Grandmother was better than no one. Ivy didn't like being alone while she slept. She never failed to miss the sound of Alice's breathing; the silence filled itself with discords.

If Mummy were here, Ivy could sleep with her, but that wasn't the case. Besides, Mummy had been dreadfully selfish about letting Ivy wander into her room at night lately. Perhaps because she thought Ivy was getting old, but it was more likely that she just wanted to cuddle with Mr. Knight instead of Ivy.

"Why, Ivy, it's time for bed." Grandmother raised her eyebrows. "You need rest. It's been a long day."

It promised to be an even longer night. Ivy wiggled her body from side to side like a little inchworm. How could she explain it? "I don't like being here."

Grandmother looked frustrated with her chest all puffed out and her jaw all tight. "I know; you've said so many times. But that doesn't change the fact that you are here, and it's for your own good."

How could this be good? Yet Ivy didn't know any argument for something being "for her own good."

"Your mother knows what's best for you—I know you trust her. She chose this place for you ... She knew it would help you." Grandmother's posture relaxed as she leaned back, folding her hands neatly on her lap. "Because she loves you, she wants you to be the best Ivy you can be."

She already was the best Ivy she could be, but of course she wouldn't say that. It might make Grandmother angry—it sounded like one of those "impertinent remarks" that Alice made, whatever that meant. "If Mummy loves me, why would she send me away?"

She hated to admit the doubt that had been coloring her thoughts of late, but it was present, teasing at the back of her mind no matter how she tried to ignore it.

"Because love sometimes means doing what *is* right, not what *seems* right." Grandmother stood. "I have to meet with Dr. McCale before bed, but I'll be sure to check on you later."

Ivy snuggled her way down deeper under the covers—without Alice, her last defense between whatever it was that lurked in the dark. "You could leave the lamp on."

"Yes, I could—and there's a fire in the grate." Grandmother clucked her tongue. "Don't you fuss."

How ridiculous—she never fussed. But she nodded anyway. "I'll try not to."

Grandmother left, and Ivy was left alone with her thoughts.

Chapter Twelve

"**S**o you're telling me that until recently she had no father in her life?" Dr. McCale demanded as if he'd been cheated out of part of his family instead of Ivy.

"Yes." Charlie's voice was steady and regimented, as always. "As I've said before, a simple case of miscommunication that momentarily wrecked lives."

"Hmm. And the mother ... was she present?"

Charlie seemed almost offended on Claire's behalf, and the lamp on Dr. McCale's desk cast strange shadows on his face. "Yes, of course."

"I know she was there, but was she loving, caring? Did she spend time with Ivy?"

"I'd say she spent more time with Ivy than most mothers do," Nora said, picking at the arm of her chair. "Or at least she made the time she had count more than most mothers do."

"Good, good." Dr. McCale scribbled away at his notes furiously. "Ivy's primary caretaker was this Nettie?"

"Yes. She was." Nora smiled. "Nettie is a wonderful woman."

"You didn't tell me much about her except that she was Mrs. Knight's maid."

"Nettie is perfect." There was no other way to describe her. Nora had always admired the woman. "She loves Ivy as much as Claire does, but she

... oh, I don't know. I suppose she never needed Ivy as much as Claire did. Or perhaps she just didn't seem to because she had Ivy all the time." How else could Nora explain it? A family dynamic was too complicated to be summed up in a few words.

"And Nettie's background is ...?"

"Just a servant," Charlie said. "She worked at Starboard Hall from the time she was perhaps ten or eleven. An industrious girl—I'd always said she'd go far. And then at school, Claire took pains to make sure she was educated, and that wasn't hard as Nettie is wonderfully intelligent." The compliments slid easily off his lips. At least they could all agree on one thing—Nettie was a stronghold in their life.

"Mm. I think I understand fairly well now." Dr. McCale leaned back on his chair, causing it to squeak slightly. "To be honest, the child has had a rather twisted life."

Nora felt herself tearing up. It couldn't be that that had made Ivy simple, could it? "Is that why ...?"

He blinked. "What? No, not at all. I believe Ivy was born the way she is."

Oh. That was both a good thing and a bad thing. "So there's no cure?"

Dr. McCale frowned and gave her an annoyed look. "I'm never sure how to answer that question. Technically, there is no way to change—to 'cure'—Ivy. She simply needs to be taught in a different way. She needs to be taught to be Ivy." Dr. McCale stood, his chair scraping across the hardwood floor. "It's dreadfully late, and I've always thought it best to get to bed early. I'll let you go now. I know all I need to—at least for now, which is why I'm glad Mrs. Chattoway will be staying with us."

Mrs. McCale also stood from her seat in the corner, speaking for the first time. "We're so glad to have Ivy here. She seems to be a dear lass, if confused at the moment. These are big changes for so small a child, and I'm sure she'll adjust."

"I'm sure she will," Charlie replied with steady confidence. He helped Nora to her feet. "She's a bright girl, really, and no one who knows her can help but love her."

Why, her boy was brimming with compliments today. Could it be he was starting to develop a heart? Nora smiled up at him, but he avoided eye contact. Of course. Never one to admit he had a tender side.

Charlie gave her a look that caused her to stop smiling and pretend to be greatly serious and unaffected. She was used to that. She'd spent her entire adult life pretending to be unaffected by things that broke her heart or built it, and she could keep it up—if that was what her loved ones wanted.

A scream jolted Ivy awake, and she sat up in bed, panting softly. Her eyes flickered around, but she could only see pitch-black darkness. Confusion flooded her—this didn't feel or smell or sound like her bedroom at home.

She wasn't home. No one she loved, absolutely no one she could count on, was here.

Another scream in the distance, and Ivy opened her own mouth to shriek in panic.

She fell back amongst the covers, but the sheets tangled around her legs, causing her to jerk and kick and cry out. What could she do? How could she get away? What was happening?

Ivy wiggled and cried. A thin line of light turned on, and then the door opened, causing a great deal of light to stream into the room. Whimpering, she covered her face with her hands against the sudden brightness, feeling the damp heat of her tears under her palms.

"Ivy!"

Yet that was not the voice she wanted to be calling her name. She wanted her Mummy. She wanted her Nettie. She wanted her Alice. Preferably in that order. And she wouldn't settle for less—no, she could not, would not.

Another scream in the distance.

Ivy dropped her hands to see Grandmother's reaction—it couldn't just be her hearing it, could it?

"What on earth?" Grandmother paused in the middle of the room, eyes flickering to the hall door. "Whatever could that be?"

Oh no. Not only could other people hear it—meaning it was a real threat—but adults didn't know what it was! Panic swirled, and Ivy felt her breaths getting shorter and quicker.

Black edged her vision.

"Ivy, Ivy! It's all right. It's nothing, I'm sure." Grandmother made her way to the bedside and placed a hand on her shoulder, but Ivy jerked back from the touch. As if Grandmother could comfort her! She didn't know a thing about Ivy. She hadn't raised Ivy or loved Ivy or comforted Ivy. What did she think she was doing? She'd only make it worse.

Like Mr. Parker. Mr. Parker always made it worse. And Mr. Knight. All the misters she knew. Probably all these new misters here, too.

Of course, Dr. McCale was a doctor, not a mister, but Ivy had never loved doctors either. There were too much poking and too many questions involved.

Grandmother tried to pull Ivy close again, but this time Ivy kicked and flailed. Thankfully, the woman had the good sense to pull back, or Ivy might've bitten her—she wasn't sure. It hadn't come up before.

She rolled onto her side, pulled her knees up to her chest, and then the tears really began. Great big, hot tears that streamed down her cheeks and wet the pillow. Grandmother tried, but Ivy stopped paying attention to her.

Then there was a man's voice and another man's voice and other voices, and they went in and out of the room and tried to talk to Ivy.

But Ivy didn't want them. She wanted her Mummy. Sadly, she couldn't tell them that and cry at the same time, so they wouldn't leave her alone.

Why couldn't they leave her alone?

At least the screams had stopped. Sometime during the maelstrom, they'd ceased, leaving Ivy alone with the sound of her own crying and the quiet, misunderstanding condolences of those around her.

People she didn't know. People who couldn't help.

They never could help, no matter what they said, no matter how they patted her shoulder or rubbed her back. They weren't Mummy.

At last the cries turned to hiccups, which allowed her to slip into a doze, and the voices drained away, and Ivy was left alone with only a sad, thin melody to keep her company.

Grandmother did up the last of Ivy's buttons and leaned back. "There. All ready for breakfast."

Still blinking and winking her sleepy eyes, Ivy nodded. She wasn't hungry, and she felt more like climbing back into bed than anything, so she didn't feel like further conversation.

She wasn't sure what had happened last night. She knew she'd had some nightmares, and she vaguely remembered a few of them. Something about a screaming girl—though perhaps those had been her own screams. She wasn't sure.

Grandmother had been worried this morning. She'd fussed, clucked, and been far too kind. Ivy loved kindness, but she wasn't quite ready for a hundred hugs from her grandmother yet.

"I hope we're not keeping anyone waiting! They eat earlier here, it would seem." Grandmother turned Ivy toward the door as if she were a doll with no capability of movement on her own. "Off we go!"

McCale House seemed more cheerful to Ivy this morning. The halls were flooded with sunlight from the windows, which were high up in this particular hallway, coming about eye level to Grandmother, which was something Ivy had never seen before. Nevertheless, despite their odd proportions, they added enough brightness to make it happier, and it allowed her chest to cease the endless painful clenching and relax.

She breathed easier as she entered the dining room, too. It was her second meal here, and she knew she could probably sit still, be quiet, and not be bothered by anyone, while all the adults and other, more energetic children droned on around her.

Greetings were issued, and Ivy let them flow around her, acknowledging good mornings with a slight dip of her head. She hoped that was the right response—she wanted to slip deep into her mind as soon as possible.

"Miss Ivy?"

She blinked. Was that her name? All the syllables were wrong, if so. She jerked her head up from her plate and met honey-gold eyes across the table.

"'Tis Ivy, 'tisn't it?" The boy cocked his head to the side. He was a big boy, who ought to know better than to say words all wrong. Probably older than Alice's Kirk, in fact.

But Ivy liked Kirk. She'd have to decide about this boy.

"Ivy," she said, her tone coming out somewhat reproving.

"Right. Ivy." He still pronounced it wrong—"ay-vee," spending far too long on the "ay" part.

"No. Ay-vee would be with an 'a' like ..." She couldn't think of a name, as Alice started with a different "a" sound.

"Angus?" the boy suggested.

"Yes. Like Angus." Though she wasn't sure that was a name, it sounded like it could be one. "Ivy is *I-vee* as in ..." Again her thoughts failed her. Perhaps she ought to read more.

"Inconsequential." A slow grin as if he was proud of that. "So it's *ih-vee* then?"

Ivy didn't even know what to say to that. She cast her eyes helplessly toward her grandmother—perhaps this boy was right.

"Jordy, leave the child alone." Dr. McCale's deep voice caused Ivy's head to jerk. "And do try to say her name properly."

Jordy leaned back on his seat. "Ach, I didna mean it. Really, Ivy's a lovely name—much better than Edith. Tha's me sister. We call her Edi."

Ivy winced. She was certainly glad that wasn't her name. "That's not good."

"Ivy!" This time it was Grandmother doing the scolding. "That's not a kind thing to say about his sister!"

"Ach, Edi wouldna mind. She doesna like her name, either." Jordy shrugged. "She's a good lass."

Ivy didn't think one's name had a thing to do with how good one was, so she just shrugged.

"An' where are ye from, Miss Ivy? Have ye any siblings?"

"Yes—Alice is my twin. She's at home—well, I suppose she's at school now." Alice attended a private boarding school somewhere to the north—or was it the south now?

"And remember little Ned!" Grandmother said cheerfully.

Ivy sighed. It wasn't as if Ned were really her brother—he was too new for that. One had brothers from the time they were born, and she hadn't had Ned that long, nor did she intend to be a sister to him now. Alice was her sister, and there was only Alice, and that was always the way it had been. Yet Ivy didn't know how to say this without sounding cross—she wasn't cross. Just greatly confused.

"What's Alice like?" Jordy took a big bite of his poached egg, then proceeded to speak around it. "Must be fun tae have a twin."

"Jordy, remember your manners," Mrs. McCale said. Her voice had the dragging adult quality that indicated she'd said it many times. Poor Jordy. Ivy couldn't remember her manners, either, sometimes.

"Alice is wonderful." There wasn't any other way to describe her. "She loves me most of all, you know. We're not alike, but that doesn't matter." At least not much. Ivy wanted to be as good and talented and special as Alice, or at least as beautiful, but that might never be.

"She sounds nice." Jordy glanced sideways at Dr. McCale as if seeking some kind of confirmation.

Dr. McCale nodded.

What did that mean?

Before Ivy could think about it too much, Jordy turned back to her. "What do ye like tae do, Miss Ivy?"

He wasn't pronouncing her name right again, but Ivy had other problems. Like thinking about what she liked to do. "I don't know."

"What do ye do when ye've a day tae yerself?" Jordy leaned forward, like he was really interested, and Ivy's stomach began squirming. How awful to not have anything to tell him.

She shrugged and took a big bite of her breakfast. He didn't ask again, and the conversation moved around the table, Jordy engaging different people.

Ivy spent the rest of breakfast quietly eating and ignoring the hectic buzzing of strangers' voices around her.

CHAPTER THIRTEEN

N ORA PLACED FIRM HANDS on her granddaughter's shoulders as they made their way to Dr. McCale's office. Without her hands, she wasn't sure Ivy wouldn't bolt. She'd disappeared into herself after Jordy McAllen stopped talking, and as of yet, her eyes hadn't recovered from that glazed look.

Poor child. After a restless night, she was still adjusting to this new environment. If only Nora knew more about how to help her! She was starting to realize that there was more to Ivy than she'd bargained for—and that revelation was both helpful and challenging.

They entered the office, and this time Dr. McCale gestured to a set of chairs and sofas positioned near the fireplace. Nora took a seat with Ivy next to her, and Mrs. McCale found one near to them.

Nora would have to get to know the woman—she was quiet and prim, but when she did speak, it was purposeful and firm. She clearly knew what she was about. Nora longed for that kind of confidence. Especially since Mrs. McCale was also surrounded by men with strong personalities.

Once Charlie, Dr. McCale, and Jordy McAllen took their seats, Dr. McCale began asking questions. Oddly enough, not of the adults—but of Ivy.

From the first simple question, Ivy squirmed. She obviously hated having to sit up in an unfamiliar room and talk about herself to strangers. Nora again found herself keeping a hold on the child for fear she'd run or burst into tears.

"Do you not like talking?" Dr. McCale cocked his head. "You don't seem to, Miss Ivy."

Ivy stilled for a moment, then nodded. "I don't."

"Why do you think that is?"

The girl's eyes went blank, and Dr. McCale leaned back.

"If you don't know, you don't have to say."

Her eyes cleared. "I don't have anything to say," she whispered, almost too low for Nora to catch it.

"That's perfectly all right." Dr. McCale turned to Jordy. "Write that down."

The boy arched his light eyebrows. "Write down tha' she has nothin' tae say?"

"Jordy." Dr. McCale gave him a firm look, and the boy hunched back over his notepad. "Now, Ivy, could you tell us ..."

Dr. McCale continued to question the girl, but most of the time, Ivy simply didn't want to answer. He let this slide, asking a different question or approaching the same one from a slightly different angle. He didn't press her, though Nora would have in his situation.

Honestly, Nora wondered if there was any stubbornness in Ivy. She had felt that Ivy held back, but perhaps that wasn't true. The child's reactions were not those of a stubborn child but a lost one and a confused one and a frightened one.

Had they been seeing her all wrong? Perhaps she was not unintelligent—just afraid. And Nora couldn't blame her for that—there was so much to be afraid of in this world. Ivy's life had not been an easy or normal one, either.

"That will do for now." Dr. McCale stood and walked to the fireplace, where he knelt and held his hands out. "Ivy, do you know what a loved girl you are?"

Her eyes flickered up, the sudden interest in them taking Nora by surprise.

"Aye, you are. I wish every child who came to McCale House were a fraction as cherished." He nodded toward his desk. "I've a whole host of letters from your mother and from your Nettie talking about your life and your talents and all the wonderful things about you, of which I am told there are many." He tapped his fingers against the mantel. "You may not see it now, Ivy, but it'll make all the difference for you."

Ivy turned her wide blue eyes to Nora and blinked twice, as if it would take a moment of staring at something boring to reorganize her thoughts. As always, those eyes reminded her of her eldest daughter, of the fear of being alone and lost.

Ivy *was* lost. She was alone and afraid. She didn't know her place in the world. Much like so many little girls—much like another little girl Nora hadn't been able to help, hadn't let herself help.

"I'll put together a schedule for you, Miss Ivy, and we'll see what we can do about finding out more about you—the things you don't know. Mr. Chattoway has a train to catch and must be leaving soon, so perhaps while he prepares himself, Jordy could take you and your grandmother on a tour of the house?"

A tour of the house? With this reckless boy? That ought to be fun. Nora was curious to see how things operated, and Jordy seemed the type to be honest—perhaps to a fault. "That would be lovely, wouldn't it, Ivy?"

No enthusiasm reflected in her granddaughter's eyes, but she did manage a little nod.

"Oh, good."

Jordy McAllen looked about as pleased about this as Ivy, but he handed Dr. McCale the notes and gestured toward the door. "Let's be goin', then."

"This hall is full o' bedrooms." Jordy turned to Ivy and her grandmother and made a sweeping motion with his arm like a man presenting an amazing spectacle. "O' course, ye've seen it, but isna it nice? See th' high windows? An' th' many oaken doors? Ah, 'tis a sight o' much renown."

Ivy didn't think it was much of a sight, but if Jordy said so. Yet Ivy wasn't sure she could trust him. Perhaps he was being silly? It was so hard to tell when someone was being silly. Other people seemed better about it, or at least they weren't as confused as Ivy. How did one know?

Grandmother seemed annoyed with Jordy. Perhaps watching other peoples' reactions was the best way to know. She'd try to remember that.

"Tha's really all there is inside th' house. It's no' special."

It wasn't special exactly, but it was neat and there were some interesting rooms. A big one a floor down with a piano and great windows, which Jordy said was often kept closed except when in use—something about windows breaking easily—and classrooms and a big library full of books.

"I didna take ye intae th' kitchen." Jordy continued. "Dr. McCale will keep tha' locked more often than no'. Ye ken, I never thought there were so many dangerous things everywhere until I talked tae him—though I've been here since I was twelve. An' tha's been all o' four years almost. So I've learned a lot."

"What exactly is it that you do here, Jordy?" Grandmother asked.

"Oh, this an' tha'." He shrugged. "Dr. McCale was just travelin' through Lorne—he'd somethin' tae do in th' Highlands; I dinna remember what. We're in Keefmore—an' tha's no' on the coast, so it was a wonder he ended up there. He stayed with me parents, since th' inn was closed for a fire ... We just got tae talkin', an' I said I'd like tae be a doctor, an' he laughed an' said, 'Then let me show ye how.'"

"That was it?"

"Aye, for Dr. McCale. Now, we had tae convince me parents—why, we're all th' way on th' other side o' Scotland! An' I'm their eldest son, tae. But I couldna get much o' an education in Keefmore, so they agreed at last."

Grandmother's posture seemed to soften. "That must have been a sacrifice for them."

Ivy wondered if it was a sacrifice for her mother to send Ivy away. Probably not. But Jordy had been, in a way, sent off. Perhaps she could learn something from him.

She watched his face as he responded—casual and cheerful.

Jordy shrugged. "Aye, I suppose so. They've got a lot o' us—Edi an' Ben an' Mick an' Liam—an' we'll have another wee one this year. Mum said so in her last letter." He hesitated. "O' course, they're younger 'n me. Edi is only fourteen, Ben an' Mick are ten an' almost nine, an' Liam is barely five." He cocked his head. "But Edi is strong, an' she can take care o' things. So they'll be all right."

Grandmother nodded. "They sound like a lovely family. What do they do, Jordy?"

"Raise sheep, mostly. Most everyone in Keefmore raises sheep for th' wool and mutton."

Ivy shuddered. The idea of mutton on her plate was always neatly separated from the idea of mutton in the field, and she simply didn't like the two being combined. Wool was all right, though.

"Anyway, tha's all o' th' house. Outside, we have a nice property, an' if we were tae bundle up, it wouldna be tae cold." Jordy's eyes moved up to the windows. Sunlight streamed through them, and there was obvious eagerness in his tone and posture.

Ivy turned to Grandmother with pleading eyes. She'd love to get out of this house, see it from the outside, in the sunshine, and determine if it was as scary as she thought it was at first glance.

Thankfully, Grandmother nodded. "Let's ask Uncle Charlie to join us."

A grin burst forth. That would be lovely.

Their walk began on a smooth pebble path that circled around the house with little offshoots through neat but bare flowerbeds. Ivy grasped Uncle Charlie's hand, but she still felt oddly at ease with this Jordy boy.

Why did she like him so much? Perhaps it was because he had such a broad smile, such a fun way of talking, and such a relaxed manner.

"It's so much more cheerful in th' spring." Jordy walked backward to face them, almost tripping over every rock and rise in the path. "Ye'll love it then. Do ye like flowers, Miss Ivy?"

Did she like flowers? Did she like biscuits or dolls? What a ridiculous question. "Of course!"

He grinned. "We'll be havin' lots o' those."

"Good." Every garden ought to have many, many flowers. That was the nice thing about Pearlbelle Park in the summer, and the bad thing about living in London.

Perhaps some changes weren't so bad after all. She'd never had flowers when she was little.

From the outside, in the sunshine, McCale House didn't look as bad as it had when they arrived yesterday. Sunshine made everything cheerier. The light brought out the brilliant greens of the grass, the hills in the distance, and it even made the empty flowerbeds and bare trees seem prettier. It sparkled off puddles in the path and made the dewdrops on every patch of moss sparkle like diamonds.

Of course, it also helped that the grounds weren't loud or crowded and that Uncle Charlie's bigness loomed over her. It ought to be scary, but really, it was more like having her own watchdog. Only this watchdog would never bite or bark.

They walked away from the house through the empty wasteland that was January. Yet the sunshine sparkled its way across bits of grass with dew on them and flavored the air with a fresh earth smell.

It wasn't bad; it was *good*. Not overwhelming, but fresh and clean. Ivy felt the stirrings of music in her heart, and she skipped a little with every step, close to laughter but not wanting to seem strange.

Ivy turned around to look at McCale House from the top of a slight rise.

She squinted—it wasn't as tall as Pearlbelle Park's mansion, but it was big.

"How many stories are there, Jordy?" she asked.

He seemed surprised at the question, but he cleared his throat. "Three. Th' ground floor, th' first floor, an' th' second floor."

"We didn't go up to the second floor, did we?" Ivy thought she would've remembered climbing another flight of stairs.

"No, we didna." Jordy hesitated, then continued. "It's mostly closed off, an' we'll go up sometimes on rainy days tae play in th' big rooms. There's a piano, ye ken—a wee one, no' so grand as th' one in th' music room."

"Why didn't we go look?" Ivy liked the idea of a quiet upper floor no one used.

"We've a wee lass up there, a few years older than ye, Ivy." Jordy sighed. "Her name is Violet, an' she's no' all bad—but she's in a bad way. Sometimes she needs special care, an' Dr. McCale has her up there with Miss Lang. None o' us ken what tae do exactly, but her parents dinna want tae take her back."

"Ah. That explains a great deal." Grandmother nodded. "How sad."

Uncle Charlie made a grumbling noise at the back of his throat, which must be an agreement sound.

It was sad. Horribly sad. "You mean she can't come out with the rest of us?" Ivy gave the mansion another long look. The other students weren't quite well, of course, but they weren't that bad off. They could have their lessons in the classrooms, sleep in bedrooms off the same hallway with the rest of them, and come out into the gardens.

This Violet must be locked up, trapped like a bird in a cage. How could one ever have any music in one's life when one wasn't free?

"Ach, no' exactly. Violet's especially bad today, but sometimes she comes down for dinner an' has lessons, an' she likes tae be outside. It's a safe place for her." He gestured around him, slowly turning toward the outer wall. "Ye see tha' fence? It keeps us in as well as others out. It's for yer safety an' Violet's an' every other child's here. We never ken if she might try runnin'. She has before."

"Tried to run away, you mean?" Grandmother's mouth turned into a perfect little *o*. "Why, she must be a wild thing!"

Jordy shifted from foot to foot. "She's no' all bad. Really, Violet can be lovely! But sometimes … Ye'll see. She's just sad is all. She talks tae me more than most, an' I dinna think she understands why she's here." He shrugged. "But then, do most o' us?"

Ivy wiggled at those words. She wasn't sure why God had placed her here or why she seemed to be so different or why other folks cared that she was so different.

Couldn't she just be Ivy? What was so wrong with that?

Yet if there were less to be afraid of, or if she could learn to be less afraid of things, it would be much better.

"Sometimes we go out on the moors together!" Jordy gestured toward a hill that rose beyond the boundary of the fences. "Just beyond tha', there's a burn … a brook, I mean. An' it's lovely. We'll take a picnic out when it gets warmer—would ye like tha', Ivy?"

She wasn't sure. Picnics were nice, but they generally included a lot of people and noisy games, which she didn't like. "I suppose." She'd give it a try, and even if she didn't like it, she'd bear it. Jordy seemed to like the idea, and she was fast deciding that he was the type of boy that was good. He might be loud and boisterous, but he wasn't *bad*.

"Ach, ye'll love it! I love it. This is tamer than our land, but 'tis no' much different."

This was tamer than where Jordy lived? Outside the fences seemed wild to her. But then, Ivy was used to London and Pearlbelle Park, which was neatly trimmed all around.

"I love th' smell o' th' open hills an' th' heather." Jordy spun on his heel. "Come on. If ye walk tae th' top, ye can see a bit o' th' burn!"

Burn must be the funny way Jordy said *brook*, only he didn't correct himself this time. Ivy picked up her pace to follow him—she loved the sound of water, and she'd like to see it.

She tugged at Uncle Charlie's hand to make him come after her, and he did. There was a chuckle in his breathing, too—he must be amused by her again, but she didn't care.

Jordy reached the peak of the little bump and pointed to the north. "There it is!"

Ivy's legs burned, but she at last came up next to him. Standing on tiptoes, she was able to see a little flowing stream of water tumbling its way down a hillside, bubbling gray water against the green and brown moss. She only saw a sliver behind a rock, but she could tell it was lovely.

Perhaps this wouldn't be such a bad place to be after all.

The next day, it became a much worse place indeed.

Uncle Charlie had to go back home to Starboard Hall, which was his estate in Yorkshire. He explained this to Ivy once, twice, three times, and still she didn't comprehend.

She'd known with her head that he was going to leave, but somehow her heart hadn't listened, and it kept making her say, "Why are you leaving me? Why don't you stay here? I love you—I want you—I need you."

However, for the first time since Ivy had made his acquaintance, Uncle Charlie seemed to have hardened his heart toward her.

"It won't be long." Just outside the door of the big house, he once again untangled her arms from his waist and placed her away from him. "There, now. Go to your grandmother."

Ivy didn't want her grandmother—she wanted him. She attempted another hug but was thwarted by his arms, which held her back away from him. Tears sprang out of nowhere, and she tried not to break down into sobs. Still, a few did leak out.

Uncle Charlie's face scrunched up as if someone had hurt him. "Now, Ivy, don't make this difficult. I've an estate to run, and once I've taken care of business, I've ... personal affairs."

"Oh?" Grandmother's voice, behind Ivy, was full of hope. "What's that, Charlie? Back to Pearlbelle Park for you?"

The look he cast Grandmother was grouchy. "If anything changes, I'm sure you'll be the last to know, Mother. Allow me to handle this, please. Do stop smirking!"

Grandmother chuckled. "There, now, Ivy—you must let Uncle Charlie go so he can find his lady love." Her voice was teasing.

Ivy didn't find that funny. She squinted up at Uncle Charlie's annoyed face and wondered why he'd want to spend time with Miss Elton, who everyone thought he should marry, when he could spend time with Ivy.

Using his distraction in her favor, she darted forward again and gave him another fierce hug. "I love you more than Miss Elton does," she whispered. "She's just your friend, but I'm your own niece."

"Oh, Ivy." Uncle Charlie bent and kissed the top of her head. "I know your heart is in the right place, but I can't stay. I love you, too, but ..." He glanced around, then got on his knee before her. "It may be that Miss Elton and I will come to an agreement," he said in the softest of voices. "I believe she wants to, and I'm starting to realize that having a family wouldn't be a bad thing."

Ivy heard Grandmother step closer. "Is he speaking of Miss Elton again, Ivy?" she asked in the cheeriest of cheery voices.

Uncle Charlie frowned. "Mother, we're having an uncle-to-niece chat. Could you please give us some space?"

Grandmother sighed, but her footsteps returned to the house.

"Now, Ivy, listen to me. I do have business I must take care of—I intend to be a good steward of what I've been given. Does that make sense?"

Ivy nodded reluctantly. Nettie had used the word *steward*—it meant "someone who takes care of their property like God would want." That was exactly like Uncle Charlie and not something she could be angry about.

"Then I want to go to Pearlbelle Park, where Miss Elton lives, and rescue her from the dread dragon Old Maidenhood." He smirked. "It's not such a dread dragon, really, and if you ever find yourself facing him, just tell him you've already a wonderful helper in the Holy Spirit, so you've no intention to go to battle. But nonetheless, I'll see if she'd like to be rescued."

Ivy stepped back, frustrated with him. "What if she wouldn't like to be rescued?"

"Then I'll leave her be and come back to you." Uncle Charlie straightened. "But let's agree that if God says to me, 'Charlie, My good man, you'd better rescue her,' that I'll not be thinking about my little niece up in Scotland but about how to best do that."

Ivy found herself making a little grunting sound just like the ones Uncle Charlie was wont to make. How could she argue with obeying God? She simply couldn't. "All right."

"Good." He held out his hand to her. "Let's shake on it, and I'll leave."

Ivy sighed, stepped forward, and shook his hand. Still, she couldn't resist one last barb at her rival. "I don't *like* Miss Elton." Only that wasn't true. Ivy didn't dislike anyone—not exactly. There were just people she didn't want to be around. But that was too complicated to say.

"Perhaps you'll like her when she's your aunt. Now, I'll say good-bye to your grandmother. Don't you get weepy on me." He ruffled her hair and stepped around her, calling to Grandmother as he went.

In a few short minutes, Ivy watched the carriage disappear down the drive. He was gone, back to his estate and then on to Miss Elton.

Now Ivy really was alone here at McCale House.

CHAPTER FOURTEEN

T HE FIRST FULL DAY of schoolwork at McCale House wasn't as hard as Ivy expected it to be. She mainly followed the schedule, which was easier than the one Nettie had planned for her years ago. Besides, the added pressure to be as smart as Alice, a standard she could never match, was eliminated.

On the other hand, she was in a classroom with the other McCale House students, and she didn't know them. Sometimes watching Felix wring his hands became more interesting than the basic reading Mrs. Davenport was trying to teach her.

Still, she kept on track as best she could, and the learning sessions were brief with what Dr. McCale called "creativity breaks" interspersed.

Grandmother seemed to find it ridiculous, and she even said so once, but she quickly shushed. Grandmother often seemed to shush.

Now they were on one of those creativity breaks, and Ivy was glad. Dr. McCale had given her an endless list of arithmetic problems. She'd struggled with them for almost half an hour, and no matter how encouraging everyone was or how simple the problems, Ivy simply didn't like numbers. They were cold and inflexible and annoying. Ivy felt no music in them. She just felt a stiffness, a formality, that she couldn't seem to get past.

If they weren't so complicated. If only she could forget about them—or better yet, do them so effortlessly that she was able to zip through and move on. Alice was good at math, and Mummy, too.

But not Ivy. Ivy didn't understand math. It seemed purposeless to her.

Yet now there was a break, and breaks weren't for thinking about what one was breaking from but rather for enjoying the reprieve. In particular, Ivy was enjoying doing a puzzle on the floor with Jordy McAllen.

Ivy had never done a puzzle before. In fact, Jordy had introduced the idea to her. This puzzle showed a scene with a meadow, and Ivy found it soothing to match the colorful flower pieces together, finding exactly how each piece fit.

"Are all the pieces different?" Ivy asked, holding up one little one. They were tiny, but they all came together to form a bigger whole.

Jordy grinned from the other side of the puzzle, his eyes sparkling. "Ye really love this, dinna ye, Miss Ivy?"

"I do!" It was one of the best things she'd ever discovered. "And it'll make a beautiful picture when we're done, won't it?"

"It will." Jordy cocked his head to the side as if to see the puzzle right side up. "At least, I think so. It's goin' tae be a meadow for sure—an' look at these brown pieces. Perhaps it's a barn. What do ye think?"

Ivy squinted. It was hard to tell when the pieces were so small. They didn't show anything by themselves—it wasn't until one started putting the pieces together that they formed a beautiful whole. "I suppose that might be it. Or some dirt. But are the pieces all different, Jordy?"

"Aye, perhaps. I dinna ken." He shrugged. "But it doesna work well if ye mess it up. At least it wouldna look nice."

Ivy nodded. That was true. She'd tried forcing a few pieces where they didn't go, and it almost never seemed to work. "I do love it, though. Will we do these often, Jordy? Perhaps we could have a puzzle time in the schedule."

A soft chuckle rose in his throat. "Perhaps. If ye like it tha' much, then tell Dr. McCale. He'll listen tae ye."

Would he? He'd seemed the listening type when Ivy had brought up her concerns, few and far between as her words could be. But she wasn't willing to trust him yet.

Everyone here was a nice sort—the teachers and Dr. and Mrs. McCale and Jordy. Jordy, especially, cheerfully told her stories about his family and friends in a Scottish village many miles away.

If only Ivy could so much as think about Mummy and Alice and Nettie without tearing up. She even thought longingly of Kirk; Jordy reminded her of him. Jordy was different than Kirk—Ivy hadn't spent a great deal of time with the stable boy, but whenever she did, she'd felt he was serious.

Jordy? He was rarely serious. But he was a boy and just a year or two older than Kirk. They looked different—though they were the same height, Jordy was stockier and had sort of orange-brown eyes, but Kirk's eyes were green. Jordy's hair was a copper gold with a bit of brown in it, while Kirk's was dark brown.

She wondered what Kirk was up to and if he still had his little dog and if he ever thought of her. He'd saved her life, after all.

Did Ivy owe Kirk a blood debt? She wasn't sure, but she'd heard Alice talking about those sorts of things before. Alice had quite the imagination sometimes, so perhaps it wasn't right, but Ivy didn't want to risk it. She'd have to ask someone who would know.

Perhaps Jordy, if she ever got up the courage.

He placed another puzzle piece down. "There! It'll only get harder now tha' we've got th' edges, though. We'll have tae really think about it."

Ivy nodded. She wasn't afraid—this puzzle was something she was sure she could conquer, little though she knew about puzzles. The messy organization of it appealed to her.

"Could you tell me more about Keefmore?" she asked. Then she blinked, surprised. She hadn't known she was going to say that until she had. Jordy's love for the town and its people was reflected in every word he spoke, and Ivy wanted more of that. It gave her a sense of security in knowing that someone could survive separation—and she liked hearing about the things people cared about.

Otherwise, she would rather just leave people alone and not ask them any questions.

"Aye, I can do tha'. Let me tell ye about th' time tha' me best mate,

Tristan, an' I almost burnt down Da's barn." Jordy launched into a reckless tale full of laughter and mistakes and fun.

"They never let me take care o' things which involved lanterns after that." He grinned. "I was a wild thing. I still can be! But Dr. McCale is tryin' tae keep me out of trouble." He shrugged. "I do me best. Sometimes it's hard tae keep calm an' go about yer day without causin' some mischief."

Ivy wasn't sure that was true. She got through all her days without causing mischief, didn't she?

Then she hesitated. Perhaps that wasn't true. Why, wasn't it mischief to run out in the middle of a snowstorm and almost get dead? Ivy wasn't sure, but that was what had happened.

Of course, Ivy hadn't intended to do that. As she looked back on it, she could scarcely remember why she had run out into that storm, and she'd had to piece a great deal of it together from the people who talked about her when they didn't think she was listening.

Oftentimes people didn't think she was listening. Oftentimes they didn't think she heard or understood. But she did, and it was sometimes scary to hear the things they said about her.

Once again she had to shush out the voices that threatened to overcome her, the little voices of servants and friends and family who hadn't known any better than to say things that hurt, that cut deep, that caused her to almost cry.

Ivy tried not to cry, though. Whenever she did, people got sympathetic. And when they got sympathetic, they surrounded her with hugs and kisses—or Mummy and Nettie did, anyway. Alice just got mad. Both of those two things—Mummy's and Nettie's being sympathetic and Alice's being angry—only made Ivy cry more, cry until she had a headache and wanted to sleep.

One more puzzle piece clicked into place. She smiled and looked up at Jordy. "Can you tell me another Keefmore story?"

"Ach, I could." He lifted a tiny puzzle piece and frowned at it. "I think this is sky. Let's put those over here."

"All right." Ivy began sorting the pile of remaining wooden shapes. "Will you, though?"

He chuckled. "Ye figured tha' one out! I could, but tha's no' what I like talkin' about. Keefmore was a part o' who I was, Miss Ivy. I'd rather move forward than back, wouldna ye?"

"No." Ivy didn't have to think about that answer. She missed the past so badly—back when she was the beloved second child of a dressmaker in London who, when she was home, only had eyes for Alice and Ivy. Back when Nettie spent all her time watching them. Back when there was no Mr. Knight, no Ned, no sick Mummy.

Jordy smiled and shook his head. "Ye dinna understand, though, Miss Ivy. Ye see, th' past will be in th' past. Th' future is all we have! Ach, nah, we dinna even have tha'. It's th' present we've got. I've me present at McCale House, an' tha'll lead tae me future as a doctor. I couldna ask for anythin' more."

"What about your family in Keefmore? And your friends? And—"

"I'll go back tae visit, aye, but I dinna expect tae ever live there again. Listen, Miss Ivy." He leaned forward conspiratorially. "Keefmore was holdin' me back. I didna even ken what th' world could offer before I left."

"But it's your home."

"Was me home."

Ivy's breaths shortened as her chest tightened. This was ridiculous! How could Jordy be so ... so unfeeling? "But your family—"

"I love me family." He cocked his head. "Are ye a'right? Remember, deep breaths."

Right. She was supposed to take long breaths whenever her chest hurt. She sucked one in.

"No' like tha'." He imitated a long drag of breath as an example. "Like tha'. Slow, steady, even. An' then again."

Ivy wanted to huff out her frustration, but instead she took the breaths, long and slow, until the pain in her chest eased. It helped, yes, but it was hard to remember. Ivy was used to ignoring the pain until it got so bad that she just couldn't breathe, and when that happened, she'd faint or cause a scene.

Perhaps if she could remember to do the breathing right, she would never faint or cause a scene again. It was a novel thought.

"Good lass. I'm proud o' ye." Jordy cocked his head. "Better?"

"Yes," she whispered, feeling small. It was silly to worry just because Jordy didn't want to go home to his family, but somehow it seemed personal to her. "I'm just sad you don't want to go home. Home is the best place, isn't it, Jordy?"

"Aye, it is. But we can be home in so many places." He settled back on the floor and began shifting through puzzle pieces again. "Sometimes what might be home for one person isna home for another, ye ken."

"What do you mean?"

"I mean tha' McCale House is me home as much as Keefmore. An' tha's a'right. It's also a'right if ye never feel as if ye could spend much time here—ye're gifted tae be able tae go home someday. No' everyone here can." He glanced over his shoulder toward Felix and Leonard. "Ye ken tha' Felix may never go home. He stands in th' way o' an inheritance—for his stepmother, his bein' here is a happy coincidence."

"Oh." Ivy wasn't sure why being at McCale House could be a happy coincidence, but Jordy seemed to understand it, so perhaps she didn't need to. "Poor Felix."

"Aye, poor Felix. He's an a'right sort—he must be a year or two older 'n ye. Have ye talked tae him?"

Ivy shuddered and shook her head. His nervous flinching and continual hand motions frightened her.

"Ye should. He's got some problems, but then, who doesna?" Jordy again began shifting his fingers through the puzzle pieces. "More barn—if it is a barn."

Ivy took the piece and placed it with the other barn-or-dirt ones. "I'll try talking to Felix. I don't know much about him."

"Tha's exactly right. Ye dinna ken much about anyone here! They all have stories—an' some o' them are sad an' some o' them are like yours."

Ivy blinked. "Isn't mine sad?" It felt sad and lonely and abandoned.

"It's no', Miss Ivy! It's hopeful." Jordy found another piece that fit and put it in place with a satisfying click. "There. We'll finish it yet."

CHAPTER FIFTEEN

I VY WENT TO BED that night more confused than she had been when she woke up. She'd spent most of the afternoon talking with Dr. McCale—about what, she wasn't sure—and nothing had happened.

Jordy assured her that McCale House was a good place for her, a hopeful place, but how could she believe him? If Dr. McCale was going to help her, he was doing it slowly, discussing Kitty and fairy-tales and Alice with her.

What good did that do? The breathing exercises helped, though she rarely remembered to do them without being reminded. But other than that, she hadn't noticed changes.

She thought about Felix Merrill. He was nice enough, though she'd only smiled at him in passing. She'd try harder tomorrow—perhaps she'd sit near him and they'd be able to talk.

If he talked. She hadn't noticed him say more than a few stuttering words to Dr. McCale. Perhaps, like Ivy, he was quiet.

Soon her confusion faded as she drifted off to sleep.

She jerked awake some hours later, eyes wide, panting for breath. For a moment, there was silence, and she thought she had dreamt it, but then the scream came again, louder this time and even more terrifying, because it seemed to Ivy that it was growing nearer.

Too frightened to cry out, she lay still in the dark room, eyes wide. She remembered last night then, with its ghostly shadows and its utter lack of

Alice, Nettie, and Mummy. Was she never to have a whole night of sleep?

Still panting, she managed to move her legs before the third scream froze her again. Her feet stuck out from under the covers, and she thought that that was some progress. However, nothing had been accomplished, save now her feet were cold.

Out of the corner of her eye, she saw a light come on under her grandmother's door. If she called, Grandmother would come. She was not Alice, Nettie, or Mummy, but she was someone, someone human, unlike the maker of the ghostly wail.

She lay still and silent. There were no more screams, and Ivy crept out of bed, not bothering with her dressing gown, though the cold wrapped around her body. Warmth tugged her back toward the bed, but she ignored its siren call. Opening the door, she found the hallway empty.

She had to know who had screamed this time. She just had to.

Creeping along it, needing to find the source of those screams, she came to the end of the hall, where a narrow staircase rose, dark and steep. Ivy swallowed hard. She couldn't enter the darkness, could she?

But if she was ever to find out who the screamer was ...

Taking a deep breath, the kind Dr. McCale wanted her to take, Ivy walked up the stairs, eyes closed, hand on the wall. She couldn't have seen anything even with her eyes open, but she decided it was better to not see anything while not trying to see anything than to not see anything when trying to see something. There was a reassuring feeling to having her eyes closed. She wasn't sure why, but it allowed her to focus more on the steps and the feel of the air around her, freeing her mind.

Finally she reached the top step. Feeling around, she found the handle to yet another door, which she opened. It creaked. Ivy jumped.

After a moment, she recovered, opened her eyes, and entered a hall lit by a lamp resting on a table. She glanced around, then hurried to the lamp, drawn to it like a moth. From there, she surveyed the corridor and found nothing spooky, nothing that could create shadows a monster could hide behind, nothing supernatural.

She didn't hear any more screaming, but there was a door with a light under it, and she eased toward it, placed a hand on the frame, and listened.

Then Ivy heard it—soft sobs, the kind that shook one's whole body in silence and let only little whimpering sounds out.

"I ... I just want it to be over. I just want to leave. Why can't ... you ... leave me alone?"

That didn't sound like the screamer. The girl who screamed had been angry, but this girl sounded broken.

"Leave ... me ... alone."

"It's all right. We're here, dearest. Shush, now. Let's wash your face. You'll feel better soon." Mrs. McCale's voice also floated through the door, gentler than Ivy had ever heard before. "Shush."

"You don't want ..." The voice broke.

Mrs. McCale clucked her tongue. "Of course we want you, dearest. Just breathe. You're all right. Just breathe."

The girl must be sad, but it was good that Mrs. McCale was there and sounded motherly. Perhaps she could help the girl feel better—though judging by the screams and the sobs, the girl wasn't ready to feel better.

Then the door opened, and Dr. McCale walked out, his body blocking the whole door so Ivy couldn't see more than a sliver of light beyond him.

He raised his eyebrows. "What are you doing here?"

"I ... I heard a scream. What ... what was it? Was it a ... a ghost?"

"Nonsense. Ghosts don't exist. If they did, we wouldn't let them in McCale House. Now, let's get you back to bed." Dr. McCale took her hand and led her down the narrow stairs.

"Who ... who was it?"

"It's none of your concern; just one of our students with a nightmare. Go to sleep, and everything will be better in the morning."

Everything wasn't better in the morning. Ivy found herself unable to work, too haunted by the frights of the night before to do much but sit in her room and stare out the window and want her loved ones.

"She can take the day to rest," Dr. McCale said in an undertone to Grandmother as they stood behind Ivy. "We'll have to watch her if she's going to be wandering into forbidden areas of the house—and we'll have to try to calm Violet more quickly if she's disturbing the other students. She's never caused this type of problem before."

"Thank you, Dr. McCale." Grandmother adjusted her position in her seat. "Is there nothing to be done for this Violet? She seems troublesome, not like the other students."

"Violet is hardly a big problem. We love her despite everything, and Emma—Mrs. McCale—and I have always held out hope that we can help her."

"Perhaps you can't," Grandmother persisted. "I just want Ivy to be safe, Dr. McCale. But if you're sure this Violet poses no threat to her, that's perfectly all right. I only want to know you're sure the child is secure and will not do anything harmful."

"She will not," Dr. McCale said. "We'll make sure of it."

On toward the afternoon, Ivy crept downstairs to find something to do. A lot of the shock of the night had worn off, and now she was tired and trembly but better.

She wondered why little things like hearing a scream in the night and going to investigate scared her so. Perhaps it was the sobs. Yes, that was definitely it. The screams had been scary, ethereal, and unsettling, but the quiet crying had been scarier. That part had told her that the poor thing was suffering and that she felt trapped here.

Like Ivy, but worse. Like Ivy, but more broken and empty.

Downstairs, she found Jordy reading a big book. He looked up with a smile and set the book on the table in front of him.

Ivy glanced around. "You're the only one in the schoolroom now?"

"Aye, everyone else is off already. Dr. McCale set me this readin'." Jordy tapped the book. "Medical. I'm tae go tae college, ye ken—in London! Or close tae it." He leaned back on the chair. "I've a lot o' catchin' up tae do."

"Oh." Ivy cocked her head. "I suppose that'll help you be a doctor."

He chuckled. "It's about th' only way tae be one."

Ivy felt her face flush. "I suppose it is." She sighed and shook her head. Nice as it would be to just talk about light, happy things, she had an important mission today. "Jordy, can I ask you a question?"

"A'right, go on." He nodded his head to a chair next to him. "I'm due for a break, at any rate, so I can talk."

Ivy slid onto the chair and laid her hands palms-up on the table. "It's just that ... you know me a little, Jordy. Do you think I could be helpful to someone?"

He pushed his book a little farther down the table. "What do ye mean? How so?"

"What if someone was hurting, and I could understand what it's like to be hurting? I feel if I were to talk to them, I could help." She wasn't sure why she felt that this was true, but she somehow knew it deep in her soul.

There was an understanding in her for the girl with the screams. There was an understanding in her for the wildness and sadness of her. Ivy didn't know what the solution to either of those were, but somehow she felt she could help.

"Perhaps." Jordy drummed his fingers on the table. "No' *perhaps* because o' ... because ye're at McCale House. But *perhaps* because it depends on th' situation. Aye, ye might be. I dinna ken."

"Hmm." Ivy folded her hands on her lap and sat still for a few moments to collect her thoughts. "So you don't think I will always be useless?"

"No' at all. Ye'll find places where ye're more useful than anyone else could be." Jordy said the words with a confident flip of his hand. "Dinna worry. Such things will come. Dr. McCale says we only have tae trust, an' God will show us th' rest in th' proper time."

"I see." So far God hadn't shown Ivy much of anything, but she'd have to trust that Jordy knew what he was talking about. "Jordy, there's a girl here. She's like me, but we haven't seen her yet. Since I got here, I mean."

Jordy's eyes widened ever so slightly, but otherwise he made no movement. "Violet Angel."

"Yes. Is she ... I mean, I hear her at night sometimes."

Jordy grunted. "Aye, she's a problem. A sweet girl, but a problem."

"Could you tell me about her?" Ivy asked. She felt she must know more, understand more to completely comprehend what was going on with Violet. If she could understand, she could help. The feeling was without explanation but persistent.

What was wrong with her? Shouldn't she be afraid? Why wasn't she terribly, terribly afraid? Fear was the normal response in most situations for Ivy. And yet she wasn't. She wanted to spend time with Violet Angel, and she wanted to learn more about her.

Jordy was slow to respond but eventually did. "She came here when she was just five years old. I dinna ken exactly why ... somethin' about her parents thinkin' she wasna all she should be. I ... I dinna think they cared much, Ivy. I think her mum might've, if Dr. McCale is right, but I dinna think that her father cared much about whether or not she was at home with them. An' tha's scary enough."

Ivy winced. The story was all too familiar—a loving mother overrun by a careless father. That was her situation, wasn't it? Though, she supposed if her mother had really wanted to keep Ivy, she would've tried harder. She shuddered, feeling that both Violet and she lived in a loveless world, where they weren't appreciated by those around them. At least not much.

"I dinna ken all o' it. I wasna here until four years ago. Dr. an' Mrs. McCale only have one child, Helen, an' Helen was a young lady by the time Violet got here. So Dr. an' Mrs. McCale raised Violet as their own—they loved her tha' much, an' they took time with her as they never took time with th' other students. An' I see tha' still. I think any other child who behaved as badly as Violet does, well, they wouldna have kept this long."

"Oh." Ivy blinked. It would seem that her position at McCale House was dependent on behavior. That was strange, for everyone here had their moments of being badly behaved.

"Oh, dinna ye worry, Ivy. I can see ye thinkin', but ye needna. Ye see, some children canna be helped. It's a new science, mental health, an' we dinna understand it. We can only help those we understand. No' tha' we understand all th' children here perfectly, but we have hope for them all. I think tha' the hardest thing for anyone tae accept here is tha' a child just has tae go back tae their parents—or be kept here without having any sort o' hope." Jordy shuddered. "We can pray for them—an' tha's all we can do in so many situations. There are limited spots here, after all."

"I see." Still, a part of her still feared being one of those children whom Dr. McCale couldn't help.

Would that mean she got sent home? Didn't that seem like the best thing ever? But Ivy couldn't imagine being sent back home because she was "hopeless." She could only go home if she were wanted, or it would be quite awful. She'd rather stay at McCale House than be sent back because she wasn't worth working with. That idea was strange to her.

"But Violet ... Violet has been here so long, an' we've tried so many things with her. We've tried to make her understand tha' we love her, but she never seems tae. I think tha' the McCales never understood what a troubled child Violet was until recently. She gets worse as she gets older rather than th' opposite. An', really, we dinna ken, Ivy. We dinna ken. We could lose her, I think, an' she would've long ago gone home if her parents wanted her. But her father insists that she's not worth having there."

"That sounds horrible," Ivy said. "I've never known someone could just ... not love their baby." At least, someone like her mother. Though, she supposed there were some grown-ups she just didn't feel sure of. Perhaps they were that type of people, the type of people who wouldn't love a precious baby girl.

"It is horrible," Jordy said. "I hate what they've done tae her. Why, the bitterness ... She is dreadfully bitter. She canna seem tae see tha' there's any hope in her life. An', tae be fair, it is hard tae see. It's no' just her attitude, though if she were tae work with us, it might help. But Violet has these fits, an' she dinna ken what she's doin'. Sometimes she doesna remember them later. She screams an' shudders uncontrollably, an' there's no' much tae be done. Dr. McCale always talks about what tae do, how tae make sure she's safe an' doesna hurt herself."

"Really?" Ivy too shuddered, scared of these new thoughts. "So she isn't ... she isn't able to help herself?" That was a scary thought. Ivy's steadier, deeper breathing was helping lessen her panic, but imagine if that didn't help! What hope would there be? Not remembering what one had done later was scary, too.

"Aye. Sometimes. We dinna always ken when Violet is bein' natural an' when Violet is bein' Violet. She's a difficult, dark child tae work with." He shrugged. "But I told ye, she talks tae me more than most, an' there's such sadness in her. I must believe that there's a possibility o' her being helped. Tha', in the end, we will save Violet Angel."

We will save Violet Angel. Ivy liked that. She wanted to believe that Violet Angel, as well as the other children at McCale House, could be saved—and that included herself. She wasn't sure exactly what *saving* would mean for all of them. She was sure that for Violet it would mean that they would be able to let her out of the upstairs. That she could come down and spend time with them.

Of course that led to Ivy's big problem. How could she spend time with Violet and help her if the girl was always locked in her upstairs room?

"Does Violet never come down?" she asked. "I did hear Dr. McCale say ..." What had he said? She couldn't remember. "That she was worse right now."

"Aye, she is. She tends tae change from week tae week." Jordy shrugged. "Ye never ken what kind o' Violet ye'll be gettin'. This morning, for instance, she was quiet an' contemplative, an' she's barely said a word tae any o' us. I ken 'cause I went tae check on her early this mornin', and she just nodded tae me. Normally she'd say something annoyin'. An' I gave her me best brogue, tae." He grinned. "Violet has an interestin' sense o' humor."

"Oh." Ivy didn't have a sense of humor, so Violet was already far ahead of her. "She's not talking?"

"No' much. But this could be good! It could mean tha' she'll rest today, an' then soon she'll be able tae come down. She has some things tae keep her entertained upstairs, so dinna ye worry. Th' piano, remember?

I mentioned it. Violet plays well, an' she's always enjoyed tha'. She reads, an' when she's no' bein' quiet like today, she'll chat with me. Tha's always fun."

"Oh." Ivy wiggled on her seat, her brain going a thousand miles an hour—or, at least, it was working quicker than she was used to. "Jordy, what do you talk about with Violet? What is she like?"

"Wha's she like? What're ye like? Tha's a hard question, tae describe someone. Why dinna ye wait until ye meet her." Jordy's eyes were fixated on the book in front of him. "I ken I've been th' one talkin', but I really do have tae finish or I'll get in trouble."

"I see." Ivy slid off the seat. "Can we talk more about Violet soon?"

"Aye, aye, we can. But dinna ye worry about her. Violet Angel will be a'right in th' end. We're doin' our best tae help her as much as we can, with the knowledge we have an' with how little Violet's helpin' us out herself."

"I see." Ivy sighed. "Thank you, Jordy. I'll be leaving, then. I think I'll go find another puzzle—maybe when you're done, you'll help me?"

"Maybe. Now run along, Miss Ivy."

CHAPTER SIXTEEN

NORA WINCED AS ONE of the students tumbled into a drift of snow.

Mrs. McCale cupped her hands over her mouth. "Jordy, be careful. You're too rough!"

Jordy McAllen waved to Mrs. McCale from a ways up the hill, jerking Felix, to his feet. They were having a calm snowball fight that mostly involved fort building, but Jordy managed to get everyone running about madly, shouting, screaming, and calling out to one another.

Great fun, but there was tumbling, a few bruised knees, and a lot of wet, cold children.

Nora agreed with Mrs. McCale's calling out to him to settle down, though she wasn't about to express it to Jordy herself. He seemed to be a wild boy, though he had his moments when Nora realized that there was intelligence and potential in him. Was that what Dr. McCale had seen in him? Nora believed so. Every day she spent at McCale House, she realized that Dr. McCale was insightful.

Ivy was next to Jordy, following him around like a little shadow determined to never leave his side for a moment. He knelt next to her and cupped her hands in his, giving her what appeared to be a serious talk—though what about, Nora couldn't begin to imagine. She supposed it must be something about the snowballs, for there wasn't much else that they could be talking about.

When Ivy knelt and began packing snow, Nora's thoughts were confirmed. They were preparing ammunition.

Heavens. Hopefully no one would get hurt.

"Ivy's made a great deal of progress, hasn't she?" Mrs. McCale adjusted her muffler. "My, it's cold."

Both of those statements were true. Though, Ivy's progress was harder to judge. "You think so?"

"Aye, it is cold."

Nora shuffled her feet like a child, feeling ashamed even as she did it. "No, about Ivy's progress."

Mrs. McCale chuckled. "Aye, I knew what you meant. Ivy is making definite progress. I think she's better off than most of the children here. Her mother's love made all the difference—it is felt and experienced even in absence."

Nora agreed with that. Though her grandchildren were not perfect, and neither was her daughter, she still believed that Claire loved the girls as much as a woman could. It was simply a matter of sometimes not being entirely mature, but who was?

"We're getting closer, too. Or Callum—my husband—says so." Mrs. McCale sighed. "He usually has a good sense for these things. If we could understand more about her, about how her mind works, we'd be there."

Nora furrowed her eyebrows. "What do you mean?"

Mrs. McCale took a deep breath. "It might not make much sense, though I'll try to explain. We're looking for a way to reach her consistently. The ability for her to work one-on-one with someone, to be met where she's at and be tutored privately, is one thing. That's what we're doing now. However, we need to find out more."

"Oh." Nora didn't understand completely. "Isn't she just a quiet child? Dr. McCale says we'll never fix her."

"Yes, Callum would say that. But what he means is that you'll never change her into something she's not. The key is to find who she is, who God created her to be. We all have talents, Mrs. Chattoway, and we all have strengths. It's just that Ivy's are hard to see." Mrs. McCale cocked her head. "I think you might understand that."

Nora blinked. Was Mrs. McCale insinuating that her mental capacities were low? She was used to that from her late husband, but she'd never heard anyone else say it. Especially not someone as pleasant as Mrs. McCale seemed to be. "What do you mean?" She wouldn't allow herself to be offended until the woman explained herself. Although even in offense, Nora rarely knew what to do.

"You don't seem confident in stating your opinions. Forgive me, Mrs. Chattoway—you'll find this forward." Mrs. McCale folded her arms across her chest. "I'm a Scotswoman, though, and I've been told all my life to speak my mind, so I've never trained my tongue as well as I ought."

Nora nodded. "Go on."

"I believe you've been smothered. I believe someone didn't let you say what you thought and told you that what you cared about, what you wanted to pursue, was not worthy. I also believe you were love-starved, and now you seek affirmation from others."

Every bone in Nora's body shuddered, then she stood still. She wasn't sure how to respond, so she turned to watch the children playing in the snow, their shouts echoing about the yard.

Jordy knelt next to Ivy again and pointed to Ella Willis, who was apparently on the opposing team. Ivy threw the snowball her way, but it fell short, and Nora chuckled. Poor dear.

She turned back to Mrs. McCale.

"I've offended you, but I can't help my observations—my husband is always making them, and he's gotten me into the habit." Mrs. McCale smoothed her hands down her skirt. "I do apologize if it came off as confrontational, as that was not my intention."

"No. That's perfectly all right." Nora cleared her throat. "I just ... was surprised. No one has said it to me before, though I feel it may be true. My husband wasn't an easy man to live with." She almost gasped at her own daring as the words came out. But should she smother the truth now that he was beyond hurting her?

No, it wasn't proper, but over the past few months, her appreciation for the truth had deepened, and she'd come to understand herself a great deal better.

The numbness had left her shortly after her husband's death, leaving devastation and anger and all kinds of other horrible emotions in its wake. Yet she didn't want to be numb again, not now that the worst was over. Now she simply had to figure out how to live.

"Aye." Mrs. McCale cocked her head. "Then what man is? I think what you mean is that he was impossible to live with, and yet you did."

Perhaps she did mean that, but she'd never put her finger on it. He'd convinced her that she deserved everything he'd done to her. That she wasn't worth his love. Jonathan tended to keep his voice low and even, sometimes using the slight singsong of one talking to an irrational child, but he rarely shouted. At their children, yes, but not at her. It was as if she weren't worth anger to him.

In his calmness, Nora had believed there was truth. Sometimes, she'd still hear the harshness of his words beneath the condescending tone, the judgment, and the lack of trust or esteem given to her.

Then she'd wonder if he'd spoken the truth. He'd been her husband—they had been close for so many years. When they were newly married, and while they were courting, he'd been kind to her, and she'd fancied herself in love. It was hard not to be—he was handsome and could be charming.

Perhaps it was because at first Jonathan had been capable of so much affection toward her, and because he had created so much longing in her, that she had not given up. Yet Mrs. McCale was right. Nora had been pushed further than she ever should have allowed. She should have left or at least put her foot down.

Certainly she knew the way he'd treated her children was unfair. He'd abused them sorely, and each one still suffered the consequences. Charlie, in his aversion to commit to marriage or fully admit his love. Claire, in her desire to bind herself to a man who'd betrayed her once, just because he'd offered her love and security. Christina, in her endless immaturity, in the way she focused on herself, perhaps feeling no one else could offer her the sympathy she desired.

That had made her angry, but she never considered herself a part of the equation. She deserved the punishment for all the times she hadn't stepped in.

"I'll think about what you've said." Nora regarded Mrs. McCale for a moment, then turned back to the children. She wasn't ready for more discussion on the topic. "Oh, Jordy's got Ivy throwing snowballs again—do you suppose he'll ever give up? She can't have much arm strength."

Mrs. McCale thankfully let their former subject drop. "Oh, he'll keep at it. Jordy's such a stubborn lad. If he sees something in Ivy, he won't let it rest. He's always wanting to fix something or someone." She sighed. "I suppose I'm the same way, and Callum, but we're all well-matched in it. Helen, my daughter, never had much of a passion for McCale House, though she respects it. But Callum and I can work as one, and Jordy helps more than you know."

Nora didn't see how Jordy helped, but she'd take Mrs. McCale's word for it.

Ivy broke away from the others and came running over, almost tripping over her own legs.

"Grandmother!" Ivy practically shouted the word. "Did you see? Jordy's teaching me how to throw, so I don't look like a silly little lass, and I almost hit that tree—which was what I'm aiming for. Jordy says I have to practice all the time." She sputtered to a stop in front of Nora. "I'll be as good a throw as him! Almost. He says he's a champion."

Mrs. McCale laughed. "Did he now?"

"Yes, of course." Ivy's eyes searched both of the women's eagerly. "He is a champion, isn't he, Mrs. McCale?"

"He says he is." Mrs. McCale accompanied this with a little snort. "Don't take him too seriously, child."

Yet Ivy's face said that she would indeed take everything Jordy said seriously. Still, she nodded before turning back to Nora. "Grandmother, will you watch?"

"I'll watch."

The child turned and dashed back to her friends, saying something about how she must have the perfect snowball, for Grandmother would be watching this time. Nora chuckled. Perhaps she'd find a way into the child's heart after all.

There was a common room upstairs that Ivy gravitated to in the evenings. It allowed her to be alone for a few minutes before prayers, and that in itself was a blessing. She also liked the open space, the little fire in the grate, and of course the grand piano.

Ivy couldn't play a note, but she could look. She could wonder. She could hope that someday someone would play it, and she could listen and let the sounds soak into her soul and somehow create a better person within her.

Music lent depth. It cleared her mind in a way nothing else ever had. At home, her mother played the piano occasionally—the one at Pearlbelle Park, that was. They hadn't had a piano in London. But she wasn't *really* good at it, and Ivy wished she could show Mummy how to make the notes emotional.

Yet Ivy couldn't do that, either. At least, she'd never tried, frightened that she'd only create a discordant crash like little Ned sitting on his father's lap and banging at the keys. That was the opposite of peace and joy, as far as Ivy was concerned. She couldn't believe anyone would play the piano who didn't know how to perfectly.

Alice certainly should never be allowed to.

Here at McCale House, no one had ever played, either. It just sat unused, sad, and lonely, and Ivy didn't know what to do about it other than to sit on the bench and keep it company.

"I have music inside, too," she whispered, "and it doesn't get played often, either."

The grand piano didn't reply, but the wooden bench did seem to receive her like an old friend. She swung her legs back and forth and looked longingly at the keys. If only, if only ... but she couldn't learn that. Perhaps she'd find another way to share the music.

Then, from above, she caught a strain of a tune. She almost jumped, worried for a moment that the piano had taken to playing itself, but no, it was coming from the top floor.

Someone was playing a piano. The notes came together to form a beautiful but eerie song. As the music went on, it gained emotion, depth. The musician clearly had something to say.

Ivy's eyes opened wide, then she closed them and concentrated on the sound, focusing on it until other sensations faded. What was the player trying to communicate? What was it? Anger, perhaps? It was intense enough. Or perhaps just frustration. No ... grief, she decided.

She didn't know who could make such music. It couldn't be Dr. McCale or his wife or any of the people who worked at McCale House. Jordy's brief mention of Violet's musical talent came to mind—and that was her floor, after all.

The music contained the same emotions as the screams had. It was like those sounds in many ways, except it was not so wild. It was contained; it was measured. It was an expression that didn't disrupt. It showed the emotion without hurting anyone or anything.

Ivy wished she could be with Violet now and show her how she felt in return, but there wasn't anything she could do. She couldn't help. She wasn't the type who could be helpful!

After a moment, Ivy stood from the piano bench and moved behind it, patting the edge of the piano as she left. She didn't want it to feel abandoned, after all, but she had something to express.

At first she just walked toward the fire, trying to expel some of the nervous energy inside her, then she began to hum, trying to keep up with the notes coming faintly from upstairs.

It matched the music inside her, so it wasn't too hard to follow, yet she felt that she could dance better than she could hum. Of course, dancing wasn't something Ivy necessarily knew how to do well, but she could certainly try with all that was within her. She twirled and swirled and tried doing things a ballerina would do. That was beyond her, but she still did her best to keep pace with the music.

It loosened something inside her like a string cut, and she found herself able to move longer than she would've thought without becoming short of breath or collapsing on the floor.

There was something about the music that was at once comforting and claiming. It touched a part of her she wasn't sure had been touched before, not exactly. There was also something else—something in her ability, alone here with the unused piano and the low light from the fire, to express herself fully. That something else made her feel free, understood, and in control of her motions and thoughts.

So she danced on, listening and humming and hearing little snippets of something that wasn't the music, wasn't her own breathing, wasn't quite earthly.

Maybe it was God, though she'd not really talked to Him on her own before. She felt ecstatic at this thought, for she'd like nothing more than to talk to God herself rather than have Nettie or Mummy or someone else do it for her.

Though, perhaps that, too, was beyond a child like her. The idea made her still for a moment, but then the music lifted again, and it called her to twirl until she became dizzy and dropped to the ground with a breathless laugh.

She crossed her legs one over the other, adjusted the skirt of her dress, and turned her face up to the ceiling. It was a normal ceiling, with a big, long crack running along it, but somehow it seemed different than it ever had before.

She sat on a rug, and her fingers felt every fiber of the carpet. She could feel the threads responding to her touch, and it wasn't itchy or overwhelming. Instead, it was a beautiful reminder that she was where she was, and those surroundings were not too much for her to handle.

She was near the fire, but there was nothing about it that made her feel overheated and therefore overwhelmed. No, not at all. The lights in the fire weren't too bright to look at, and the cool colors of the room appealed to her in a way they hadn't before.

Even the grand piano seemed more cheerful, as if it had come into its own and understood its purpose in life. The keys looked inviting, though Ivy was too exhausted to think of playing it now.

She knew without a doubt that she would play, and she would hear such sounds and feel such sensations again.

Was it God? Was it just a dream? Or was it real? It must be; Ivy pinched herself and felt it. This was reality, and reality was suddenly a great deal less dull than she remembered.

The song upstairs had come to a conclusion, and Ivy rose to her feet and turned in a complete circle, taking in the room.

Though she felt vaguely that she ought to be confused by her feelings of happiness and contentedness, she wasn't. Instead, she remained calm and relaxed as if she might fall asleep.

"Thank you," she whispered, not sure to whom. She wanted to say more, but the simple words were enough. "Thank you."

CHAPTER SEVENTEEN

NORA SLIPPED OUT OF the doorway and hurried down the hall. She'd only come to bring the child to her bedroom for the night and prepare her for sleep, but she couldn't help but watch.

She couldn't imagine what had been going through Ivy's head as she listened to the ghostly music drifting down from Violet Angel's room and danced to it. Of course, the music hadn't been so much ghostly as threaded with emotion, but it was hard to tell the difference at times.

Nora wasn't a great musician, though she could play enough to pass at parties in her youth. Still, she recognized the powerful effect that music could have on some—and that Ivy was the type who needed an outlet.

Mrs. McCale had spoken of finding a way to reach Ivy. Could this be what they were speaking of? Could this be what touched the child's soul and drew her out?

The child had seemed freer and more active than ever before. Was there hope? Surely there must be!

Nora hastened her way down the halls to Dr. McCale's study. He'd mentioned that once the children were on their way to their rooms for the night, he'd settle in there and read.

She rapped lightly on the door and waited.

"Come in."

Nora opened the door and stepped into the dark, quiet room, lit only by a low fire. It would seem that the McCales found comfort in a dim room. Nora found it odd, and it reminded her of the condition Jonathan liked to keep their house in. Still, she supposed it might seem cozy to some. It didn't to her. Now that Jonathan was gone, she kept Starboard Hall as light as possible, and she loved staying at Pearlbelle Park. Her daughter's estate was beautifully lit.

"Dr. McCale?" She approached the desk, where the man sat, a book discarded in front of him. "I'm so sorry to bother you, but I discovered some information I think you'll be interested in."

"I'm not bothered." He nodded his head toward the chair opposite him. "Emma, would you like to join us?"

Nora glanced over her shoulder to find that Mrs. McCale was snuggled up on a chair by the fire. However, at Dr. McCale's words, she rose and drew a chair near, smiling slightly at Nora.

"What is it, then? Hopefully nothing's wrong."

"No, quite the opposite." Nora took a deep breath. "Just now, Ivy was in the upstairs common room—the one with the grand piano. I saw her stand up from the bench and dance around the room, listening to the music coming from ... from the floor above."

Dr. McCale raised his eyebrows. "That is different. Did she know you were there?"

"No, I don't believe so."

"Hmm." Dr. McCale drummed his fingers on the desk. "Her mother mentioned nothing about Ivy's dancing to me."

"No. She never has—she's never done much of anything." At least, not as far as Nora knew. She'd tried to understand Ivy from the moment she'd met her, but so far she hadn't succeeded as well as she would like to. "And the look on her face ..." If only she could explain a little better. It was hard to describe to one who hadn't seen it with one's own eyes, but Ivy had seemed so happy.

"I see." Dr. McCale placed his hands on the desk and folded them. "You think this might be something important, then?"

"Yes, I do." Nora struggled again for words, then forced them out. "I think perhaps it's ... perhaps it's how we can reach her."

"Music?"

"Exactly. Come to think of it, she's always shown an aversion to loud noises and an affinity to beautiful ones. Perhaps music can touch her soul." She hoped that didn't sound too ridiculous.

"Wonderful." Dr. McCale leaned back on his chair to pull out a drawer and then a pad of paper. He snatched up a pen and began scribbling. "It's worth a try. I'll write down some things we can do."

Mrs. McCale rose from her seat and came to stand at her husband's elbow. She glanced at his frantic writing, then up at Nora with a smile. "That's how we reached Violet, actually. It still works sometimes, when other things don't. She's always calmer after she's been playing the piano—she's probably in a better mood tonight."

"Besides, Violet is talented—and we don't know that Ivy won't be as talented." Dr. McCale pushed the paper away. "Emma, you'll have to write her out a better lesson plan, but those are my ideas. It'll all depend on her, of course."

"Of course." Mrs. McCale accepted the paper, glanced over it, and nodded. "Starting tomorrow?"

"Aye." He leaned back on his chair again. "You know, Mrs. Chattoway, Violet Angel may have saved Ivy, in a way."

Mrs. McCale laughed, but she also nodded. "Stranger things have happened! We affect people without meaning to all the time, and Violet is no exception."

"Very true." Dr. McCale drummed his fingers against the desk. "I'm supposed to check in with the teachers about student progress reports in a few minutes here, and I'll definitely get their thoughts on this. Emma, will you come?"

"Aye."

"Mrs. Chattoway, is Ivy settled for the night?"

"Not yet." Nora swallowed, realizing she'd abandoned the little thing to wander around on the first floor. "I'll go put her to bed."

"Good. She'll have a busy day tomorrow!"

Early the next morning, Dr. McCale led Ivy away from the other students, upstairs to the room with the piano and the fire. Ivy had come to love this place, and she wasn't sure she wanted it tainted by school, but she submitted without question.

Dr. McCale walked across the room to the piano and pulled the bench out. "Sit down, Ivy."

Ivy jerked back. Though sitting there wasn't an issue, touching the keys or, worse yet, pushing them down was. She shook her head emphatically to let him know that it would definitely not be a good idea. "I don't play."

Dr. McCale repeated the inviting gesture, nodding his head toward the keys this time. "That's why I want to teach you. I'm no master, but I know enough to get you started, then we can decide who will finish the rest of your tutelage."

No. She couldn't. She *wouldn't*. Even given the beauty of the music the night before—or perhaps it was because of the beauty of the music the night before—she could not play, not when she would only botch it as badly as little Ned. Or Alice. She couldn't do better than Alice, and Alice was horrific. "I don't want to learn."

He seemed unconvinced. "Why not?"

Ivy thought about this for a moment. There was no reasonable reply. Saying that she thought her bad playing would disrespect the music hidden deep within the gorgeous grand piano seemed silly. What could she say that would make sense? She shrugged, imitating Alice's bored expression as best she could. "I don't like to."

"How do you know until you try?"

"I … I don't know." It was a fair argument, and she wasn't sure how to explain her desire to keep music in its pure and proper place.

Dr. McCale's face was gentle. "Now, Ivy, just give it a try. For me. I'd be so disappointed if you didn't!"

Ivy winced. She didn't want to disappoint him—perhaps she could try. But surely he'd see immediately how dreadful the noise was and let her stop.

She sat down on the piano bench and rested her hands on the keyboard, then glanced up at Dr. McCale for guidance. Surely he wouldn't just throw her into this without any instruction.

She couldn't do this.

"Go on."

Ivy sighed. She'd just have to show him what a bad idea this was. Closing her eyes as tight as she could and preparing herself for the horrible noise to follow, she pressed down on all the keys she could at once.

She almost moaned aloud at the horrible sound. The poor piano! She whispered, "I'm sorry," under her breath, but that didn't seem like enough to make up for it.

How could he make her do this to the piano?

"Don't be sorry. Try again. Play fewer keys—perhaps just pick one or two." There was a chuckle in Dr. McCale's voice, as if he found this to be a laughing matter. How insensitive of him. This was anything but funny!

Not wanting to be difficult, Ivy pressed just one. After trying a few different keys, she pressed another, and then a third. In no time, she found three that sounded wonderful together.

At least there was that much.

"That's it." Dr. McCale knelt next to the bench. "See what a beautiful sound you can make? You just have to go slow and steady."

Slow and steady, slow and steady. All right. She could try. It wouldn't be beautiful, but perhaps it wouldn't kill her inside to do it if she listened to every key as she pressed it.

"Shall I leave you to it?" Dr. McCale asked.

She nodded. She needed quiet to figure this out and having a person there disturbed her. If she was to get this right, it must be done by herself.

Ivy barely felt Dr. McCale leave the room. She was too focused on the music, on each note that created a better whole.

She found sounds that she was familiar with and began to turn them into a song, a hesitant song that was barely anything.

It turned into a melody she'd heard inside herself all her life but never been able to express. It was then that she paused to wipe tears from her eyes, and a sob escaped from her throat.

She'd done it. No, it wasn't perfect, and it was just one note at a time, but she'd done it. Ivy had discovered a way to share the songs inside her without dishonoring the entire musical world.

Ivy played all through the morning, and they had to pull her away to eat lunch. She was back right afterward, dragging Dr. McCale with her to explain how music worked. When he had to leave to tend to other things, she turned back to the piano to try again.

"If you learn to read, Ivy, you can read music theory books." Dr. McCale turned at the door. "So perhaps you won't be so stubborn about that anymore."

He was right—she certainly wouldn't be. She'd put her everything into this, for it must be her everything.

Again, she whispered, "Thank you." No response yet, but she somehow believed that it was important to thank last night's music and her reaction to it.

This would change everything.

"Ivy, come away from the piano for a moment!" Grandmother stood in the doorway of the room with the grand piano, arms folded across her chest. "You've been at it for hours."

Of course Ivy had been at it for hours! No one but Dr. McCale seemed to understand it, though—he always let her play the piano when she wasn't doing the schoolwork he made her do every day before she began. Sometimes she'd wake up before the birds and start playing. No one seemed to care for this much, however.

It had been six weeks since the night Ivy discovered the power of music. Since then, she'd poured herself into that and the only other thing that seemed to offer her hope of learning all the many details she must learn about music—reading.

Dr. McCale insisted that there was more to reading than simply learning music theory, but Ivy didn't see the purpose beyond that.

Music was everything.

"Grandmother, do I have to?" Ivy called over her shoulder. "Please don't make me. I don't have long before dinner, and I want to finish this!" Dr. McCale had given her some simple sheet music, which she'd quickly learned how to read and flown through.

Every day she learned new things one could read on sheet music, and Dr. McCale had made a "cheat sheet," which talked about what everything meant and what it did—notes, rests, time signatures, and everything else. Music seemed to have its own language—forte, pianissimo, tempo, fermata, octave. Pretty words, she thought, but not very familiar to her before these last weeks. Now these words were her life.

Today Ivy wanted to get through a more complicated piece she'd found that she was having to discover measure by measure.

"When I tell you what I've got, you'll be glad to take a break."

Sheet music, Ivy hoped, or a music theory book with simpler language than the one Dr. McCale had presented to her. Either way, she wouldn't be excited until she heard what it was that Grandmother thought would excite her.

Grandmother sighed, obviously disappointed Ivy didn't immediately react. "It's a letter from your mother for you."

Ivy blinked. That was exciting indeed! She found herself jumping up from the bench and dashing across the floor. She'd only received one letter from her mother before, and it'd been boring, simple things about how glad she was that Ivy was at McCale House and how nice it would be for Ivy to learn things there.

In no time, Ivy had the envelope in her hands. She opened it and removed the three sheets of paper, delighted by the length of the letter. She then sat down on the floor and began reading, slowly sounding out every word, though she did find it easier to understand the letter with her mind made clear by the music.

Thankfully, Mummy had written in an unadorned script, so Ivy could read it relatively easily.

> *My Dearest Girl,*
>
> *How I miss you, my darling! You have been such a light in my world. I wish you were here, but I know you are receiving the care you need at McCale House. I hope to come visit you sometime this autumn.*
>
> *I would like to see you in late August, but I might be ill early in that month, though you're not to worry, and I can't come for some time afterward. However, I hope you will write to me, perhaps with your grandmother's assistance. Your last note was treasured, though I wish you would try to write it yourself rather than have someone else take the words d own!*
>
> *It is difficult to be separated like this. I know it must be hard on you, but remember that I love you, and this parting is necessary. I've been praying for you continually.*
>
> *I hope you're remembering to say your prayers and reflect on God's Word every evening. Obey Dr. McCale and everyone in a position of authority at McCale House, including your grandmother.*

Mummy went on to write of the happenings at Pearlbelle Park, describing little things like Ned's asking after her and how Kitty seemed a little grumpier—though that could honestly be due to anything from her cream being too warm to her fur being petted the wrong way.

She chatted about Alice going back to school, and how they'd host a few of Alice's friends there for the summer. Uncle Charlie had returned to Pearlbelle Park to "see some friends there," which Ivy supposed might mean he was spending time with Miss Elton. Ivy didn't want him to, but there seemed to be no stopping it.

It made Ivy sad-happy, a strange combination that bit at the back of her brain and forced her to reevaluate her feelings. It was good that she was missed but bad that she wasn't there. It was good that her mother had filled her in but bad that she wasn't able to see and experience these things for herself. Good that Uncle Charlie was happy but bad that the happiness might come at the expense of more of his time and attention.

At the end of the letter was a post script written in a different handwriting, a little messier and therefore harder to read, but Ivy soon managed to translate.

> *Dear Ivy,*
>
> *I must add a quick note to say, as your mother has, that we miss you greatly here and are eager to see you again.*
>
> *You are a beautiful young lady, and I know you can succeed at whatever you put your mind to. I love you, even if I haven't been the best at showing it. I believe there is a lot more to you than meets the eye, and I can't wait to see it come to light!*
>
> *With love, your father, Philip E. Knight*

Ivy swallowed. She didn't know what to think about that. Though her mother and Alice were both in love with Mr. Knight, Ivy still couldn't see the reason for him. He was simply there, an addition to her life that she never would adjust to.

She passed the letter back to Grandmother. "Thank you. I like hearing from her. Can we write a reply? I ... I'll try to write it myself."

"That would be wonderful."

CHAPTER EIGHTEEN

March 1874

MARCH ARRIVED WITH A rush of color and sunlight, and the warmth of the garden was irresistible. Thankfully, now that the snow had melted, Dr. McCale was encouraging the students to go outside every day and get plenty of fresh air and exercise.

Ivy couldn't be happier. Her feet skipped as she walked down one of the paths between flower beds that now sported occasional sprouts. She took in deep breaths of the earthy scent drifting up from them. The sky was full of birds singing and chirping, and every so often she caught sight of one zipping to and fro. There were many trees, and she'd yet to find a nest, but she hoped to soon. Jordy had mentioned they had a few larks that built around the house.

Jordy left to show Felix a bush that was sprouting leaves—apparently, Felix liked plants—and Ivy found herself alone. She didn't care. It gave her mind time to rest.

She came around a bend and found a bench—and there was a girl sitting on it. She paused, squinting. It was not a girl she had seen before. Not a servant, not a student, not a teacher.

Perhaps it was—no, it couldn't be. She was still locked away upstairs.

Unless they'd let her out.

The girl was sitting up straight, almost stiffly, staring directly in front of her. Long, tangled dark hair was tucked behind her ears and flipped over her shoulders. She wore a simple brown dress, and her fingers nervously wore at the right sleeve, pushing it up and down her arm.

As Ivy approached, the girl looked up, then stood. She was as straight standing as she was sitting, slim to almost frailty, but two heads taller than Ivy. Her face was pale save for dark circles under her blue eyes.

The two stared at each other for a few moments, then the girl spoke.

"I suppose I'll have to go now." Her voice dragged like a moan, drawling in an odd way that definitely wasn't happy.

Ivy shook her head, the girl's voice waking her up. "Why?" She didn't know what else to say. Her mind was still catching up to the fact that this was the girl—the sobber, the screamer, the piano player, the one Ivy wished she could understand and did understand all at once.

"I don't particularly like the looks of you, and I don't want to talk. But," she added, "Dr. McCale wouldn't like that. He'd like it if I said, 'Do sit down and talk with me.' So do. Why not? Isn't my life meant to be controlled by the whims of the masses?" She sank down on the bench with a deep sigh.

Ivy walked over to the bench and sat down next to the girl. "I'm Ivy. I'm twelve." She hesitantly extended her hand, believing that was what was to be done when meeting a stranger.

The girl cringed away from her. "Violet. Fourteen. I don't care to shake hands—or to be touched at all—so don't."

Ivy's hand dropped. "I shan't." Until they got to know each other better, that would suit her just fine. Not that hugs weren't nice, but they were so much more pleasant with loved ones.

Violet squinted at her, looking her up and down like a specimen under glass. "Do you intend to sit here for a long time?"

"No. Yes. I mean, do I?" Ivy's stomach tightened, and she remembered to suck in a deep breath. Why did this girl hate her already? They'd hardly been introduced.

Violet shrugged. "I honestly don't care what you do."

"Oh." Confusion came then. Didn't Violet want her to leave? Though, it occurred to Ivy that Violet was a little confused herself.

"I suppose you're here because you're ... how does Dr. McCale put it? Mentally undeveloped?" A slight eye roll accompanied these words.

Ivy hesitated, folding her arms tightly over her stomach. "I'm here to learn. I can play the piano now."

Violet raised her eyebrows. "That's nothing. So can I. Anything else?"

She wiggled from side to side on the bench, and even a deep breath didn't dispel the tightness growing in her abdomen. "I can read better. Dr. McCale says I can learn other things if I don't get overwhelmed, but I get overwhelmed a lot."

"Hmm. That's what he says about me, only I'm likely worse than you—unless you're running away, too."

"You ran away ... to the garden?" Ivy asked, glancing around. This seemed like a mild place to "run away" to. She wasn't sure it even counted as running away.

Violet glanced over her shoulder. "Yes. I'm not to go outside unless someone's with me, but I don't like people, so why would I want someone to come with me?"

"I don't know," Ivy admitted. "Maybe you should learn to like people? I don't mind them. Some of them, anyway. But I don't have all the ones I don't mind anymore." Ivy dropped her eyes to her lap. Sometimes the sadness was almost gone, but other times she felt it quite deeply, and she had to make an effort not to cry. She wasn't used to weeping in front of strangers.

"Indeed. I'm sorry." Violet seemed to hesitate before continuing. "That's how the world works, I'm afraid. I have no one. I imagine you have a family who loves you or else you wouldn't be here; I have a family who hates me, and so I am here. Though, I suppose they couldn't have known I'd rather have died in Bedlam than live at McCale House."

Sympathy rose in Ivy's chest, blotting out her own grief. "I'm terribly sorry. I hope you'll leave sometime soon."

Violet shook her head, eyes glued straight in front of her, unblinking.

"No. I'll spend the rest of my life here. I've heard them say so. I'm a hopeless case."

Ivy squinted. "But you seem all right. I don't know a lot about what people call normal, but you don't seem any different from the rest of them." At least she could talk, and other than rubbing her arm, she seemed calm.

"That's because I'm calm today. I'm at my best. Tomorrow or next hour or next minute, I'll be back to what I normally am. I never know how long I can handle things."

"Handle things?" Even as she said it, Ivy knew what Violet meant. There was a certain limit that one arrived at—and it was different for every person—and once that limit was reached, it was almost impossible to go back.

"I've heard them talking about me. You'll probably hear them talking about you if you listen. But I don't care and neither should you." Violet abruptly stood, then lowered herself back onto the bench, her fingers catching the edge and gripping it. "I'm not here to be the way other people want me to be. I'm not even going to try. I don't think I could be normal if I wanted to be, which I don't."

After Ivy recovered from the shock of Violet's abrupt movements, she replied. "I'm going to try to be what they want me to be. But I don't think Dr. McCale wants us to be anything different than who we are at our best."

"Perhaps," Violet said, and she was starting to say more when a good-natured "Hullo!" was heard from up the path.

"We've all been looking for you, Violet," said Jordy McAllen, smiling broadly. "Will you come back with me? Or would you rather we stay here? It doesn't matter as long as we know where you are. You mustn't wander off like that."

The girl's eyes livened at the sight of Jordy, sparkling in a quiet, special way that made Ivy wonder. Violet rose and stepped toward him, almost seeming to reach for his hand, but stopped herself. They left together, Jordy saying something about her getting lost on the property.

Ivy watched Jordy and Violet disappear over the rise on the way back to the house, but she sat there in silence for a while longer. The birds were still chirping, the sun was still shining, but Ivy's thoughts were taking her far away from the bright spring day around her.

Violet Angel was hurting. That much was true. But she wasn't the monster Ivy had been frightened of while she screamed, and she wasn't as broken, perhaps, as Ivy had thought when she'd heard the sobs.

Who was Violet Angel? Why did she behave the way she behaved? How could Ivy help her?

As of yet, there were no answers, but Ivy was determined to find them. She had to help. Somehow, she had to!

Ivy narrowed her eyes at the sheet music in front of her, a slightly more complicated piece that she'd only had for a few days. She thought she understood how it worked, but there was always that moment of uncertainty.

She placed her fingers on the keys and pressed them down, a few at a time as the notes on the paper directed. A beautiful tune began to bloom under her fingers, and a smile slipped over her lips.

She was doing it. Really doing it!

"I slipped out again."

Ivy's hands slid off the keyboard, and she turned to find Violet Angel standing directly behind her.

"Can you read the music? You're playing with a degree of accuracy."

"I can read it," Ivy said, not without a sense of pride. But then she realized that she didn't know enough to be proud, and she changed her phrasing. "That is, I can read most of it. I don't understand it all."

"I see." Violet took a seat on the bench next to her and placed her own hands on the keys. "It's simple." She played the first few bars quickly.

"There. That's all there is to it. Let's see you try again."

Ivy hesitantly placed her hands on the keys, feeling the cool texture of the ivory. She played it correctly, but much slower, or at least she thought it was correct. Her eyes rose to Violet's when she finished.

"That was all right, but I'm better." Violet leaned back. "We'll have to go over it a few more times."

Have to? As in there was no choice but to? But Ivy agreed—there was a lot of practice to be done. She leaned forward and picked out the correct positioning for her fingers, arching her hands like Mrs. McCale had told her, and began to play.

Violet made her stop and go over different bars over and over again. Ivy didn't protest. She wasn't sure what to say to Violet.

Sitting in this room, with the girl at her side playing the music with such grace and feeling whenever she felt obliged to take over from Ivy—which was often—reminded her of a few things. That this room was where she'd heard Violet play. That Violet was the one who had helped her discover the beauty of music. That she wanted to help Violet in return.

Some of these thoughts made Ivy hesitate, made her make little mistakes in the piece, but Violet made her try again and again until she could play the music with her eyes closed and her mind elsewhere.

Which was nice. The ability to play while not thinking allowed a distance that let her thoughts flow freely. Though her senses were engaged, her mind was not, so it was allowed to form clearer thoughts.

Clearer thoughts became clearer words, and she whispered, "You saved me, Violet."

Violet dropped her hands from the keys. "I did not."

"Yes, you did. You just didn't know it. A few weeks ago ... you saved me." Beyond that, she hadn't thought of an explanation.

"I see." Violet tapped her chin. "I'll accept that. Not sure how I managed it, but I believe you. Of course, I must say, I might not have if I had known I was doing it at the time."

Ivy blinked. Violet wouldn't help someone if the opportunity to do so was presented? Ivy couldn't imagine ever feeling like that. "Why not?"

"Because I don't like helping people." She picked at a few keys, played an eerie chord. "No one has ever helped me, after all."

Ivy hesitated, then screwed up her courage and spoke the words she'd been trying to discover for some time now. "I could help you."

Violet's eyebrows shot up quicker than Ivy could blink. "Oh, have we a reformer in our midst?"

"N-no." Ivy wasn't sure what a reformer was, but she didn't think she was that. "I just like helping people, and you helped me—really, you did!—so I thought—"

"Try to stop thinking, dear. It'll hurt your head." Violet smiled, though it wasn't exactly a happy smile—more pleased with herself than anything. "Do you often think you can help people?"

"Not often. Just ... just once, actually." Ivy wiggled, causing the bench to squeak. She caught the piano, just in case the bench decided to collapse on her, but that caused a discordant clash as her fingers smashed the keys.

Violet winced. "Don't do that."

"I know." She hated it, too. "But it's just that ... I don't know why, but I feel as if we could be friends, and we could talk ... talk about music, like we did today. And then maybe you'd feel better?"

A soft chuckle issued from the older girl's throat, causing a bit of a shudder to trickle its way up Ivy's spine, ending at the back of her neck. "Oh, Ivy. What a lump of sugar you are."

Was that a compliment? Ivy couldn't tell, even after examining Violet's face closely. "Thank you?"

"You did well to put it as a query, my dear little trifle." Violet stood from the bench and ran her fingers over a few keys, though of course when she did it, it sounded nice, a little trill of sound. "*Trifle* is a good name for you. A bit sickening, a bit pointless, and likely someday you'll be more than a bit intoxicating. You have the looks for it. But in the end, you're just a trifling little thing." She smirked.

Ivy blinked. She hadn't caught half of that, but she could tell it wasn't entirely complimentary. She'd have to sort through the bad and cling to the good, such as there was, or she'd never be Violet's friend.

"Yes, my little Trifle ..." Violet walked over toward the fireplace, unlit though it was, and knelt near it. "I suppose we could talk music a bit. If I feel up to it, which I don't know I shall, and if I don't become too sickened by your candied flowers before then."

"All right." There seemed to be a lot of *ifs* involved, but Ivy was willing to accept them as long as it wasn't *no*. "When shall we meet again?"

Violet rose to her feet. "Don't you worry about that, Trifle. I'll find you." With that, she quit the room, leaving Ivy staring after her.

CHAPTER NINETEEN

April 1874

E VERY SUNDAY, ALL THE students of McCale House who were able went to church in Edinburgh. It was a grand church with arches and far, far too many people.

As usual, Ivy struggled with sitting still at first, but she soon drifted into dreamland. She stared blankly at the pulpit until it was time to go home. Grandmother would ramble on about the sermon later anyway, trying to "help" Ivy learn, so she would get the idea.

After church, the group returned to McCale House. Ivy was tired, and Dr. McCale suggested she have a light lunch in her room and take a nap.

Later in the afternoon, perhaps an hour or so before tea, Ivy again went walking in the garden and found Violet Angel sitting on her favorite bench. She was thoughtful today, her hands folded neatly on her lap, staring at the sky which was melting into a late afternoon blue that mirrored the color of her eyes.

"Hello, Violet," said Ivy.

"Hello." Violet kept her eyes glued on the sky, refusing to glance down.

After standing on tiptoes and walking toward her to catch her eye, Ivy gave up and took a seat on the bench next to Violet. "How are you?"

"I never thought you'd ask such a silly question," Violet said with a light laugh. "The only answer I could possibly reply with is 'I'm well, thank you. How are you?' I'm never well. At least, that's what they tell me."

"Is that why you don't go to church?"

Violet laughed, a many-toned, raucous giggle. "No, my little Trifle. It's because they think I'm mad."

Ivy winced. That wasn't kind. She swallowed hard, hoping that it wasn't true. "Are you?"

"Sometimes."

Ivy blinked. If Violet was only sometimes mad, then that was better than nothing. "Couldn't you have gone to church today? You seem all right."

"I am, but I don't want to go to church. It's nonsense, and I don't care for nonsense except my own."

Ivy's chest compressed all of a sudden, and she struggled to catch her breath. "What do you mean? Of course it's not nonsense!" How horrid of someone to say that—and how untrue!

"Why do you think that?"

"Because Nettie said so! And the Bible says so." These two were enough to convince Ivy of anything. Nettie was always right, and of course the Bible was, too.

"The Bible is just a book, and Nettie is just a person."

Ivy's mouth dropped at these sacrileges. "But God said—"

Violet held up her hand. "Ivy. There is no God."

Breath coming in short pants, she jerked to face the older girl. She had to take a deep breath to settle herself down, but once she did, her words were clearer. "Of course there is. The world and everything in it was made by God."

A chuckle emerged from Violet's throat once again, causing a shudder to beeline its way down Ivy's back. "Oh, that I had your confidence in what people tell me. Not that I want it much anyway, Trifle—people are inconsistent and unworthy of trust, if you haven't noticed. Have you any more flashes of sunlight to shine on my gray world?"

Ivy blinked. "What do you mean?"

Violet shrugged, barely moving her shoulders as if the action weren't worth her full effort. "Any more wisdom to impart?"

"Oh." Perhaps she could tell Violet the full story and she would understand? Stories helped Ivy understand. "God made the world perfect, but He put us people in it, and He loves us. Because He loved us, He gave the first humans a choice—to obey Him, or not to. They wouldn't obey Him, so the world couldn't be perfect anymore, and from then on the world was ... corrupted." These words weren't her own, but they were good enough. Let Violet make light of her mentors—Ivy knew and trusted them, and what they said was true.

"Mm. How fascinating. Well. I know there's more to it." She made a movement with her hand to encourage Ivy to continue.

She was glad to do just that. "Of course there is, for God loves us, remember? So He sacrificed His Son and covered us with His glory so we could be near Him forever."

"How wonderful." Violet's voice dripped like syrup, too sweet.

Ivy swallowed. Really? "I think so, too."

Violet jerked to her feet, wrapping her arms around herself, and her eyes flew here and there, as if searching for something in the empty air around her. "Thank you, Ivy." Now her words trembled, dipping and diving like a swallow on the breeze. "I'll see you later."

Confused, Ivy watched Violet go. It was as if she'd been affected by Ivy's words, yet not. She laughed at what Ivy said and then her eyes started hurting.

What a strange girl Violet was. All the more reason to be her friend.

A scream pierced the air, and Ivy jolted up. For a moment she lay there panting, wondering if it had been a nightmare, but the scream came again—wild and out of control.

This time she didn't hesitate. Her feet hit the floor, and she ran for the door, not even bothering to collect her dressing gown or slippers.

In the hallway, her cold bare feet pattered against the wood. She raced up the stairs, not minding the steep darkness of them. She had a mission, and without thinking, she was able to accomplish it unafraid.

At last she reached the door to Violet's room. There was a light under it, and Miss Lang's voice already echoed, soothingly, through it.

"Ivy?" Dr. McCale's voice came up the stairs behind her—he must have heard Violet, too. "What are you doing up?"

She ignored him, opened the door, and rushed in.

Violet stood by her bed, her arms wrapped around herself, half bent over as if her stomach hurt. A little whimper escaped from her lips, and she slid to the floor and screamed again.

"Violet, dear." Miss Lang sighed and knelt next to her. "Come here. Let's ... let's calm down and take a sip of tea. It'll settle your nerves."

"I-I can't. I won't! Don't make me—stop touching me! I want ... I want ..." Her voice was lost in a sob, and Ivy stepped forward.

"Can I help?"

Both Violet and Miss Lang froze. Miss Lang looked from Ivy to, she presumed, Dr. McCale behind her—and then shrugged and stepped back from Violet.

"Violet, it's your friend, Ivy," Miss Lang crooned.

Violet straightened, to her full height and regarded Ivy with bloodshot, wild eyes. "Trifle," she whispered.

"Hmm?" Miss Lang cocked her head. "What's that? Trifle?"

Dr. McCale cleared his throat. "Never mind that, Miss Lang. Why don't you run along and get a few hours of sleep? I can handle this—Emma was coming to replace you in half an hour anyway."

Miss Lang hesitated, then nodded and quit the room into the adjoining chamber. After the door clicked shut, Violet relaxed.

Ivy took a few more hesitant steps across the chamber. "Violet, it's me. What is it? Why do you scream? Are you all right?"

Violet clenched her fists. "It ... it's ..." She lowered herself onto the edge of the bed and pressed her hands to her forehead. "It's over now."

"Was it a nightmare?" Ivy suggested.

"Yes—I think that was it."

Dr. McCale came up beside Ivy. "Why don't you let Ivy chat with you, Violet?"

Ivy glanced up. Did he, too, think she could be a help? He made a forward gesture, and Ivy crept to the edge of the bed and sat down next to Violet.

Violet remained still, her hands over her face and her breaths ragged. Ivy put her arm around Violet and gave her a hug, and the older girl didn't protest—was that a good sign or a bad one? Violet did seem to hate touch, so maybe she'd given up, but perhaps that was a façade. Who knew?

Only Violet and God, Ivy imagined.

"I ... I *hate* being here." Violet leaned somewhat heavily on Ivy. "I don't like it. I want to go ... oh, I don't know where I want to go. There's nowhere to go!"

There wasn't. Ivy leaned her head on Violet's shoulder and sighed. "I know, Violet. But it's not so bad! Everyone here is so nice, and you have your own piano—I haven't even my own like you have up here—so that's nice. And there's a lovely yard to go out into—"

"It's a ... a cage."

"Is it?" Ivy cocked her head. "It's an awfully big cage, then. And anyways, Jordy says we'll go on a picnic this spring out on the hill—the walls are just there to keep us safe."

"Oh, Ivy ..." Violet heaved another little sob. "It's to keep us in. It's to keep us captive. To keep the rest of the world ... to keep us from hurting them."

Ivy narrowed her eyes and looked up to Dr. McCale. "Is that why there are walls?"

He shook his head. "The walls were here when we bought the property, but we really can't have you all wandering away—there are too many cliffs and animals and people and other things we can't trust on the moors.

They're for safety."

"See?" Ivy released Violet and scooted back on the bed, toward the pillow. "Just to keep us safe. Isn't that nice, dearest?" She made her voice just like Mummy's. "Come up here. We'll talk about it." She was getting sleepy now that the shock of the screams in the night had worn off, but she was determined not to sleep until Violet did.

If that ever happened. Violet didn't seem sleepy, despite the big, dark circles under her eyes.

What could she do to get poor Violet settled in for the night? What did her mother do when it was time for bed but no one wanted to sleep? Oh, she remembered.

"Can I tell you a bedtime story?"

Violet, too, slid back on the bed, all the way to the headboard, where she leaned back with a defeated sigh. "I suppose so, Trifle. Though I've not had a bedtime story in a long time—if you haven't noticed, I'm too old for those."

Ivy smiled. "You're never too old for a bedtime story, Violet! Now, let me think. Shall I tell you about the Snow Queen or a princess who—"

Violet's eyes sparkled slightly. "Oh, always tell me about a queen rather than a princess, Trifle. Give me someone I can respect."

Ivy wrinkled her nose. She wasn't all too sure she respected this particular queen, but she'd tell the story if Violet wanted to hear it. She sat still for a moment, remembering how Nettie had begun, then she started the story.

"Let me see. Once upon a time, in a faraway land a long time ago, there was an evil troll—"

Violet cleared her throat. "Who was also the devil."

Ivy blinked. Of all things! "Wherever do you get these ideas, Violet? Let me tell the story." It was her turn to talk, after all.

"Who told it to you?"

"Oh, Nettie."

Violet giggled. "That explains it. Go on, Trifle."

"The troll, who was probably not the devil—although he does have some strange powers—had a magic mirror. Like in Snow White, only not that at all. This magic mirror doesn't show all the good things in people. It just shows the *bad* things—and it shows them big and scary!"

"How frightening." Violet curled up on her side and propped her head on her hand. "Sounds like a great many people I know."

Dr. McCale chuckled behind them, startling Ivy, who had forgotten he was there. "Sounds like you two have it under control. Mrs. McCale will be up in a few moments—I'll leave you to it."

Violet nodded and waved him away. "Go on."

"The troll and his underlings used the mirror to distort the world, but one day, they dropped it. It fell to earth and shattered into a billion pieces, some smaller than the smallest bit of sand. The splinters blew all over the earth and got into people's hearts and eyes. If a splinter got into your eyes, it'd turn them into a mirror that saw only the bad and ugly in people and things—and it froze hearts like blocks of ice."

"I'm surprised Nettie told you this." Violet smirked. "I do so love a moral allegory. Seems most people have those splinters in them still, Trifle."

Ivy winced. "Perhaps." But she knew so many beautiful things and beautiful people in this world that she doubted it. "Years and years passed. There were two friends who lived next door to each other, Kai and Gerda. They had a flower garden, and they grew roses. Their grandmother told them a story—it was about a Snow Queen who ruled an army of snowflakes—"

"Snow bees."

Ivy narrowed her eyes. "Violet, that's just silly. Now can I just tell the story, please?"

"Very well, but Nettie is trimming it down."

"She had an army of snowflakes. The grandmother told them that she could be seen wherever the snowflakes clustered the most. One day, while looking out the window, Kai caught sight of the Snow Queen. She beckoned to him, as if asking him to follow, but he was frightened, so he wouldn't."

Violet rolled her eyes. "Good for him. Even I know not to follow strangers."

Ivy glared. "Can I—"

"Yes, yes, I'm being quiet."

"But that's just it—you're not!"

"Whatever. Go on about the mirror splinters."

Ivy cocked her head. "How did you know? Yes, that summer, while he was playing in the garden, Kai got a splinter in his eye! He became mean and nasty, and he only saw the ugly things in this world. He didn't care about Gerda anymore—after all, he only saw the bad and ugly in her, even though there wasn't much to see.

"That winter, Kai caught sight of the Snow Queen again—only this time he followed her out of the city. She kissed him—"

"My, you didn't tell me it was going to be *that* kind of story!"

Ivy moaned. The story was never going to end at this rate. "It's not. These were *magic* kisses."

Violet flopped on her back and grinned at the ceiling. "If someone tells you kisses are magic, don't believe them. You'll get yourself in more trouble than you can handle, Trifle."

"Perhaps they are." Ivy wasn't really intending to kiss anyone until she was good and ready, though, so she was willing to wait and find out. "These kisses were. The first one made it so he wouldn't get cold—and the second so he would forget Gerda and his family. If the queen kissed him a third time, he'd die, but she didn't."

"Thank goodness."

"The Snow Queen took Kai away to her castle, and the whole village believed he drowned in the river. But Gerda didn't believe it—that next summer, she asked the river—"

Violet snorted. "Could you back up and explain a bit?"

"About what?"

"The talking river!"

"It's a fairytale. I don't have to explain. Now, Gerda found out from the river that Kai didn't drown, so she continued her search."

"Ah, young love. So naïve. More than likely he found a prettier Gerda to keep him busy."

"Violet, you—"

"I'm shushing."

"But you're not!"

Violet mimed buttoning her lips. "Mow my am," she mumbled.

"All right." Ivy took a deep breath. "Where was I? Oh, right. Gerda searched and searched for Kai, and she ran into some trouble on the way, which I shan't get into since it's so late."

"But Ivy, if you don't tell about the trouble, mentioning the rose garden earlier on has no purpose!"

"Violet, please. At last, after many adventures, Gerda met a reindeer named Bae, who knew where Kai was. On the way there, they stopped at a few places. At one home, a Finnish woman told Bae that Gerda was the only one who can save Kai—do you know how?"

Violet just flipped her hand in a "get on with it" movement.

"Because she was so good and pure and innocent. She was the only one who could remove the splinters from Kai's eyes. At last, Gerda reached the Snow Queen's palace and found her way to Kai, who was imprisoned on a lake of ice until he could form fragments on ice together into a word she'd given him to spell."

"Dear boy just needed a few more years of school." Violet snickered.

Ivy ignored her. "Gerda ran to Kai and kissed him—see, Violet, that was a good kiss! It melted the mirror splinter in his eye, and he remembered her. They danced together, and the splinters of ice shifted to spell the word—eternity."

"Why *eternity*?"

"Oh, I don't know. Then they escaped from the Snow Queen's lair and"—Ivy yawned—"lived happily ever after. Oh, and it's summer, and the world was a much better place. The end."

Violet adjusted the pillow under her head. "I wish them many children and whatever else it is that people want in a marriage, though I can't imagine wanting anything of the sort."

Ivy blinked. "Oh, I think they're just best of friends, Violet—not sweethearts. Kai and Gerda, I mean. It's about friendship, you know."

"Ah, the innocence." Violet rested her head on the pillow. "I'm settled now. Thank you for the lovely, censored version of the Snow Queen."

"What's *censored*?"

"Never mind. Will you stay here with me tonight? Just … just until I fall asleep, at least." Violet seemed to be struggling with a yawn or two herself.

"Yes, I can do that."

"It's not because I care about you—just because I'd hate for you to open the door and let anything in from those drafty halls." Violet rolled over with her back to Ivy. "Now it's your turn to stop talking, Trifle."

"Oh, all right." That wasn't a challenge at this hour. Ivy settled down under the covers and was soon fast asleep.

CHAPTER TWENTY

"I T'S PRACTICALLY A MIRACLE." Dr. McCale leaned toward Nora with his eyes twinkling. "To think, that little wisp of a thing taming our resident beast."

Mrs. McCale's hand went to her husband's arm, a gentle rebuke. "Callum, Violet is not a beast."

Nora wasn't sure she agreed, but she didn't want to seem cruel, so she said nothing as she eased herself onto the chair across from Dr. McCale. She'd heard in the morning that Ivy had slipped out during the night to be with Violet and had calmed another of her tantrums.

Since then, Violet had remained close to Ivy's side, even venturing down to do some schoolwork. Ivy didn't seem to mind her shadow—she chatted with Violet continually, and though the older girl's replies were nothing short of toxic, the dear thing hardly seemed to notice.

Ivy really was a gem.

"Violet has never been calmed that quickly after an episode—or a nightmare." Dr. McCale rested his arms on the desk in front of him. "I'd like to know what it is about Ivy that so appeals to Violet. She's so cruel to the other students—she's cruel to Ivy, too, but somehow it doesn't seem to matter. Somehow their friendship works."

"I think it's because Ivy is so innocent and gentle, so unassuming." Mrs. McCale smiled. "She's a dear one, Mrs. Chattoway, and no mistaking it!

Violet told me Ivy told her a story, and though she joked about it, it must have meant a lot to her. The Snow Queen, you know, with the shattered mirror."

"Oh." Dr. McCale nodded. "I wonder if that meant something to Violet. It is a familiar theme to her life, after all. Especially these last two years. You must believe Violet wasn't always like this, Mrs. Chattoway. Actually, she was quite the opposite for many years."

"Yes, she was a dear." Mrs. McCale sighed, obvious sadness in her eyes. "She was a frightened, troubled little girl, but after a while, she seemed to adjust to McCale House. She learned quickly, and her intelligence is incredible—you wouldn't know it, but she's almost a genius."

"She is bright. Well-read, too. I believe she's read every book in the house more than once, and we have a large library." A smile appeared on Dr. McCale's face. "I wouldn't say this about anything else in regards to Violet, but we are two birds of a feather when it comes to reading."

"Yes, you are." Mrs. McCale nodded. "But ... you know how difficult it is to become a woman, Mrs. Chattoway—"

Dr. McCale cleared his throat. "I am still here."

"You'll bear it. It wasn't just that, of course—that was when her moods started shifting drastically, but I don't think it's a simple matter of maturing. I think it's more than that." Mrs. McCale cocked her head. "You'd agree, Callum, wouldn't you?"

"Yes, yes, I would." He stood. "I have other duties to attend to that I'm delaying for this, but I suppose I just wanted to express that your granddaughter has been a great help, at least today. It's been weeks since Violet has behaved this well."

After Dr. McCale left the room, Mrs. McCale turned to Nora. "I can see you're skeptical of Violet, but now that Callum's gone, I'd like to tell you more about her."

"Oh?" Nora shifted on her seat, gripping the arms. She did have a bit of a hard heart toward the child, but then, she was afraid that Violet would hurt Ivy. It seemed within the realm of belief given that Ivy was so innocent and Violet so unpredictable.

"Yes. Callum wouldn't like my saying this—he thinks I get too attached to the children. But would any woman with a heart in her breast do anything less? They're little things, often, when they come here. Violet was the youngest we've ever had—just five, and her father ... Mr. Angel was hard toward her. I think he wanted a son first." Mrs. McCale shrugged. "I detested the man. He's not come to see the child, or allowed Mrs. Angel to come—that I'm simply guessing at, though. Mrs. Angel does write occasionally, to us not to Violet, and says things such as, 'I would like to come, but my husband thinks it's not for the best.' With a husband as you seem to have had, Mrs. Chattoway, you understand."

Nora nodded. It was wrong of Mrs. Angel to give in to it, but Nora did understand. Men could be a powerful force for evil in this world if they weren't what God had created them to be—restrained, gentle, protective, and loving above all else.

She'd known such men. Dr. McCale seemed to be a good one, though he was a little brusque at times. Her Charlie was like that—he might have a rough exterior, or pretend to, but beneath that, he was everything he ought to be.

"Apparently, Mr. Angel sent Violet away because she was having fits and 'acting strange,' but I suspect that there was also a disdain for her and her behavior and impatience with her lack of growth. She was a small child, physically, and she wasn't speaking when she arrived—she could not be convinced to talk, only to scream." Mrs. McCale stood and began sorting papers on her husband's desk into piles. "I think there was also a certain amount of neglect. Mrs. Angel seemed pleasant if light-headed—pardon my saying so, but there it is. She's probably more interested in her next party than her children. And Mr. Angel is a cold man."

A cold man. Three little words that spoke pages to Nora's soul. "I see. But Violet did bloom at McCale House for a time?"

Mrs. McCale smiled. "Violet 'blooming' is appropriate, but I wouldn't call it that. She began to speak, slowly, though with a slur. Eventually, she caught on, and now, of course, you can't tell. After she began reading, it was all we could do to make her sleep. That's still an issue at times." Her lips quirked. "But then, she doesn't really seem to need a lot of sleep."

"Yes." Nora shifted in her seat. "So you must have practically raised her."

"Aye." Mrs. McCale shrugged. "My only child, Helen, who is married now with a babe on the way, was too old to need my cuddles by then. I wished we'd had more children, but we couldn't. I was glad to take Violet on and mother her. Callum doesn't believe it's practical to get overly attached—but as I said, I have a heart, and I'm not afraid of that fact. She was sweet, in her own way, and so precocious once she adjusted to McCale House.

"But she's changed. She's not our Violet, exactly, which is difficult. When she's with Ivy, I see a glimpse of the Violet I was familiar with, who would share her thoughts with me and keep control of herself. I'm not sure how much is put on and how much is unstoppable—but I believe if Violet would lose some of her fear and understand that we still love her and want to help her, she would be able to find some comfort, at least."

"I see." Nora sighed. "I'm sorry. You're right—we don't know how much of Violet is put on for show and how much is real."

"She is legitimately frightened sometimes—I know her anxiety eats at her. And she has so many nightmares and fears. Right now music is the only thing that seems to comfort her. Even reading tends to make her seem depressed and lonely." Mrs. McCale shook her head. "We'll keep trying, and perhaps Ivy will show us how to help Violet. I think that Ivy will benefit as much as Violet does from this friendship. She's learning to communicate with someone rather difficult and to be helpful in that relationship. That's a skill she'll not soon forget."

"That's true." Nora had never thought of that. Perhaps Violet offered as much to Ivy, in a roundabout way, as Ivy offered to Violet. It was worth thinking about.

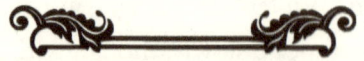

May 1874

Ivy's laughter hit the warm air in uncontrollable giggles, almost bending her over. Seeing Jordy stagger around with a white handkerchief tied over his eyes was enough to make her die of amusement.

"See, an' now I ken where ye're at." Jordy stopped and put his hands on his hips, imitating Mrs. McCale rather obviously. "Ye dinna seem tae understand th' game."

"I understand." Ivy backed up from him, taking small, gentle steps on the soft green grass of the McCale House lawns, barefoot to eliminate extra noise. "I'm sorry. You just look so silly!"

"I suppose I do." He reached up to adjust his blindfold.

"No peeking!" Violet called from behind him. "Hands down, McAllen."

He sighed and dropped his hands to his sides. "Ye've got it tae tight, Violet."

"It's supposed to be tight." Violet walked up right behind Jordy and tapped his back.

He whirled around, but somehow his feet got tangled up under him, and he fell on his backside with a shout.

This time both Violet and Ivy laughed. But Violet shouldn't have, for Jordy lunged in her direction, caught her skirts, and jerked her to the ground.

"Got ye!" he said, triumphantly. "Now it's just Ivy, an' ye'll be 'it' next, Violet."

Violet thrashed her legs twice, then lay still, defeated. "Well then, get Ivy, and I'll catch you both twice as fast. I've better ears than you."

Jordy propped himself up on his elbow, once again reaching up to adjust his mask.

"Jordy!"

"I'm just straightening it! An' ye havena better ears than me."

"Aye, I have," Violet said, imitating his accent perfectly. "An' anyway, ye're such a clumsy oaf tha' I've twice th' chance ye do o' winnin'."

"Dinna." But Jordy jumped to his feet, seeming content to let the argument go. "Now where are you, Ivy?"

She wouldn't speak now. She wouldn't. Though, with just three players, there was only so long one could delay the game—yet she wasn't content to let it end so soon. She stepped back, but her foot caught on a root from a nearby tree, and she gasped softly at the twinge to her ankle.

"There ye are."

She jumped back, further twisting her ankle, but she'd made the mistake of moving close when he fell over. Even still, he was upon her in two lunges.

He caught her arm and jerked her toward him. "Ha! An' now I've got ye both. But it's Violet's turn, no' yers, Ivy, so I suppose ye've won."

Once the excitement was over, the pain in Ivy's ankle caught up to her. "I hurt myself," she whispered.

"Hmm?" Jordy pushed the blindfold up, causing his hair to stick up oddly. "How?"

"My ankle."

Jordy's eyes darkened. "I'm sorry! What happened?"

"I tripped over the root, trying to get away."

"Ah, I see." He helped her sit down on the grass and examined her ankle. "Looks like it was just a twinge, an' it's no' swollen, but let's sit down for a moment." He plopped down next to her. "Violet, how does it feel tae have lost?"

Violet strutted over to them. "It was only once. You'll lose many more times before the day's over. If there were more people, it'd be easier."

"Aye, tha's true, but it doesna change th' fact that ye lost." His eyes twinkled. "Now, admit it, Vi—ye're human like th' rest o' us."

She rolled her eyes as she lowered herself onto the ground on Jordy's other side. "Such a proud lad ye are, McAllen."

"Aye, an' I've a reason tae be. How's yer ankle, Ivy?"

"Getting better." It turned out Jordy was right; the pain was fading fast. "I just want to catch my breath."

"A'right. An' I've got tae convince Violet tha' I'm perfect in every way, so I've time tae rest."

"As if ye ever could!" Violet said, still sticking to her Scots accent, which was rapidly disintegrating into something pirate-y. "I've no need for ye."

Jordy turned to Ivy, pretending not to be paying any attention to Violet. "Ach, Ivy, she doesna admit it, but she loves me."

There was an oddly serious light in Violet's eyes as she replied, "Perhaps I do," but Dr. McCale's voice was heard calling them back to the manor house, and there wasn't time to think about it.

"There you three are! I'd started to think you'd run off. Ivy, your grandmother has some letters she wants you to read."

It was always lovely to get more letters from Mummy, so Ivy raced back to the house. She found her grandmother already settled on one of the small sitting rooms with a few letters in her hands.

"There you are! Would you like to read it for yourself?"

Ivy nodded eagerly, holding her hand out for the letter.

> *My Ivy,*
>
> *My dearest, can you believe how long it's been? It won't be long before we're able to see each other again.*
>
> *What news I have from Pearlbelle Park! Nettie has a new little baby at her house now. It's a girl, and they have decided to call her Ella—she was christened Elinor Hope Jameson last week.*
>
> *Now, there will be another baby here in a few short months, and after he arrives, I shall feel better, and I can come to see you. Perhaps you can even come home!*
>
> *I'm sorry that it can't be now, but your father feels it's best to not remove you from school until we are able to go see you. That can't be until September, at the earliest.*
>
> *I'm sure you shall love this baby, and of course you'll love Nettie's Ella as much as you love Malcolm. Our baby may be a little sister or perhaps another little brother like Ned, which I know you'll like.*

Ivy wrinkled her nose. Why did her mother think that Ivy could reconcile herself to another young brother or sister? Ned was already more trouble than he was worth, and the newcomer was sure to take everyone's love even further from her. Didn't Mummy know this?

Yet the letter continued on for a few more paragraphs, praising the benefits of being an older sister and how nice it would be to have a little one looking up to Ivy, loving her and giving her someone else to love.

Utter nonsense, in Ivy's opinion. Babies were all right, in their proper place, but their family already had as many as one could wish for.

Your father misses you, of course, and Uncle Charlie mentions you when he comes to visit. He's been at Pearlbelle Park a great deal lately. I don't believe in gossip, dearest, but it would seem that, perhaps, we will have a wedding here soon!

In other news, that young stable boy who helped you, Kirk Manning, will be starting at a boy's school soon. Your father thought it was a fitting reward, and his mother feels that he ought to have an education.

Alice expressed some concerns in a letter to us that his family would be unsupported if he left, but given that we own the land they live on, we can definitely see that they're supported. So it will work out splendidly.

That's about all the news here from Pearlbelle Park! I love you and pray God will bless you every day with His wisdom and care.

Your mother,

Claire Knight

Ivy put down the letter with a little sigh. At least her mother was happy, even if Ivy was far away from her and not able to properly experience it. She missed everyone there greatly. She was even starting to wish she could see Mr. Knight or Mr. Parker, just to be reminded that her mother was a real person who lived at a real place with real people.

Yet it was only until September, and she could—must—bear it until then.

Not that there weren't nice things, wondrous things, about McCale House. A bit of a smile flickered across her lips, refusing to be put down, when she thought of them. Violet and Jordy and Dr. and Mrs. McCale and music and reading ...

Perhaps her mother had been right, after all, about sending her here. There were so many beautiful things to discover.

CHAPTER TWENTY-ONE

A BEAUTIFUL SONG BLOOMED under Ivy's fingers as she trailed them over the keys, following her own instinct more than the sheet music in front of her. It was such a lovely piece, the tune by Beethoven, and she wanted to keep it going on forever.

At last, though, she knew she must bring it to a conclusion, and she did, with a chord which she made trail out as long as she could.

Her fingers slipped from the keys, and she glanced at Violet. "Was that better?"

"Mm ... a bit. There were a few times when your fingers hesitated. You want to feel as if your fingers flow from key to key without hesitation, restraint, or haste."

That was a lovely way of describing it. Ivy sighed. "Do you think I'll ever be perfect?"

"Probably not, but you'll be better than me in another month. There's a lot of natural talent in you."

Ivy wiggled in pleasure. It was rare that Violet complimented her or anyone—in fact, this might be only the second time she'd heard the older girl say something positive about her. Yet there it was. An actual compliment. Ivy had natural talent. She would exceed Violet in talent, and the beautiful music that gave her so much joy would be even more beautiful with every day that passed.

There was a rightness about playing the piano, as if she knew that she was doing what she was meant to be doing, what she ought to be doing.

"I wonder if God can use piano playing," she murmured. "You know, for something other than fun."

Violet shrugged. "I know music has an effect on people in a deep, almost incomprehensible way. I've felt its effect on me. But no, I don't think God really uses anyone for anything—much less people like us."

Ivy cringed. "I don't think that's true." It wasn't what Nettie and Mummy said, and it wasn't what the Bible said. "You can't actually believe that, Violet."

Violet sighed. "Yes, I do, my dear Trifle. I believe it with every fiber of my being, because I know it to be true."

Ivy gritted her teeth. She wished it were easier to convince Violet of the truths she'd known all her life, but it wasn't. She always tried to talk about God around Violet and convince her that He was real, He was loving, and He wanted Violet. However, no matter what she said, Violet put her off—and sometimes she'd say horrid, bitter things.

Ivy had been spending time with Violet for many months now, and it was starting to get sad how little she'd changed her friend.

Yet she couldn't stop trying.

"God loves you so much." Ivy cocked her head. "He loves everyone, and He wants us, too. You know, like in—oh, I forget where, but it says, 'But as many as received Him, to them gave He power to become the sons of God, even to them that believe on His name.' Isn't that lovely?"

Violet shrugged. "No one would want me, Ivy. Not now, not ever. People think of me as a demon, as soulless, as mindless."

"That's not true! People here at McCale House love you." Ivy turned to Violet with a huff. "And I love you! But it doesn't matter what people think about you—only what God thinks of you. He loves you, and wants you, and willingly sacrificed Himself so you can come to Him!"

Violet stood and walked to the fireplace, then over to the windows, restlessly moving her hands above her to touch the mantel and the windowsill. She didn't reply, so Ivy felt compelled to speak again.

"You do believe that God exists, don't you, Violet? You don't really believe all that nonsense that says He doesn't exist?"

"I don't know, Ivy … All I know is that God is not a part of my life. It doesn't much matter to me whether or not He's real—only that He makes no difference in my reality."

"That's not true, either!" How could she convince Violet of this fact? Hesitancy swirled through her soul, but then she got an idea. She jumped to her feet and started for the door. "Come to my room."

"I don't want—"

"Violet, please?"

Violet sighed and began to follow. "I'll humor you this once, Trifle, but don't expect me to be at your beck and call all the time."

In her room, Ivy pulled her small Bible out of the drawer beside her bed and opened it. She almost never read it by herself, but she did have a treasure tucked between the pages—a dozen or so notecards, printed in Nettie's pristine handwriting with Bible verses.

She cradled the verses in her hands for a moment. She'd never really used them, but she was glad she had them now. Certainly these would serve to convince Violet.

"See?" She turned to her friend, holding out the cards. "Would you read them aloud? You're better with the harder words than me."

Violet sighed and accepted the cards. She shuffled them in her hands as she lowered herself down on the edge of Ivy's bed. "This is just silly, Ivy."

"No, it's not! It's the Bible. See how beautiful those words are?" She hopped up next to Violet. "You've got to believe them, Violet."

"I don't have to," Violet said with another roll of her eyes, by Ivy's count her fourth of the day. Nonetheless, she sat down and read the first card aloud. "'But they that wait upon the Lord shall renew their strength; they shall mount up with wings as eagles; they shall run, and not be weary; and they shall walk, and not faint.' Isaiah 40:31." A bit of a smile flickered over her face. "I admit I've always been partial to that one."

Ivy blinked. "What? You've read it before?"

Violet dropped the card onto the bed beside her. "I've read them all, Ivy.

Every last verse of the Bible, several times through. In between book orders, I get bored, and there seems to be always something new to discover in the Bible. Not that I believe a word of it."

Ivy couldn't help gawking at Violet; she really couldn't. It was strange to her that Violet could read so much of the Bible and still not take anything from it! To Ivy, the more she read the Bible, the more she understood, and the more she felt inspired to follow God. For Violet, it didn't seem to help, though Ivy supposed she already was a Christian, and Violet wasn't. Perhaps that made a difference.

Nevertheless, Ivy wouldn't give up on Violet. Not now, not while she had the ability to make a difference.

"Please read the next one," she begged.

Violet did—and the next and the next, until she'd tossed all of the stack onto the bed beside her. She made little comments about each of them, most jocular, but sometimes there was true understanding or even an insight Ivy had never thought of.

"This was a good selection. Your Nettie knows what she's doing, I think," Violet declared softly, sliding off the bed. There was actual respect in her tone, a surprising amount of it. "I'll be on my way now."

"Are you sure you wouldn't like to ... to talk some more?" Ivy asked. There was hope brewing in her soul. Violet's willingness to read the verses, and her new knowledge of her friend's reading, had inspired her.

"No ... not yet. Perhaps some other day." She turned at the door. "You'll tell me another story sometime, won't you, Trifle?"

"Of course I will!" Ivy promised.

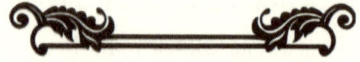

Jordy cupped a handful of water and splashed it toward Ivy. She gasped and fell back onto the bank with a little shriek.

"Jordy! I could've fallen in." She grasped the rock behind her.

He laughed and rose from his kneeling position beside the brook. "Ach, an' what would tha' hurt?"

"I'd get all wet." She pulled herself to her feet. "Violet, tell Jordy how cold it is!"

"It's not that cold," Violet said, removing her hand from the stream. "And anyway, you'd be rushed home and coddled. Not much to worry about."

Ivy didn't think either of them was taking this situation with the seriousness it deserved. However, Jordy and Violet hopped up and followed Ivy away from the stream.

"We'll be havin' our lunch soon, but there's somethin' I want tae show ye both first," Jordy said.

Ivy glanced toward the picnic cloths and other residents of McCale House to the east, then nodded. "All right, but let's go quickly."

Away from the party, they followed Jordy on a little side path that led to a steep embankment. Below, a small waterfall raged, falling twenty or thirty feet.

"See how beautiful?" Jordy gestured to the cliff's edge. "No' tae close, lassies, but ye can see from here!"

Violet smirked. "Is that all you brought us here for, Jordy? I've seen this before."

"Aye, but Ivy hasna, an' ye can enjoy it again." Jordy crossed his arms behind his head and leaned back. "Lovely, isna it?"

"I like it," Ivy said. She closed her eyes for a moment, concentrating on the feeling of the mist on her face and the roar of the water tumbling over the rocks.

"I'm going back."

Ivy opened her eyes and turned to Violet. "We'll come soon."

Violet shrugged and started away. "I'll see you later, Trifle—remember, you promised to tell me another story."

Jordy's eyes popped open. "Trifle, Vi? As in ..." He smirked. "Tipsy laird?"

Violet grinned over her shoulder and picked up her pace. Soon she disappeared around a pile of rocks.

Jordy chuckled. "Ye have quite a friend there, Ivy. My, how ye've tamed th' beast! I couldna be happier, an' th' McCales couldna, either."

Ivy laughed. "Do you really think so?"

"Aye." Jordy stood. "Let's go back. Keep up th' good work, though!"

Of course she would. Violet was her friend—she could never give up on her. "I will."

Nora adjusted her skirt as she sat on the picnic blanket. Not far from her, Ivy sat with Jordy McAllen, Violet Angel, and a few other students.

Violet hadn't said a word that Nora had heard. Rather, she simply focused on eating, but she was there with the other students, and occasionally a smile appeared. Nora couldn't help but feel lighthearted whenever she saw those smiles.

"You know, I've seen such a wondrous change in Violet." Miss Lang, who sat across from Nora on the blanket, nodded her head toward the little group of students. "She's open now in a way I've not seen her be before. She wasn't always this bad, but she's always been distant from the other students. Now Ivy is drawing her to them, showing her the value of friendship." She shook her head with a slight smile. "I've never seen anything like it."

"I agree." Mrs. McCale, who sat nearby, nodded. "Violet has changed, and I believe it to be primarily because of Ivy's influence."

Nora's heart lightened. Of course Ivy's influence was a major factor. But more and more, she felt it wasn't fair to say that Violet was the only one benefiting from the friendship. "Of course, Violet has helped Ivy, too. All of McCale House has helped Ivy! I think it's a good thing we came here."

"I'm glad you think so." A chuckle emerged from Mrs. McCale's throat. "That means we're doing what we wanted to with this place, even though the changes are slow to come. We'll keep trying to help these children. We may not always succeed, but we will continue to try."

"Of course. You're doing something truly worthy here. I don't believe everyone is able to say that about their lives—that they did something good, something to be proud of." Nora spoke with the passion of one who knew the reality of having done nothing truly good. At least, not anything she could think of.

"Aye. I suppose that's true. Or at least we're able to see some of the good we do, though not all of it." Mrs. McCale turned her water glass around in her hand, her thumb brushing condensation from the side. "It's not always clear that we're doing anything worthwhile. It's especially hard on Callum—he gets so much criticism for his work. I think he often doesn't see what his research will mean for the rest of the country."

"Yes, I think looking at the big picture helps," said Miss Lang. "When you look at the individual students—for instance, when you look at Violet—it's so easy to say, 'We haven't helped.' We can continue working with her, praying for her, but in the end, we won't likely give her what most would term a normal life. Yet we have helped in ways we can't see, and we gain more knowledge on how to help her every day."

"Exactly." Mrs. McCale tipped her glass at Miss Lang. "And that knowledge can be given to others, who can apply it to people like her. It takes time, and we in ourselves are not powerful enough to change anyone. God is the only one who can really do that."

Miss Lang nodded. "But would we want to try to remove that unique essence that makes these children who they are? Just so they could be 'normal,' just so they could conform? That wouldn't do."

"No, it wouldn't." Mrs. McCale adjusted her position to reach into one of the picnic baskets. "I say we hand out biscuits and start herding them back. It's getting on toward evening."

While Mrs. McCale and Miss Lang focused on passing out the biscuits, Nora leaned back to watch.

She did feel that the McCales were doing something noble, not only in helping her granddaughter but in helping all the children here.

Violet did seem to be a great deal more intelligent, sensitive, and complex than Nora had imagined. She was just a lost young woman, and who could help but want to help her?

Yes, McCale House was doing what it could. Violet was more likely to harm herself than anyone else, and that must be prevented. Perhaps, with prayer, the child might even recover from some of her ... alarming tendencies.

One never knew how God might choose to help someone. Perhaps He might heal Violet—and if not, the McCale House staff would do all they could to help Violet live a normal life and seek God's comfort.

Nora rose to help Mrs. McCale pack baskets. She wasn't used to this kind of work—in fact, she hadn't gone on a picnic since she was a child—but she wanted to feel useful.

"You don't have to do that, Mrs. Chattoway." Mrs. McCale placed a few cups toward the bottom of the basket. "I can do this myself."

"I'd like to help—it's the least I can do." She often did little when she ought to be doing a great deal.

Mrs. McCale paused for a moment, then gestured to the blanket. "We'll fold this next, then. Take the other end."

Nora quickly did as she was told, and they straightened together to shake out the blanket, ridding it of crumbs and bits of grass, moss, and soil.

"Mrs. Chattoway, I feel as if sometime we should talk together. I ... I don't know if there's anything I can do to reassure you, but my husband has made me sensitive—perhaps overly so—to other peoples' emotional needs, and I can't—that is, I would like to speak to you. You are a Christian woman, aren't you?"

Nora took a moment to mull these words over before nodding. "I am. I

... I drifted away from God until these last few years, but I've been trying to renew my relationship with Him as I realized how far I'd drifted from His love and strength."

"Mm-hmm." Mrs. McCale tucked the blanket into a basket. "We don't need to have a conversation about this right away, but I feel there are some things I could say to you. I might want to pray about it first, and perhaps find certain Bible verses. For now, I would like to say that you are loved and valued by God. You seem to have been badly used by your husband. There is no excuse for that. God didn't create women to be abused by their husbands."

Nora swallowed the lump in her throat and kept her breathing light and even. She didn't want her outward reactions to be too extreme. "Of course. I ... I do realize his behavior wasn't perfect."

"Very well. I'll—"

Just then, Ivy came running up with a question about something Jordy had said to her, and Nora turned from Mrs. McCale to her granddaughter.

The chat would have to wait until later.

CHAPTER TWENTY-TWO

July 1874

D ESPITE MRS. MCCALE'S INSISTENCE at the picnic, it took several more weeks for her to actually initiate the conversation.

However, Nora did have to admire Mrs. McCale's way of handlings things. She'd invited Nora to her private sitting room for a cup of tea and encouraged her to bring a Bible. Nora liked the normalness of the formal invitation.

It was late afternoon, and the room had a cozy glow from the setting sun permeating its small area. Mrs. McCale had placed a small table, complete with purple flowers in a vase on top, and two chairs near the window. Nora hoped she'd be invited into this little room more often.

"Will you take a seat?" Mrs. McCale gestured to one of the chairs. "I am sorry if it feels like I've pinned you down and forced you to talk to me. It's just in my nature to make things happen—ask Callum; he'll tell you how often he has to rein me in. I'm never one to ignore my intuition. Since suggesting this conversation, though, I've done a great deal of prayer and Bible-reading."

"That's always a good sign," Nora said as she lowered herself onto the chair across from Mrs. McCale. She didn't know what else to say. She wanted to assure Mrs. McCale that she would appreciate her thoughts, but all she felt was a kind of numbness combined with a pinch of anxiety. Her chest tightened, and she breathed rapidly.

"Mrs. Chattoway—may I call you Nora?"

"Oh! Of ... of course." Nora swallowed, trying to suppress her nervousness.

"Then you should call me Emma." Mrs. McCale's firm way of speaking and serious expression reminded Nora of Alice in that moment, and she had to smile in response.

"Very well."

"Thank you. Now, will you consider telling me a few details of your marriage and what your relationship with your husband truly was like? I know these sorts of things usually go undiscussed, as per proper society." She leaned forward. "But, Nora, I say that telling a woman that she's to bottle up abuse received from her husband is one of the most dangerous societal expectations. Your husband has passed on. There is no reason for you to withhold the truth, and there is nothing to be ashamed of."

Yes. Nothing to be ashamed of—that was true. Yet talking of past hurts wasn't exactly the easiest thing in the world. "I ... I know there isn't. Not in God's eyes, at least. But I don't think I would know ... that is, I don't know how to explain."

Mrs. McCale cocked her head. "Would it help if I asked questions?"

Technically, that meant Nora wouldn't be entirely in control of the story, which made her feel oddly reassured. She nodded.

"All right. We'll start with the basics. Did your husband ever beat you?"

Well. Mrs. McCale definitely got right to the point. Though, really, what did Nora expect? "I ... no. Not exactly."

The woman across the table winced. "Did he strike you? Physically force you to do something you didn't want to do?"

Yes. But it took a few moments of sipping her tea for Nora to raise the courage to nod. She'd not told anyone about that—she'd barely admitted it to herself.

"All right. That must have been frightening." Mrs. McCale's gentle voice and eyes coaxed Nora to share more.

It wasn't as easy as that. It had been something more than frightening. It had been a horror-filled existence, which Nora had thought normal at the time. She'd assumed it was his prerogative—or, at the least, he had always been in the right and she in the wrong.

Yet that wasn't true. She'd seen the damage he'd caused. It hurt, and she knew that she had not behaved in a godly way in submitting to him. Far from it—he was a bad man, whom she had enabled.

She blinked. There she was, blaming herself again. Was she responsible for his manipulation? Perhaps. Perhaps ... not.

"I was afraid," she said at last, alarmed by her thoughts. She would shut them down and move on quickly now. "But I should have done more. I should have saved my children from that life. I ... I failed." Her throat tightened, and unexpected tears flooded her eyes. She'd thought herself too old and tired to weep—yet here she was, about to.

Her claim seemed to Nora to be an undeniable truth, but instead of agreeing with her, Mrs. McCale shook her head. "You did not fail. You were the victim. I've talked to other women, who have been in similar situations—and few, if any, are able to defy their husbands. Though submission is a requirement of Christian marriage, most women forget that that doesn't mean 'allow your husband to hurt you.' It can't be that way in a healthy marriage."

Nora nodded but said nothing. Her deep, low breaths were the only things keeping her head even vaguely clear.

"You mustn't grow bitter about it any more than you can help, but I hope you do realize that you ... you didn't deserve to be manipulated by him. You didn't deserve any sort of abuse or neglect. You didn't deserve any of that, because that's not what true marriage is."

Nora knew that now. If only someone had told her that in the early days of her marriage. She might not have listened, but it would have been nice to hear.

Still, she didn't need more advice along this line. It had nothing to do with her now except to encourage her to move on from her past, something she was doing more and more every day.

"Where did you intend this conversation to go, Emma?" She wanted to maintain some dignity in this situation, or at least she wanted to try to.

"I simply want to offer any help I can. I can just see you're hurting, and besides prayer, I want to see what I can do. I jotted down a list of some favorite Bible verses ..."

Nora offered a wobbly smile. "All of God's Word is helpful."

Mrs. McCale nodded. "Agreed." She lifted her Bible from her lap, withdrew a slip of paper, and extended it across the table. "Would you rather read them by yourself or here? We could discuss them now or later."

Nora blinked. She had an option? Oh, of course she did. She was an adult woman, independent and able to do what she wanted. "I would rather read them by myself." She took the slip of paper and tucked it in her own Bible. It would be a welcome read later on, when she had alone time with God.

"Is there anything else you'd like to talk about?" Mrs. McCale asked. "Or anything else I can do?"

Nora clasped her hands over her Bible. "I need a friend and a chance for casual conversation and perhaps someone to talk things over with—in time."

Mrs. McCale nodded thoughtfully. "Very well. Perhaps we could do this every day—on every day that it's convenient. Since the other teachers are younger than I, it would be lovely to chat with a woman close to my own age while you're here."

Nora swallowed. So she would be needed, too? She couldn't communicate with words what that meant to her. "Thank you. I might not be here much long—"

"Which is exactly what letters are for." Mrs. McCale's voice was firm. "We'll keep in touch. You're a sweet woman, and there aren't enough of those in this world."

Nora wasn't sure exactly how she felt about being called "sweet;" it felt a little condescending, but it was a sincerely meant compliment. "Thank you, Emma. We'll have to do that." Maybe, with Mrs. McCale's help, she could at last learn to rest in her worth in Christ and in His love.

August 1874

The screams in the night woke Ivy again. It had been many weeks since this happened—hopeful weeks when Violet improved, little by little, becoming almost pleasant.

She still seemed to hang back from the other students, but at least she was spending time with Ivy and Jordy, and she wanted to talk more about the important things. Ivy used every opportunity she could to bring God up, and though Violet might joke, she also seemed to have a begrudging respect for Ivy's faith.

Ivy hadn't had to get up in the night because of Violet's screams since that last time when she'd told her about the Snow Queen. Now she did, flying out from under the covers and toward the stairs.

This time, she realized people were already there as soon as she threw open the door—Dr. and Mrs. McCale, Miss Lang, and another teacher. And Violet was standing on the bed, eyes wilder than Ivy had ever seen them before.

"Violet!" Ivy called. "Violet, what are you doing?"

Everyone was standing by as if they didn't know how to approach Violet, but they all froze at Ivy's words.

"Ivy, don't." Dr. McCale stepped to her side and grabbed her shoulders. "She's not conscious right now. She might hurt—"

"Let her try, Callum." Mrs. McCale took a step back from the bed. "Let her try."

Ivy swallowed. Violet might hurt her? But she didn't let herself think—she approached the bed, her hand out. "Violet, it's me. Are you having a nightmare? We're here to help, Violet. We—"

Violet leaped off the bed toward Ivy, and Dr. Goodington grabbed her around the waist and pulled her back. Violet jerked against him, flailing and shrieking. Her face was hideous, twisted and contorted, and her screams were more enraged than fearful now, more monster than human.

Ivy turned and ran out of the room.

Sometime later, Mrs. McCale came, and Ivy's grandmother was woken up, too. They both tried to comfort her, but Ivy couldn't help thinking ... what if?

What if Violet had really hurt Ivy? What if she hadn't been pretending when she said all those cruel things? What if Violet hated Ivy and God and everyone, just like she said? What if ... what if Violet was really a monster?

What if Ivy couldn't help her, couldn't change her?

Ivy kept trying to play the piece, but the song wouldn't come. Over and over she ran her fingers over the keys in familiar patterns, and it failed to come out the way she wanted.

Frustrated tears blinded her, and she had to stop playing to wipe them away and sniffle and snuffle and feel sorry for herself.

Was Violet still her friend? She didn't think so.

After a great deal more quiet tears and a few more failed attempts at playing, she slid off the bench and went to sit at the hearth. There was no fire, but she still felt drawn to sit there before the grate, a place where warmth had been and would be again if there was need for it.

She heard footsteps behind her and glanced over her shoulder to see Jordy McAllen watching her from the door. She scowled and turned back to the bare fireplace, not wanting him to see the tears on her cheeks.

He approached without a word, and she felt him lower himself down on the other side of the hearth, his big body making a thud. Perhaps he was a clumsy—she'd often heard that boys were.

The silence stretched on, and even Ivy, a lover of quiet, started to feel uneasy. But still he didn't speak, didn't comment on the situation.

When Ivy herself was about to say something, his voice cracked the air. "Ye needna feel sae bad, Ivy. I heard wha' happened, an' I ken why ye'd feel sae bad. But ye dinna need tae."

Ivy rubbed her sleeve under her nose and over her eyes, then turned to face him. "She was ... she wasn't like herself. She wasn't like Violet. Not at all."

"I ken tha'. An' tha's why ye needna feel sae bad. Sometimes there's no' much we can do with Violet other than tae love her when she's no' feelin' well. Tha's what Mrs. McCale said. She says ... someday maybe some brave scientist will go beyond what we can, an' ken how tae help her, but until then, all we can give is our love."

Ivy shifted, her stomach a hard, tight knot. "I ... I just ... I wish she would ... I'm sorry that she has to be that way. She didn't know me, though. What good is love if you don't know someone?"

"Ach, Ivy, I dinna ken. I think she feels it, though—feels when we love her even though she's had a fit or a nightmare or whatever they are. An' she kens when we dinna think o' them as all she is, tae."

"Yes ..." Violet did seem to be the insightful sort. "Do you think ... *I* think she'd be better if she had God, you know?"

Jordy shrugged and shook his head. "There're many here who are Christians, Ivy. Felix, for instance. An' it doesna take it away. Does being a Christian take away yer pains an' sufferin'? Does God promise us happiness here on earth?"

Ivy shook her head. "N-no. But He does make everything so much easier to bear. And ... then there is hope."

"Aye." A smile flickered across his lips. "Tha's th' key, isna it? Hope for th' future, hope for perfection in Heaven, even if now couldna be any worse."

"Exactly." Ivy shuddered. "Nettie says she doesn't know how people survive on earth without that hope. And I think so, too. No wonder Violet feels horribly ... but if she could just trust God ..." It would make everything better.

"But Violet will still have th' fits, Ivy. Dinna ye doubt it. God could heal her, aye, but it would be unlikely for Him tae do tha' on earth. It would be a miracle, and we can pray for miracles, but we canna always expect them. Tha's no proof o' God's love or no'—He keeps His own calendar."

Now Jordy sounded just like Nettie. She wondered how he did it—all her good words about that seemed to come out muddled. "You're right. So do you think ... Jordy, is it wrong to want more for Violet?" Ivy swallowed. "More than ... more than she is now, I mean?"

Jordy shrugged. "It isna true tha' ye can change her. First, ye canna change her mind tae be different than it is ... Second, ye canna change her soul. Ye canna make her be a Christian—she must make tha' decision for herself. So on th' first, I would say ye can pray and beg God, same as ye would beg for yerself or anyone at McCale House ... but ye canna treat her differently because o' tha'. We all have our demons. An' on th' second, ye can pray an' ye can tell her th' truth an' ye can show her what it's like to live like a Christian—but more? Nah, it isna yer job tae do, Ivy, nor could ye."

Ivy nodded slowly, taking this all in. "So what now?"

"Continue on as ye've always done." He jumped to his feet and held out his hand. "Now take me hand, bonnie—we'll get ye back tae th' piano and release some o' th' sadness I see in yer eyes, a'right?"

Ivy's frustration rose once again. "I can't."

"Ye canna?" Jordy laughed. "So says th' best pianist in this house. Wha' do ye mean, 'ye canna'? Aye, ye can." Again, he offered his hand, but Ivy shook her head.

"I can't. I've been trying all morning, but ... it just won't come."

"Hmm." Jordy flopped down next to her again. "Let's pray about it, then ye'll try again."

That didn't seem like it would help much, but Ivy nodded nonetheless.

It was probably rude or unholy or something to turn down a prayer when offered.

"Dear Lord," Jordy began, "please let Ivy play th' piano again, with th' heart an' th' gifts Ye gave tae her. An' help her understand how tae best help Violet. Take Violet into Yer arms an' bless her. In Jesus' name, amen."

"Amen," Ivy echoed. She opened her eyes. "That was short, and I don't feel any different."

"Short is best." He jumped up again, this time grabbing her hands and yanking her to her feet. "A'right. Let's see."

Ivy followed him to the piano and took a seat on the bench. A few deep breaths and she placed her hands on the keys. This time, her fingers weren't trembling. She slowly worked herself through bar after bar, taking deep breaths in between, and it seemed to come easier.

"There, tha's lovely." Jordy knelt next to the piano. "Can ye play somethin' more lively?" He grinned. "Perhaps I'll show ye how tae dance."

"With whom?" Ivy giggled. "If I'm playing, and no one else is here."

"Ach, I'll figure tha' out. Ye play." He jumped up and stepped into the middle of the floor. "Have ye anything a bit Scots, woman?"

She laughed again. "I suppose so." She tried a few bars and then let her fingers roll into a lively tune that Violet had showed her earlier, all trills and rolls and staccatos.

"There ye go!" Jordy shouted. He began dancing a little jig that involved more than a few over-exaggerated kicks, plenty of arm waving, and some enthusiastic yells.

Ivy had to stop playing a few times because her sides hurt from laughing, but by the time Jordy had collapsed to the floor, telling her his legs had surely fallen off and his head was likely to roll with them, she could play as well as she ever had.

CHAPTER TWENTY-THREE

IT WAS A FEW days before Ivy saw Violet again. She was back to normal as far as Ivy could tell. She sat pensively on her favorite bench in the garden, hands folded on her lap, eyes fixated on some distant point.

The only difference from when they'd met here before was that Mrs. McCale sat a short distance away, reading a book, occasionally glancing up to check on the two.

"Violet?" Ivy stood in front of the bench, trying to look and sound as non-threatening and gentle as possible. She wasn't sure what that meant coming from her, but she was at least careful not to put her hands on her hips or fold them across her chest. To Ivy, that was somewhat threatening.

Yet despite this forethought to her manner of approach, there was no response from Violet.

"I've missed you."

Still no response.

"I have things to share. Remember how I told you my mummy was getting another baby, and you said that meant she was ... was with child?" She still wasn't entirely sure what that meant, but she had an idea, and it was strange as anything. "She's not anymore—that is, I got a letter, and it was born. It's a boy, and they've named him Caleb Arthur."

Not a word.

"He's a miracle, Mummy says, because he came too early."

Violet's eyebrows arched. "I came too early."

"Did you?" Ivy hesitantly took a seat on the edge of the bench, being careful to hold herself so she could spring up at a moment's notice. Despite all her good intentions, she was frightened of Violet now.

"Yes. Just a few weeks." A smile fluttered across her lips. "But I didn't die. I still haven't died. Pity that."

"I ... I don't think it's a pity." Ivy swallowed. "I-I love you. I'm glad you're alive."

"Really?" A strange look crossed Violet's face. "Even after—" She stopped herself and seemed to swallow. "That is—" For the first time since Ivy had met her, Violet seemed befuddled.

Ivy understood. That was every day for her. "I still love you no matter what. Because ... because love doesn't need to go away just because of what someone did. That's not how God's love works, and that's not how our love should work."

"I-I don't know what happened." Violet's voice stuttered and twisted over every word. "I never do afterward. I can't tell anyone why, because I don't know. I wish they wouldn't ask me why."

Ivy considered this for a moment. "That makes sense. After all, you can't be expected to tell everyone what you're thinking. Some things don't have words to go with them."

Violet nodded her agreement of this fact.

"I wish that you wouldn't scream so much, though, Violet." Ivy cleared her throat. "It's frightening. I don't like being frightened."

Then Violet did smile, as if this statement was more than amusing. Yet her expression seemed sincere. Ivy didn't detect a trace of what Jordy called "Vi's sass." "I'm sorry. I won't if I can remember. Sometimes ... sometimes I don't remember much while I'm like that."

"Like a bad dream," Ivy said. "Or any kind of dream, I suppose."

"Yes," Violet said. "You know you've had one, but you don't know exactly what it was about. You just remember waking up in bed, screaming and afraid ..." She stopped. "Ivy, I think this is the most I've ever talked with anyone about this."

Ivy blinked. Violet hadn't said this to anyone else? How did she expect people to understand her if she didn't share such things? "Not even Dr. McCale? I talk to Dr. McCale sometimes. He knows a lot of things, and he can fix almost any problem."

Violet shuddered, wrapping her arms around herself. "No, of course not him. He's the one who keeps me here. I don't want to be here."

Fair enough. "Where do you want to be?"

"I ... I don't know. But when I get there, I won't come back. It'll be so much nicer than this place." Violet raised her chin and set her jaw. "I'll never have to be alone."

"You don't have to be alone here," Ivy protested. *At least not while I'm living at McCale House, which I may be for a long time to come.*

"Yes, you do, if you're like me." Violet scowled. "You don't have to be alone. You can be with the other boys and girls who stay here, and with all the teachers and with ... with *Jordy*." The envy that flashed across Violet's face and poured from her words made Ivy shudder. "I must stay in my room unless someone is watching me. I get away often, though, and someday they won't catch me."

None of this made any sense. Did Violet believe it did? Yet Ivy would give her the benefit of the doubt. "But if you don't know where you're going, how can you leave?"

Violet scoffed. "Anywhere would be better than McCale House. I'd rather live in a slum by myself than at McCale House with the crazies."

"We're not crazies! Jordy says so. And McCale House is so beautiful." Ivy gestured to the landscape around her. "Isn't it?"

"Perhaps, but beauty isn't everything." Violet flipped her hand back and forth impatiently. "I'm sick of talking about this. Can you tell me a story now, Trifle?"

Ivy tried not to be frustrated with Violet, but it was so hard. Their conversation was just getting somewhere, and now she wanted to talk about something else? However, Ivy did like stories. What was one she knew well? "I could tell you about ... about the time God helped a girl become a queen—that's even better than a princess—and saved her people.

That was always my favorite."

Violet sighed. "Esther? That's hardly a story, but very well."

"All right, then. Once upon a time," Ivy began, "there was a girl named Esther. She lived thousands of years ago—or at least hundreds; I can't remember what Nettie said exactly—in a land called ... Persia, I think. Or Babylon. I always get those two mixed up. She wasn't really Persian ... or Babylonian ... though."

"It was Persia, Trifle; she wasn't *Persian*."

"Yes. She was Jewish, and the Jewish people had been captured by ... yes, I'm sure it was Persia ... and taken to live in a foreign land, and they didn't much care for it.

"The king of Persia had a wife who wouldn't obey him, and the king's royal advisers told him to find a new queen. So he sent out a decree for all the beautiful women in the kingdom to be gathered together so he could choose himself a new bride. Anyway, the king took one look at Esther and married her."

"Wait a moment." Violet had a cruel smile about her lips that Ivy didn't like. "Didn't you say God made Esther queen?"

"He did."

"No, He didn't. It just happened."

"But God is in control of everything."

"But, Ivy, you're forgetting this marvelous *choice* I've heard so much about. How do you reconcile the two?"

Ivy sat still for a moment, refusing to answer. This wasn't something she understood, either—how God created a world and breathed life in every facet of it and then let humans choose whether or not to follow Him. It was deeper than her, and even Nettie admitted to not comprehending the details. "Of course we can choose to obey God and to be His children, but that's a different sort of thing entirely. Anyway, I don't think even grown-ups understand all the way. You've just got to believe!"

Violet made no comment on this, so Ivy continued on.

"Now, Esther and the king got married, and then some of the king's enemies wanted to kill him, and Esther's uncle, Mordecai, warned the king, and the king wanted to honor him. But the king's friend Haman was angry at Mordecai, so he—"

"Wait! Why was he angry, Ivy? You're forgetting important plot points."

"Because Mordecai wouldn't bow before him. He was a Jew, just like Esther, and he wouldn't bow to a fellow who didn't believe in his God—the true God. I think that was it, anyway. Now, Haman wanted to kill Mordecai—"

"Rather vengeful person."

"But he didn't know that Mordecai was in favor with the king—"

"Doesn't know much about the affairs of the kingdom, does this Haman?"

"The king summoned him, and Haman came. The king asked Haman what he'd give to the man the king wanted to honor, and Haman thought—"

"Conceited fellow."

"—that he meant him, so he told the king he should parade the man through the streets wearing fancy clothes."

"Very manly."

Ivy threw her hands up, defeated. "Violet, will you please stop that? I can't concentrate. I haven't had anyone tell me this story in a long time."

"Very well. I'll be quiet."

"All right, then. So Mordecai got that honor, and Haman was furious. He had a tall gallows built to hang Mordecai on, and he decided to kill all the Jews, too, for good measure."

"Let's not be too uppity. We had the same idea once, too."

"Oh, please stop, Violet! I want to finish the story! This is the best part. It's romantic, too."

"I never much cared for romance. It's unrealistic."

"No, it isn't! Let me finish now. Haman sent a proclamation throughout the kingdom about how he was going to kill all the Jews. Esther found out through Mordecai, and Mordecai made her promise to talk to the king and see if she couldn't get him not to kill her people. Esther agreed, but it would be dangerous for her to try. Nobody—and I mean not even Esther, his own wife—could go into the presence of the king without being called for. If they did, they'd be executed. Esther hadn't been called for, but she was willing to sacrifice her life for her people."

"How noble."

"It was *very* noble. So Esther put on her prettiest dress and went to see the king. She was afraid, probably, but God helped her be brave, and she walked right up to him.

"Everyone thought the king was going to kill her, but he didn't. He just asked her what she wanted. She said she wanted him to come have a banquet in her part of the castle. Everyone thought it was silly to risk your life to ask the king to come to a dinner party, but he agreed to attend the banquet, and the next night, he came. Haman came along, too.

"On that night, she wanted a second favor, and the king said all right. She asked for them to come tomorrow night for another feast. And they came. Esther asked for another favor, and this time the king said, 'You can have anything you want, up to half of my kingdom.' So Esther told him how she was a Jew, and Haman was going to kill her people along with Mordecai, who had saved the king's life.

"The king was angry. He had Haman hung on the gallows he'd prepared for Mordecai. And Queen Esther and the king lived happily ever after."

"The end?" Violet suggested, rising.

"No, not quite. Nettie always finished up by telling me how it all leads back to Jesus."

Violet cocked her head. "How's that?"

"If God's people—if God's 'precious seed'—had been killed, there wouldn't have been any Jesus. Esther saved us all, really."

"Good for her."

"Of course, she couldn't have done it without God's helping her," Ivy added. "Nobody can do anything good without God, even if they don't know it. And Nettie would always say, when she finished telling me this story, that the whole Bible is about Jesus. That's what the Bible is for. To tell the world about Jesus. That's what Christians are for, too. Because God won't rest until He's made sure everyone has that choice you talked about earlier."

Violet chuckled as if this were funny. Ivy couldn't understand all the things Violet laughed about, for they never made sense. "Well, Trifle, you'll have to tell me more someday. About Jesus and all that. He does sound like a pleasant fellow, and I do like the idea of having a choice in *something*."

Ivy's heart immediately lightened. "I can tell you all about Jesus, Violet. Everything! Or as much as I know. It's not really important how much of a choice we have or not, though, Nettie says, because the most important thing is surrendering to Him, and—"

Violet held up her hand against Ivy's word storm. "Tell me about it later, Trifle. I'm tired now."

She walked away, off into the gardens, and Ivy jumped to her feet and practically galloped into the house.

She found Jordy in the library, studying another boring, thick medical book. "Jordy! Jordy! I told Violet a Bible story, and she wants to talk about Jesus someday. Actually *talk* about Him! She said so herself. Jordy, do you think she's understanding?"

Jordy jumped up and pulled her into a hug. "Good, brave lass! If anyone can make her understand, it's ye, Ivy, an' yer big heart for th' world. God's got her in His sights, an' no mistakin' it."

Ivy beamed and danced and laughed a little. She believed God had Violet in His sights, too.

CHAPTER TWENTY-FOUR

"W ILL YOU COME TO my room, Ivy?" Violet stood in the doorway of Ivy's music room, her eyebrows furrowed. "You've never been there before, but I think it's time."

Ivy blinked and jumped off the piano bench. "But I have been to your room before, Violet. Several times."

"No ... not that room." Violet glanced over her shoulder. "Come on. I'll show you. It's ... it's just ... more *me* than my bedroom."

Ivy followed Violet up the stairs. They passed the door to the bedroom Ivy had visited so many times and walked down the hall to the end, where a closed door faced them.

Violet half-turned to Ivy with her hand on the doorknob. "I don't let people come in here, you know. Other than Miss Lang, who must. And sometimes the McCales come in, but they know I don't like it. I don't *ask* anyone to come in—not even Jordy."

"Oh." Anticipation rose in Ivy's chest like a tidal wave, but she wasn't sure how to express it with words. "That's ... I'd love to see it."

Violet smirked. "And I'll show you." She opened the door and stepped to the side.

It was a spacious room, somewhat circular in nature, with great curtains covering the windows, casting everything in a deep gloom. Ivy was able to decipher the outline of a small piano, a sofa, a fireplace with a stone mantel, and a table with what appeared to be random knick-knacks resting on it.

Violet closed the door behind them, causing even more darkness to pervade. But before Ivy could be scared, Violet dashed past her and began drawing the curtains.

As the drapes were pulled back, the room began to be flooded in light. Ivy noticed that between the glass of the four big windows and the room were bars, or rather thin grates that caused the light to dapple in strange patterns.

Ivy swallowed. That was frightening. She could see why Violet kept the drapes drawn. But without the sunlight, the room was so dark.

Now Ivy was able to make out bookcases, many of them, so crowded with books that they were stacked one on top of the other haphazardly instead of arranged in neat lines. In piles on the floor by the shelves were more books, enough that Ivy had no clue how anyone would have time to read them all.

It was a beautiful place nonetheless, even given the clutter and the bars. The sunlight dappled over a doily and yet more books on the top of the piano, a table covered with books, paper, pens, sheet music, and what looked to be some toys—a carved horse, a doll clothed in a pretty dress lying on her side, and a stuffed duckling. By the fire was a big armchair with a pillow and a blanket thrown across the seat, and another blanket was balled on the floor next to it. There was even a vase full of flowers on the mantle.

So, yes, it was messy, but Ivy didn't mind messy if it was comfortable, and it *was* comfortable.

Yet Ivy didn't understand why it would be a secret. There wasn't anything particularly exciting or interesting about the room. She supposed the secret, the specialness of it, must be more due to Violet's preferences than anything. It belonged to her and only her. Ivy could understand that—even if she was disappointed that Violet didn't have a unicorn stored up here or something along those lines.

"I like it," Ivy said.

Violet glanced around her with a pleased little nod. "I thought you would. It's quiet and mine, and, really, how many things are both of those in this world?"

Not many, at least as far as Ivy had been able to discover. She shook her head.

"Exactly." Violet sighed. "I've had to beg for every book, and for the piano to be moved up here—it was downstairs in the parlor doing nothing for no one—and I still haven't gotten all the shelves I need. But, honestly, sometimes I stack all the books in a big circle around me, and that's nice, so I'm not sure I want shelves."

Ivy nodded. There was something nice about being surrounded by the things you loved. That's why families were invented, she decided. Though, of course, Ivy hadn't enough family to be surrounded by them.

Or, perhaps, she had. Now that Mummy had her baby, she thought it might not be so bad. Mummy did use such pleasant words to describe him—precious and beautiful and beloved. Perhaps Ned was all those things, too—and Mr. Knight ... She'd have to think about him still. But it was worth reconsidering.

Violet gestured toward a pair of chairs that sat in front of a window. "Dr. McCale will sit there and ask me to sit next to him and talk. I won't. But you could come and tell me a story, now, couldn't you, Trifle?"

"Yes, I can." Ivy took a deep breath. She wanted to share more with Violet than she ever had before, but it would be challenging. It certainly was frightening. However, friendship meant love, and love meant truth, and she couldn't separate the three. "I think today we should talk about a Baby Boy who was born in Bethlehem."

Violet sighed and flopped down onto one of the chairs. "Oh, dear. I knew it wouldn't be long in coming."

Ivy was surprised the girl offered no further protestation. She took the other seat and folded her hands on her lap. "It starts with a young lady named Mary."

"Does it now?" Violet scowled. "She sounds sanctimonious already."

"Really, it starts at the beginning of time with Adam and Eve." Ivy realized as she said these words that there was a lot more to the story than she'd bargained for. How could she get it all across?

God, give me the words. Please. I need them so, and Violet needs them even more than I do.

She launched into her tale then, not letting herself hesitate to overthink a phrase or complicate a sentiment. On and on the story went, from Adam and Eve through Abraham through Joseph and Moses and all of the Israelites' failures and successes.

At last she arrived back where she'd wanted to start, with Mary, an ordinary girl with an incredible job. She liked this part—how Nettie explained that God used normal people—she always emphasized, when she told the story, "people like Ivy"—to do incredible things.

Of course, Ivy always wondered if she'd be as faithful and good as Mary. She believed she might be, if God gave her the strength to do so. It was hard to know such things, having never been in a similar situation.

Then baby Jesus arrived and grew up, and His teaching was seen as heretical. Ivy struggled even more with the words as the leaders closed in on Him, but she remembered Nettie had said that they only succeeded in capturing Him when it was time.

The time came. Ivy took a while to get the words out about the crucifixion. Strangely enough, Violet remained silent through this part. She let Ivy work through the words, let her process every horrible thing.

But Ivy could smile once it was over, for He rose from the dead on the third day. How could anything possibly be better than that?

She arrived at the conclusion, and she found that the words flowed easily now into the silence of the room. "And He died for us, Violet. Don't you see that? He died for all of us—you, me, Jordy, the McCales. Every last one of us! We've been offered a perfect gift—we can be cleansed from our sins and gathered into His arms and offered His comfort and strength through this life. But, Violet, we have to accept this gift!"

Ivy suddenly was shaken out of her fervor, as if something in her had said, "Time to stop talking," and she noticed there were tears in Violet's eyes.

"Violet?" Ivy hopped up and raced to kneel next to her chair. "Oh,

Violet, don't cry! I'm sorry. It's true, though—do you see it?"

"N-not at all." Violet swiped at her face with her sleeve. "I-I'm just ... I'll be all right." She straightened, throwing back her shoulders, and brushing her loose hair back with both hands. "There, now. I was a bit ... sorry, I must've had something in my eyes."

"No." Ivy shook her head firmly. "You were crying."

"Leave me my little lies, Ivy." Violet sniffed. "I'll be all right."

"Violet, what do you think? Don't you believe? Violet, you must, for—"

Yet the older girl held up her hand. "No, not now. That was more than enough for today. Thank you for explaining it. Somehow the things you say are clear, Ivy, when nothing else is. But I don't want to talk about it now. May I have this room to myself?"

That was a polite way to ask someone to get out, especially for Violet. Ivy sensed that she'd done what she could.

"All right." She stood and stepped backward. "I'll see you later?"

Violet waved her off, already curling into herself, into her façade. "Yes, yes. Good-bye, Trifle."

August 1874

It was a beautiful afternoon at McCale House, and Nora couldn't stop looking out the window. Going on a walk seemed a happy eventuality, but she'd have to do it soon if she wanted to be on time for tea, which she certainly did.

She walked downstairs to the schoolroom in search of a suitable companion—and, as if God had decreed it, there was Ivy sitting on a chair and staring out of the window, her legs swinging back and forth, face blank of emotion.

"Ivy, have you anything to do?"

Ivy jumped, then turned to Nora with hope in her eyes. "Not anything!"

"Oh, that's too bad. Where are your friends?" She glanced around the empty library. "Jordy? Violet? Felix?"

"Felix is reading, and Violet says I'm too much trouble today." Ivy winced. "I don't know why. And Dr. McCale told Jordy that if he didn't catch up on his studying today, he'd have to sleep in the stables tonight—I don't think he meant it, but Jordy has to study anyway."

Nora nodded. "What about playing your piano?"

Ivy shook her head. "I did, but I've done that for almost all week."

How strange that the child had gone from wanting nothing to do to craving something to do! Though it was true that Dr. McCale had been giving the children a holiday to "refresh their dear, young minds," and Ivy was no longer used to this lack of occupation, even if that is how she had lived for so many years.

"I've a solution to that, Ivy. Why don't we go on a walk together? We could go outside the property if we ask Dr. McCale for a key to the gate. It seems like it's a lovely, cool afternoon, and I think we'd both enjoy it."

Ivy's eyes immediately filled with light. "That would be nice, Grandmother. Let's go now!"

"I'll tell Dr. McCale where we're off to—we'll have to make sure to get back in time for tea, but we'll walk fast and not too far, and it'll be fun!" Already excited by this little break from routine, Nora started off to tell Dr. McCale.

It was only a quarter of an hour later that they were walking down the driveway toward the big gate at the entry to the property. At first, there was only silence between Nora and Ivy, but after a bit, Nora thought of something to ask her granddaughter.

"How are your studies going, dear?"

Ivy shrugged. "Very well. Dr. McCale could tell you—but I don't think it's too hard. I enjoy the reading most, you know, other than music. Music is … music isn't really studying. I just do it."

Nora laughed. That was true—Ivy just did it, and effortlessly at that. But that didn't change the fact that it was an impressive accomplishment. "You are miraculous in that respect, Ivy. We're all impressed with you—and I'm proud."

Ivy beamed, but then she cast her eyes down and shook her head. "I can't help but be good at it, I suppose, though I would like to be better. I think God lets certain people be better at certain things. Or that's what Jordy says. Jordy says he likes to make people laugh, and Violet is good at remembering everything she reads, and I'm good at music, and Felix is good at math—I didn't know Felix was good at math until Jordy told me, though. I suppose some people don't show off how they're good at something as much as other people, do they? I think it's so interesting."

Nora blinked. That was the most she'd ever heard Ivy say before at once. The child really was blossoming in every way. It was strange how every day she became more of the person God must have created her to be, showing that Dr. McCale was right about her uniqueness and, therefore, the uniqueness of every child here. Quite possibly, Dr. McCale was a genius. That was the only way Nora knew to put it.

When silence again threatened, and the driveway seemed to stretch on forever, Nora cleared her throat to speak again. "You said you enjoy reading now, Ivy? How odd, for you didn't seem to like it before."

Ivy cocked her head and looked up at Nora with a quizzical expression. "I'd forgotten I didn't like it. I think the change was because I realized reading is about stories."

"Ah, yes." Ivy did like stories. "What are you reading now?"

"*The Pilgrim's Progress*. Dr. McCale says 'every child needs to suffer through it once,' but I like it, so it's not 'suffering through it.' Why do you think he doesn't like it, Grandmother?" Ivy looked almost offended on the book's behalf.

Nora laughed. "I don't know, Ivy. I've heard more people who love it than not—I read it myself as a child."

"Really? What else did you read?" Ivy's eyes were bright with interest. "I wish I knew of more books, but there aren't so many other than readers.

Not until I'm older, Dr. McCale said."

Indeed, that was true. Nora couldn't think of many books, which weren't for instruction, she'd read as a child.

"I read *Aesop's Fables*, I suppose." Nora cocked her head. "Those were fun. And I read some 'classics,' but they were all horrid books my governess assigned me. Nothing interesting. I didn't really enjoy reading until I was a young woman."

Then she'd invested heavily in Gothic romances, the kind with broody heroes and vapid heroines and sweeping moors. They weren't the kind of fantasies she wanted Ivy indulging in, now or ever. It had colored her own impressions of romance in an unfavorable way.

She'd read better books as an adult, when her children were small. Dickens, the Brontë sisters, and other similar books had kept her sane. But it would be a long time before those were appropriate for Ivy. Still, she would remember to share them when the time came, along with Shakespeare and philosophers and historians—she felt Ivy would thoroughly enjoy them all.

They reached the edge of the property and unlocked the gate that let them out onto the stone bridge. Below, water trickled, quiet now as the summer sun caused more and more of it to disappear.

Nora stepped toward the edge, mindful to block Ivy from the fright of being too close. However, Ivy stepped around Nora and glanced down herself.

"There's not much of a river there," Ivy observed.

No, there wasn't. She watched as Ivy stood a safe distance from the edge and then backed up and walked on ahead of her across the bridge.

The dear girl really was conquering her fears. Yes, she'd be all right. One way or another, she'd be all right.

She wondered which romance novels Ivy might enjoy. She wanted the girl to read the kind that spoke the truth about love and the future a woman could expect from a marriage filled with love. She felt that, again, the Brontë sisters were fairly safe, and there were a few other authors she could think of, yet they were few and far between.

Romances were so often romanticized, emphasizing all the wrong things about the relationship between a man and a woman, creating unrealistic expectations which, if clung to, could cause damage in a marriage.

Yes, she would have to make sure Ivy, and her other granddaughters, knew what was right and what was wrong. For Nora had not known, and that had been a part of her downfall.

Of course, that might not come up in Ivy's life. She drew alongside Ivy and glanced down at her. "Ivy, do you want a husband and children?" Might as well ask.

Ivy blinked. Nora got the idea that no one had ever asked her that before. "I don't think so," Ivy said slowly. "Just Mummy and Alice and Kitty—oh, and good friends, like Jordy and Violet, who make me smile. Because then we can help each other. It's nice to have friends who help. Jordy helps me, and Violet helps me a little, and I help them back."

Nora had to chuckle at these words. At the tender age of twelve, Ivy had grasped the root of a good friendship—a relationship in which both persons built each other up. She should've known that as a twelve-year-old. "That's exactly right, Ivy. You should always have friends like that."

Ivy cocked her head. "Jordy says I can help people, too, just as I am. That I help Violet."

"Of course you do! You've a bright future ahead of you, Ivy."

The girl flushed and glanced down. There were a few moments of pleasant silence as they walked along, then Ivy raised her eyes to Nora's face. "Have you a bright future ahead of you, Grandmother? What will you do?"

What would Nora do? She'd thought of that as little as possible lately, preferring to focus on the present. Lord willing, she had a number of years left on earth ... and what she would do with them had always been up in the air.

"I think so," she said. "I intend to spend all the time I have left on earth with my children and their families, which I think will be splendid. But I don't worry about that too much—right now, it's just you and me, and we're having a good time here, aren't we?"

Ivy wrinkled her brow. "Yes, I suppose so. I ... I didn't ever not like you, Grandmother. But now I think we are friends. Though—" She frowned. "I suppose only you are helping me, and I'm not helping you."

Nora felt tears fill her eyes. Oh, the dear child! She pulled Ivy into an impromptu hug, and for once, the child didn't try to wiggle away. "Ivy, you help me every day! Why, it's an honor to be here with you."

"Is it?" Yet Ivy remained close. "I'm glad."

After another moment, Nora stepped back. "Let's go back to McCale House. It's getting late."

Ivy nodded, and they started back toward the gates.

CHAPTER TWENTY-FIVE

Early September 1874

G RANDMOTHER AND IVY HAD gone on many walks together, but this one was different. They were coming around the house from the gardens when Ivy saw two carriages pull up in front. She hesitated, not sure if she wanted to walk around the front way if there were strangers coming. "Who's that?" she asked.

"I don't know," Grandmother said. "I see a gentleman getting out of the first—oh my! It's your father." She picked up her pace, and Ivy was dragged along after her.

Mr. Knight held out his hand to assist a lady down, making a comment about unexpected arrivals. The lady laughed, and Ivy knew that laugh. She left Grandmother behind and began to run.

"Mummy, Mummy, Mummy!"

Mummy turned and held her arms out; Ivy almost knocked her over. After a minute, Mummy held Ivy back and looked her up and down. "Why, darling, you've grown an inch, I think."

Grandmother huffed up behind Ivy. "Yes, she's tall now, isn't she?"

"Yes!" Mummy tangled her fingers in Ivy's hair. "How beautiful you are! I'd forgotten."

Ivy snuggled back against Mummy's shoulder, and thankfully she wasn't pushed back this time. The adults talked around her, excited words about how they hadn't been expected for another few weeks. She heard other people dismount from the carriages.

There was a soft fussing noise, and Mummy drew away. "I brought someone special with me, Ivy."

Ivy blinked up at a servant she didn't recognize with a curious bundle in her arms. How was this maid special? She seemed ordinary.

Mummy took the bundle from the maid and turned back the edge. "This is your brother, Caleb," she said in a soft, still voice.

Ivy peered into a funny little face. It was screwed up, and he made grunting noises like a piglet. She looked up at her mother in confusion. "He's not pretty."

Mummy laughed. "I think he's pretty. But he's fussy now—his naps have been interrupted with all these carriage changes." She passed him back to the maid and turned to Grandmother. "Yes, the McCales did know that we were coming, but I wanted to surprise Ivy."

"We've Ned with us, too," said Mr. Knight. "And the Angels."

Ivy froze. She didn't care much about Ned, but Violet's parents? How strange that they had come. What had made them, after all these years?

Mrs. Angel was as lovely as ever, and Mr. Angel as stone-like. Knowing more about them now, she was even less impressed than she'd been before.

Yet she had more important things to worry about. "I must show you my music, Mummy! I told you about it, but I couldn't show you, remember? I can play it now."

"Play?" Mummy blinked. "Oh, the piano. You did mention that—Mrs. Angel was right about your talent, wasn't she?"

Ivy sighed. She didn't want to think about Mrs. Angel now. She dragged her mother into the house, straight to the parlor, bypassing the McCales without a word.

"This is the piano," Ivy said, resting her hands on the keys.

"Oh," said Mummy, raising her eyebrows. "Where is your music?"

"It's on the shelf over there, but it isn't as pretty as my own," Ivy said, "so I'd rather play that for you."

Ivy took a deep breath and put her hands on the keys.

The notes bloomed under her fingertips, cascading one after the other in a seamless melody. After a few bars, she glanced over her shoulder at her mother.

Mummy's mouth formed a perfect *o*, and her eyes were wide. "Ivy. I didn't realize that you were … that you could …" Her voice trailed off, confusion turning her face dark. "You're talented."

Ivy flushed under her mother's praise and returned to her playing. She needed the music to process her mother's arrival, the Angels' presence, and the fact that, perhaps, this meant she would be leaving McCale House soon.

"Ivy?"

At the sound of Violet's voice, Ivy dropped her fingers from the keys and whirled to face her friend. "You came to listen? Did you like it?"

Violet's eyes darted warily around the room. By now the McCales had come in, along with the Angels, and they spoke quietly while Mr. Knight and Mummy stood near the piano, listening to Ivy's playing.

"Who are these people?" Her voice held a hostility Ivy hadn't heard in months.

"My parents and yours."

Violet took a step back. "What are they doing here?"

Mrs. Angel moved toward her daughter. "Violet, dear, we came especially to see you." Even as Violet stepped back once more, Mrs. Angel stepped forward, searching the young woman's face. "Will you sit down with me, Violet? Will you talk to me? I want to get to know you. It's been so long … so very long."

Violet's eyes sparked, and Ivy could see the tick in her jaw, in her restless hands that clung to the skirt of the nightgown she wore. "I will never come near you, and I will never talk to you. I hate you."

"Now, Violet." Dr. McCale reached a hand out to her. "Behave yourself."

"I will not behave myself." Violet's voice was almost a scream, her words coming in sharp, loud gasps as she jerked toward the door. "I hate her, and

I hate you, and I hate everyone in this room!"

Ivy flinched.

Violet turned and ran.

No one followed her.

Ivy obeyed Dr. McCale's order to let Violet have some time to herself, but she couldn't play anymore—not even from the sheet music. It just wouldn't come out, so she went to sit with her mother in a private room, where they could talk and she was kissed and petted and told she was so talented, so special.

"Like Alice?" Ivy asked.

"I've never heard Alice play the piano well, despite my repeated attempts to teach her to do so and the lessons she's had at Miss Selle's," Mummy said.

Ivy shook her head. Her mother hadn't understood what Ivy was getting at, though she'd do her best to explain better. "Alice is talented."

"She draws, and she has an excellent seat on a horse, yes."

"And I am, too?"

Mummy's brow furrowed, deep lines appearing across her forehead. "I don't know. Can you draw? I know you don't like horses."

Ivy nibbled at her bottom lip. How could she get her point across? "That's not what matters."

"What does matter?"

Ivy swallowed. Being special but not different. Being wanted and needed. Being loved for who she was and not just because she happened to be Mummy's little girl. "Being talented ... like Alice."

Then Mummy's eyes filled with light, and she snuggled Ivy closer against her side with a sigh. "Darling, you will never be Alice, and I wouldn't have it any other way."

"But … I want to be Alice!" Beautiful, talented, carefree, intelligent, and forceful. All these things were what made a woman, and Ivy so badly wanted to be more than a child someday. She wanted to grow into an adult who could make a difference in this world—for herself, others, and most especially for God.

Mummy buried her face in Ivy's hair. "Don't ever let me hear you say that again, Ivy Adeline Knight. You are Ivy, and I never want you to be anyone else. Do you understand me?"

"Yes." She thought she did at least. "But you sent me here because you wanted me to be normal, didn't you?"

"No, darling—I sent you here because I wanted you to be Ivy." She pressed a kiss to her forehead. "And I see that you've become her, so I couldn't be happier. You've your music and friends, and Dr. McCale mentioned that your schoolwork has improved—I can't wait to see how far you've come!"

"I can read," Ivy whispered. "Almost as well as Alice, I think."

Mummy rolled her eyes. "That isn't a contest, dear. Alice does so hate to read!"

They chatted on for some time afterward about different things Ivy had done and how life would be different and yet the same at Pearlbelle Park.

Ivy wasn't sure how she felt about going home. Before it had always seemed years away, distant, but her ultimate goal. Now she wasn't sure she'd like to leave. Not with all her friends here and how much she could learn … and Violet, of course. How she would hate to leave Violet.

Chapter Twenty-Six

WHEN SHE FELT VIOLET had been gone long enough to be ready to accept reason, Ivy left her mother to find her. After searching the house, she walked through the gardens and came back puzzled.

She found Dr. McCale sorting through files in his office, probably collecting records on Ivy and Violet to show their parents—she did see several folders with her name on them.

"Where is Violet?" she asked.

"In her room," Dr. McCale replied without turning to her.

"No, she isn't."

He paused and glanced over her shoulder. "What? Then she must be sitting on her favorite bench in the garden. Though, who would want to be outdoors? The wind's picking up."

Panic rose in Ivy's chest, and she took deep breaths, but it didn't help much. "She's not in the garden. I looked!"

"Calm down, Ivy." Dr. McCale crossed the room and knelt in front of her, taking her hand. "Breathe in, breathe out. We'll find her. I'll have Dr. Goodington look around the property. She couldn't have gotten out of it."

Perhaps that was true, but Ivy couldn't help but worry. Dr. McCale left the room, and Ivy followed close on his heels.

Within half an hour, the teachers at McCale House were out searching for Violet. Faces were showing concern, and Ivy struggled to remain calm.

Jordy ran up to her and grabbed her arm. "Ivy, think. Where could she have gone?"

For a moment, she stood still, eyes half-closed, trying to remember. Then, in a flash, Ivy knew. She grabbed his arm and dragged him toward the gate of the estate.

Once out of the gate, which was locked but could be pulled back on its chain enough that they could squeeze through, Ivy crossed the bridge and followed the road she'd gone on for several picnics and walks, still holding Jordy's hand, until she came to a much narrower one that jutted off, probably made by cows or sheep.

Ivy didn't know why, but something pushed her to follow this path, and she was never one to ignore her instincts, so she hurried up it. As she walked, she heard the roaring sound of rushing water and picked up her pace as she felt that the noise must have soothed and drawn Violet as it did her. The path was narrow, rutted, and steep. It wore Ivy out, and so she was panting when she came to the crest.

There was a ledge overlooking a large creek, which tumbled over the rocks at a speed uncommon for mid-September, even accounting for the heavy rainfall of late. Violet stood there, staring down at the water, which fell over twenty feet there in a wild, tumultuous waterfall that caused the roaring Ivy had heard. Rubbing her arms against the biting wind, Ivy called out to her friend.

"Violet! Won't you come back and talk? Oh, Violet, please?" Ivy started toward her, but Jordy held her back and gave a slight shake of his head.

"Aye, come back."

"Have you ever felt hopeless?" Violet asked, ignoring Ivy's plea. "As if you'll never change to be as you want to be. As if people will never stop looking at you as if you're some circus exhibit?"

"I don't think so, no." Ivy scrunched up her nose as she considered this.

"I feel that way now. It's so hard, Ivy. You aren't like I am. I could always tell you weren't. You're different, you're simple, but, unlike me, your weaknesses can be strengths, and when I look at you, I think to myself, 'there's a girl who could have a life, an impact, a meaning.' Look at you, already such a musician, with a strong faith and a loving family. You'll be adored and cared for forever."

Ivy thought for a minute before she replied. "You can have faith, too, Violet."

"I doubt it. I'm a terrible person." Violet leaned over the cliff. "How easy it would be, Ivy. One step, and so the end."

"You mean ... jumping off the cliff?" Ivy asked. Her eyes widened, and she glanced worriedly at Jordy. "Why, Violet! You'd die."

"I know. I want to. I just haven't the courage."

Jordy folded his arms across his chest, and his chin lowered. "It would be cowardly, no' courageous."

"Neither of you know." Violet shook her head. "Neither of you know what it's like. It's horrible. I can't live like this—I can't."

"But you can! You already are. Violet, please." Ivy took another hesitant step toward her. "Come back with us. Come meet your parents—I'll stay with you when you talk, and you don't have to talk to them long. Maybe they've changed."

Violet's eyes closed. "People don't change."

"But you have." Ivy blinked back tears and took another step. "Violet, you ... you're my best friend. I love you. Ever since I've come, I've seen you change—you're so much nicer now. Step away and come home with Jordy and me."

"Tha's right," Jordy said from behind her. "Violet, ye've become almost pleasant. Please, dinna give up on yerself!"

Ivy edged her feet closer. She was now less than a yard away from Violet, but she was afraid to draw nearer. Still, Violet didn't move away or tell her to step back. "You wouldn't really jump, would you?" She held out her hand. "You wouldn't."

Violet's eyes opened, and she jerked to find Ivy so close, but she offered no further reaction. "I might."

"No ..." Ivy let her voice trail off as she took one final step and placed her hand on Violet's arm. "You wouldn't. You know your life is valuable. It's what I've been telling you, isn't it?"

Violet shook her head, slow swings back and forth. "I-I don't know ... You don't know what you're ..." Her voice was tight with little hiccups about the edges. "I ..."

Ivy took a step backward, and Violet followed her. Without a word, Ivy put her arms around Violet and hugged her close. "It's going to work out." She gave her the hardest squeeze she could muster and sighed. "We'll go home, all right? I'll be there with you. You don't have to be afraid."

Violet dropped her head on Ivy's shoulder. "I-I can't ... I can't go back. They don't want me. *No one* wants me."

"Tha's th' furthest thing from th' truth." Jordy's voice was close now, and Ivy felt him draw to their side. "Ye ken we all want ye, Violet. Tha's why ye're here. Th' McCales, Ivy, me, th' other teachers. We just want tae help."

"But ... you ... can't." Violet's breath came in little sobs. "You can't ... fix me. No one ... no one can."

"Oh, Vi, no one but God can 'fix' anyone." Jordy placed a light hand on Ivy's shoulder, and she looked up to see him meeting Violet's eyes, his firm and hers teary. "We dinna have tha' power on earth. But Vi, we can love, an' we can do what we can tae help, an' we can try tae encourage ye tae draw closer tae Him. He can at least make this time here bearable an' offer ye a Heavenly Father more loving an' caring than yer own could ever be."

"I don't believe He can," Violet whispered.

"Let Him help ye believe." Jordy stepped away and nodded back in the direction of McCale House. "Come on. There'll be rain in a minna. Let's go home."

Violet hiccupped and drew back from Ivy. Thankfully, Grandmother had tucked a handkerchief into Ivy's pocket that morning, and she took it out and passed it to Violet.

"Th-thank you," Violet stuttered.

"Let's go down tae th' burn—lower, I mean—an' ye can wash yer face."

Still trembling, but her breaths firmer with every moment, Violet nodded and followed Jordy and Ivy down the hill.

CHAPTER TWENTY-SEVEN

IT HAD BEEN A long time since Mummy had tucked Ivy into bed, and it didn't feel like a necessity anymore. However, it was nice to have her sitting there, talking in a soft voice and saying comforting things.

"It sounds as if you've had a wonderful time here, Ivy." Mummy looked more than pleased, a smile never far from her lips or laughter from her voice.

Ivy *had* had a wonderful time—not always, but often. "Yes, I suppose I have. I'm glad Mr. Knight brought you here today, though, because I missed you most of anyone."

Mummy winced. "Ivy, I wish you could refer to your father as 'Papa' or something similar. I think it hurts him that you can't accept him into your life."

Ivy wrinkled her nose. Didn't Mummy understand that she just wasn't sure of Mr. Knight? There might not be any getting used to him, either. He'd stolen so many things from her. Though, perhaps, she could learn to cope with that. She'd adjusted to many things at McCale House—and there was no use in clinging to bitterness over what she could not prevent. He did make Mummy happy, and Ivy should love anyone who made Mummy happy, even if sometimes that meant Mummy was distracted.

The door opened, and Mr. Knight came in. Perhaps he'd known they were thinking about him. He greeted Mummy and Ivy with a smile and a nod, saying something about coming in to help Ivy get settled.

That was caring enough, though Ivy had been settled at McCale House since March or April, so there wasn't really any need for it.

Still, it got her thinking. Was he safe? Was he gentle; was he kind? She could never decide. Now he sat on the edge of the bed near Mummy, a neutral expression on his face, as if his mind was elsewhere. That seemed a fairly normal, non-monstrous thing to be doing—but one could never tell with men. They were unpredictable, if Mr. Parker was any sort of a standard.

"Are you going to tell me a story, Mummy?" Ivy asked, deciding to put all thoughts of her father aside for a time.

"Oh, I don't know, darling." Mummy pressed a kiss to Ivy's forehead. "I don't really feel up to making one up just now. Trains give me a headache, and little Caleb was so fussy." He was currently asleep in a basket in the adjoining room, where Grandmother had always slept, but Ivy knew now that Caleb had a surprising lung capacity for such a small thing. She almost had to respect him for it.

"What do you mean, making one up?" Mr. Knight's eyes twinkled.

Mummy's brow furrowed. "A story, Philip. Weren't you listening?"

"I was, but *you* don't make up stories, Claire. You take them straight out of books. You memorize and repeat."

A frown played about Mummy's mouth. "And your point is?"

"You have no imagination."

Mummy laughed and shook her head. "I do. I just respect the Brothers Grimm and the Bible too much to make my own frail attempts at story-telling."

"I could make up a wonderful story right off the top of my head." Mr. Knight puffed up his chest. "I had a little sister once, remember? Let me try. That is, if Ivy's willing?"

They turned to her together. Ivy looked between her parents—saw hope in Mummy's eyes and wistfulness in Mr. Knight's—and nodded. She could give this to them, though she doubted that it'd be much of a story.

"Then I will." Mr. Knight shifted to sit at the end of the bed and leaned slightly against the post. "Let me see. What do you like stories to be about, Ivy?"

"Princesses," Ivy said. They always made things better. "I like *Rapunzel* best."

"Then I'll tell you *Rapunzel*."

Mummy tapped on Ivy's shoulder so she'd sit up. "I thought you were going to make one up."

"I am, but I'm basing it off things Ivy appreciates; ergo, we shall have Rapunzel."

"Do you even know the story of Rapunzel?"

He looked offended. "I know it well, assuming it's the one about the princess with the long hair."

Mummy laughed and began dividing Ivy's hair to braid. "That's the one."

"I thought so." He glanced up at the canopy above him to think, then returned his gaze to Ivy's. "Now, Ivy, I'm a little out of practice. Actually, I was never in practice—so you'll have to be patient with me. But I have a nice story in mind, and I think you'll like it."

"All right."

"It starts once upon a time, like any other story. Now, you're used to hearing about the princess first, but today I'd like to turn your attention to the prince."

"The prince?" Who cared about the prince? He was always there, always heroic, but never interesting. The princess was the one Ivy wanted to hear about.

He nodded. "Yes. Prince Charming. He's unfortunately a minor character in all the stories that revolve around him, and I mean to fix that. Now, once upon a time, there was a young prince named Charming. The problem was, he was misnamed."

"Misnamed?"

"Yes. He wasn't charming. In fact, he was awkward and stupid and, more times than not, he'd end up tripping over his own words or his own feet, for that matter. It took him a while to grow into his legs; I'm not sure he ever did. One day, he decided to go out in the world to seek his fortune. So he traveled to a faraway land—"

"On his horse."

"This land was across the sea, but once he got there, he did borrow a horse. It wasn't white, though; it was chestnut."

Ivy nodded. The prince had good taste. "Good."

Mr. Knight laughed. "As I was saying, the prince was visiting a neighboring kingdom. Of course, there was a beautiful princess living there, as there always is in these stories. Now, you've heard of some pretty princesses in your time, I'm sure, Ivy, but this princess was different. She … she was so beautiful that looking at her was like looking at the stars. It struck you with awe, and poor Prince Not-So-Very-Charming had no chance with her."

Ivy knew how that went. Fate must interfere in these cases. "But he was the prince, and she was the princess."

"Exactly. It had to be, even if it didn't look like it could. So it was."

Mummy finished braiding Ivy's hair, and Ivy again slumped back on the pillow. The story was about to get interesting. "And …?"

"They were married."

Shocked, Ivy sat up. At first she wondered if he was mistaken, but then she got to thinking. A Prince Not-So-Very-Charming? A country across the sea? A beautiful princess? It sounded too familiar for words, and Ivy began to wonder about it. Slowly, she said, "That's not how these stories go, Papa." There. Test the waters. She'd watch his face and see. Alice liked to do surprising things to secure peoples' honesty—Ivy could do that, too.

For a long moment, Mr. Knight didn't say anything. "Oh, it isn't?"

Sometimes the man could be too dense for words. "No! They don't marry until the end. That couldn't be the end. I thought you were telling me about Rapunzel!"

"I've changed my mind. This story is more interesting to me."

Mummy stood up from the bed and went to the window, staring at the darkness. Perhaps she was upset with the lack of proper storytelling procedures, too. Ivy watched her for a moment, then turned back to her father with a little huff.

Yes, this was definitely personal. And Mr. Knight definitely thought he was fooling her. However, he was also trying, and she could call a man who tried "Papa." There were so many other grudges Ivy could hold other than that one. "Oh, all right. Go on, then."

"Something terrible happened. The prince was sent back to his own country. He had no choice but to go. He promised her his eternal devotion and then he left, and the princess was taken far away and locked in a tower."

"But why?"

"A selfish, cruel man made it be so."

Oh. Ivy had not met her grandfather, but it sounded like she didn't want to. Yet she'd let this charade continue. It was almost endearing but equally as frustrating. "You mean a wicked witch."

"No, I mean a selfish, cruel man." He scooted up closer to the head of the bed and tapped her nose lightly with his fingertip. "This is my story. It's not like the stories you're used to hearing."

Ivy sighed. "Oh, all right. I don't understand, though. Why would the selfish, cruel man do that?"

"He didn't like the prince. He wasn't charming, remember? And this man thought such a beautiful princess as she shouldn't be tied to such a fumbling, stupid prince."

"That makes sense, I suppose. What happened next? The prince came back as soon as he could, didn't he?" She pinned him with a gaze she hoped would make him squirm.

"He would have—but there was a war."

"A war?"

"Yes. A war, and the prince had to fight for his country."

"That's good, I suppose. Princes are supposed to do heroic things like that."

"It didn't feel heroic to the prince. It felt horrific. War ..." He took a deep breath, and his eyes attached to the wall above her head. "War is a terrible thing, Ivy."

"But he went to her after he was done fighting, didn't he?"

Mr. Knight looked back to her and winced. "It's hard to understand why the prince acted the way the prince acted after this. You remember, he was a stupid prince, and he wasn't really used to princesses loving him. He didn't remember that a princess never breaks her promises."

Ivy narrowed her eyes. "What do you mean?"

"I mean, he thought the princess didn't love him anymore."

Why, the idiot—! "But she was the princess, and he was the prince, Papa!"

"I know ... but he thought, 'Maybe I'm not the prince after all.' He'd written to her, and there'd been no reply. He thought that if the princess really loved him, she would find a way to get word to him. He thought the princess must have found another prince, a better prince, a prince worthy of such a princess as she."

Comprehension swept through the rest of her confusion, and Ivy struggled through all her thoughts. It wasn't really Prince Charming, and the princess wasn't really Rapunzel. She glanced at her mother. Mummy still wasn't looking at her, at them, and Ivy shuddered a little.

Yes, Ivy knew. But Mr. Knight hadn't. Suddenly, a great many things made sense. "He just didn't understand," she whispered.

"No, he didn't. He didn't understand. Perhaps it was stupid of him to doubt her, but he did. Then he met a young lady—she was sixteen and naïve—who he probably spent more time with than he should have. But he was hurt, she was kind, and ..." He sighed. "I still don't know how he could've been so stupid."

Ivy folded her arms across her chest. "The prince *should have* gone to see his princess after the war."

"Yes, but ... but he thought he couldn't risk seeing her in the arms of another prince. He thought he couldn't stand that; he thought it would kill him. So the prince waited—and he wrote letter after letter after letter." His brow wrinkled. "Where was I going with this?"

Ivy sighed. "The prince was in his country, and the princess was in the tower, and the war was over, and there was a young lady who was in love with the prince."

He blinked. "Oh, the princess isn't in the tower anymore."

"What do you mean?"

"She escaped. She got out, and she ran away to a big town and began working, sewing for the people who would once have kissed her toes."

"Oh." Ivy should have known that, but the idea of a princess escaping from a tower without a prince was novel to her. She supposed that was what had happened, though.

"Now, the prince ... he did something wrong, Ivy, and he will regret it all his life in some ways—though not in others. He convinced himself that the princess had another prince, and he married the young lady I mentioned earlier."

"Oh, Papa!" Ivy closed her eyes, feeling almost tearful. It wasn't fair. It just wasn't. Why had he left them? Why hadn't he come? He should have come—and then everything would have been all right.

Mr. Knight put an arm around her shoulders and hugged her. "I know, darling. I know. I'm sorry."

Ivy sniffled and pressed him back. "Will there be a happy ending?"

His Adam's apple jerked as he swallowed. "There will be. The prince ... he returned to the princess's country with his new wife and baby. Of course you know the princess had had twins."

Ivy nodded. She didn't feel like commenting on it.

"He couldn't do anything about it. I don't know if you—well, of course you do. You know what it is to be completely helpless, unable to fix something no matter how hard you try." He took her hand. "The prince was married to the young lady, and he couldn't very well be married to the princess, too. He had a son with her, and a life, and it seemed hopeless. It was hopeless, and, honestly, Ivy, the way it turned out wasn't ideal."

She looked away from him. His eyes were too gentle and his voice too sad. "I know how it turned out," she whispered. "I know. She *died*. She wasn't my friend, but it's sad that she died."

"Yes, the young lady died, leaving him alone with his son." Mr. Knight sat up. His eyes were misty. "And, sometime later, when everything was proper, he married the princess. They could be a family again. They could live at the castle again. And that's about as close to 'happily ever after' as the world lets you get sometimes."

Ivy's heart twisted. Was that really a happy ending, though? It had never felt like one. "Papa, it's not really—that is, I don't like the way it ended."

"I know. I can tell." He lightly touched her cheek, then leaned back. "Claire? Are you all right?"

Mummy nodded. "Just tired." But when she turned around, there were tears on her cheeks.

Ivy hopped out of bed and ran to her. "Mummy?"

"I'm all right, darling. I'm all right." She hugged Ivy close. "We're going to keep becoming a family, though. I promise. We're trying, Ivy. We haven't reached our perfect ending, but we're trying with what we have."

Ivy snuggled against Mummy and took a deep breath. "I'm trying, too."

"Good. When we go home, we'll show you—"

Mummy went on, but Ivy's mind became distant. Go home? Ivy couldn't go home. Not when Violet was still unsure. Her friend was on the verge of becoming a child of God, but she had so much to learn—and she needed so much love.

Ivy couldn't leave Violet. She couldn't.

"Mummy?"

After a moment of surprise at the interruption, Mummy nodded. "Yes, dear?"

"I don't want to go home yet. I ... I can't. Not until Violet ... well, I need another year here. Please?"

Mummy and Mr. Knight stared at each other.

"You don't want to go home?" Mummy murmured.

"No." Would she be able to explain? She took a deep breath and tried. "Mummy, Violet needs me to stay and help her. And ... and I want to learn more from the McCales. I'm not finished here yet. I know it. And Grandmother ... Grandmother wouldn't mind staying with me. She likes it here, and she and Mrs. McCale are great friends now."

Confusion coloring her face, Mummy turned to Mr. Knight with a little shrug.

"I ... I could come home for a while and visit, and then I could come home for Christmas, and you could get me next autumn, perhaps." She glanced between them. "Please, Mummy. Please, Papa."

"I ... I suppose we could ... discuss it with Dr. McCale and your grandmother." Mr. Knight shrugged, his eyes hopeless. "Claire, what do you think?"

"I think ... I think that if Ivy feels it is best, and if she really wants to stay and help Violet Angel, perhaps we shouldn't stop her." Mummy moved toward the bed and sat down next to Mr. Knight. "Ivy, are you sure?"

She nodded firmly. "I am sure."

"Then we'll try to keep you here. I'm not sure what the McCales would think about that." Mummy sighed. "Though, I can't say I'll like it. Perhaps we can stay longer, Philip?"

"Perhaps. Or you can—I'll see what can be done."

"All right." Mummy took a deep breath. "Ivy, it's time for bed. We'll discuss this further in the morning."

That was as close to a "yes" as Ivy knew she would get tonight. She hopped back into bed and was tucked in, kissed, and her parents turned to leave.

"Papa?"

Mr. Knight paused in the doorway. "What?"

"I know you are the prince now."

A smile almost split his face in two. "Why, thank you, Ivy."

"You're welcome." She rolled over, pulled the covers up to her chin, and focused on falling asleep.

CHAPTER TWENTY-EIGHT

T HE MORNING AFTER CLAIRE and Philip arrived at McCale House, Claire asked Nora for a moment of her time after breakfast. Apparently, there was something they needed to discuss "immediately."

Hopefully nothing was wrong, though she couldn't think what could be. Everything seemed fine, but Claire had become a master at hiding her emotions.

Nora followed her daughter to one of the parlors, and they both took a seat.

Claire cleared her throat. "I want to ask a large favor of you, and I'm not sure how to start. It would seem that Ivy wants nothing more than to stay here, at McCale House. She has friends here, and she seems comfortable. Much as ..." She stopped, her face twisted. "Much as I'd like to take her home, it seems she could benefit from more time here, and that is her wish."

Nora blinked. How could this be true? Yes, she knew Ivy had enjoyed these last several months at McCale House, but that was one thing, and being willing to stay there when she was allowed to go home to her mummy was quite another. "She wants to stay."

"She does." Claire's blue eyes met Nora's evenly, intense and questioning all at once. "And if you are willing, I would like you to stay with her. You ... you have a way with the child, and I can't be away from home now that there's both Caleb and Ned to take care of. I need to be at Pearlbelle."

Nora nodded. Yes, Claire needed to be home—that much was true. Still, Ivy didn't seem to care much for Nora. They were friends now, but surely the child would be upset to continue spending time with her old grandmother when she could have her mother.

"Ivy loves you. She told me so this morning—what she said was 'Grandmother makes me smile.'" That made Claire smile, too, for her lips twitched upward. "Still, that's what she meant. I think she would love to have you here, but I do realize you probably had plans."

"No plans," Nora said quickly. "None." At least, none as important as Ivy and none that made her want to give up this precious time in Scotland with good friends and plenty of quiet time with God. Besides, with Charlie now engaged to Lois Elton and sure to marry her this Christmas, she'd want to stay away from Starboard Hall and let the newlyweds adjust to each other.

"Good." Though Claire could never do something as human and vulnerable as sigh in relief—at least, not that Nora was aware of—her shoulders did slump in a way that told Nora this took a load off her mind.

Nora cocked her head. "You want to go home, then? Be at Pearbelle Park?"

"That's where Philip is." Claire chuckled. "I can raise the boys best there, too. I've a lot to learn about little men, though at least I know more about babies than the first time. I don't think Philip would like me to be in Scotland when he must be in Kent, either."

That was true, but since when had Claire deferred to her husband—or anyone—regardless of the importance of the decision?

"Philip's a good man." Nora folded her hands on her lap and regarded her daughter closely. "He loves you and loves his family. However, I've not seen much in him that I respected—and I've often wondered if you do."

Claire stood. "We shouldn't leave Ivy for too long. I won't have long enough with her as it is, though we'll come for both of you before Christmas. I think we'll be at Starboard Hall this year, if we're all able to travel. Charlie and Lois might be married by then, so I think they'd like to host it."

Nora thought that would be lovely, but she wasn't talking about her son right now. She wanted to talk about her elder daughter. "You didn't answer me."

Claire glanced over her shoulder. "You didn't ask a question."

No, she hadn't, but she'd been having a conversation, and normally in conversations people spoke back and forth about a subject until a resolution was arrived at. "Do you respect Philip Knight more than you did when I left you this past January? You seem to, in the way you treat him and the way you speak of him. I believe he is trying, and I think you see that now. So do you?"

"Yes." Claire folded her arms across her chest. "He has stood by my side for this last year without fail, and together we can build a good life. He only needed a chance to prove that. Mother, my strength doesn't lie in myself anymore. It lies in God—and, after Him, in my husband."

"So then you'll be all right." Nora almost whispered the words, but Claire must have caught them, for she gave her an odd look, one brow arched slightly higher than the other.

"Yes. Philip and I are fine. We always were going to be."

"Thank God for that." Perhaps Claire hadn't just attached herself to Philip because she wanted security, because she was vulnerable after her father's rejection.

And if Claire could move on to establish healthy relationships, so could Charlie. And so could Christina.

And so could Nora.

She followed Claire out of the room. Ivy waited just outside the door, wiggling from side to side. Her face lit up when she saw them.

"We have to show Mummy all the prettiest places in the garden." Her words slid one over the other, trembling with excitement. "Can we go now, Grandmother? Mummy, will you come?"

"Of course," Claire and Nora said in unison.

The sun was dipping below the horizon by the time Ivy found her way to Violet. Mrs. Angel had tried to spend time with Ivy's friend earlier in the day, and Violet had spoken with Mr. Angel and her at dinner, but other than that, they didn't really seem to want much to do with each other.

Ivy wondered if, perhaps, Violet wouldn't have a perfectly happy ending. Though that made her sad, she supposed the world couldn't be perfect—only Heaven really could be.

Still, she was glad she had God on her side ... and, Lord willing, Violet would have Him on her side, too.

Violet was in Ivy's music room, sitting on the piano bench but not playing. Instead, she stared at the ceiling, her eyes somewhat vacant, her breathing deep and even.

"Violet?"

Her friend flinched, then glanced over her shoulder. "Come in. Where have you been? Enjoying your family?" Her sentences were short, clipped, a staccato melody full of anxiety and regret.

"I've been with my mummy and with Mr.—with Papa. I had to show them McCale House. They'll only be here a few days."

"Oh." Violet stood and glided across the room to the window. "When will you be leaving?"

"They'll be leaving in three days." Ivy took a deep breath. "And I'll be staying until next September."

Violet whirled around, eyes wide. Quickly, she shook her head, seeming to force the surprise from her expression. "Next September? Then you're not ..."

Ivy shook her head. "N-no. I'm staying with Grandmother. I wanted to stay because I ... I love you, Violet. You're my best friend. I know you're not ready to be a Christian yet, but I want you to be, and I thought if I stayed—"

Violet turned back to the window, her arms wrapped around herself. "I-I ..." Her shoulders shook. "Ivy, all you've been wanting to do since you came here was go home."

"I know." Ivy stepped quietly across the room and placed her hand on Violet's back. "But I think you're more important than that."

Violet made a sniffling sound, and her shoulders hunched. "N-no one ... loves me ... like that."

Was she crying? It seemed so. Ivy stood close and cocked her head, but Violet kept her face turned away. "I'm just Ivy. I suppose ... I suppose Nettie would say that God loves you more than I ever could. Or anyone."

A chuckle emerged from deep in Violet's throat, a rough sound. "Of course Nettie would say that. But would it be true?"

Ivy didn't have the words to reassure Violet of what she believed. She wasn't even sure if it would do any good for her to stay here. However, she wouldn't leave until she'd given it her best chance. "We'll have to find that out together."

A moment of silence passed, then Violet nodded. "We'll do exactly that, Trifle—exactly that."

EPILOGUE

One Year Later
September 1875

IT WAS ALWAYS SAD saying good-bye to friends and loved ones, and that was precisely what Ivy was doing on this brisk September day.

She hugged Jordy tightly for a long moment, then leaned back with a smile. "Will you write?"

He shrugged and shifted his weight from one foot to the other. "I'll be goin' tae college in London soon, an' I'm no writer."

"Please?"

A grin slipped through. "I'll try. Th' McCales have yer address?"

"Yes." She stepped around him to Violet, who was leaning against the side of the door, trying to look unaffected. But Violet and Ivy had been such close friends for the last two years that Ivy knew it wasn't true.

"I'll miss you, Violet," she murmured, "and I know you will write."

Violet rolled her eyes. "Who has time to write? Honestly, Trifle, I don't think—"

Ivy gave Violet a quick hug. "I know you will!"

A heavy sigh brushed her ear. "Of course I will."

After these last, most important good-byes were out of the way, Ivy turned to her parents, who were waiting in the carriage. She squared her shoulders and stepped up, but as soon as she was in, she turned.

The door of the carriage slammed shut, and Ivy poked her head out of the open window and waved. "Good-bye!"

Jordy waved enthusiastically even though they were still only yards from each other, while Violet pretended to be heading back into the house. Dear Violet. She might be a child of God now, but she had a long way to go—and learning to be all right with being positive when one could was one of those things.

It had been a long year. Ivy wasn't sure what it would be like to be home at Pearlbelle Park. However, she felt more confident now.

Dr. McCale said she was a bright young lady with a brilliant future ahead of her, and somehow she believed him.

The carriage went through the gates and over the bridge and out over the familiar moors—toward Edinburgh and the train station.

Ivy finally brought her head into the carriage and turned to her mother. "I'll visit sometime."

"Of course you will." Mummy held open her arms, and Ivy went to give her another hug, though she didn't even try to crawl onto her lap. That was a long ways behind her.

Grandmother shuffled through her bag for her knitting. "Do you like Jackie a bit more than you liked Caleb when he was a babe, Ivy?"

Ivy nodded. She'd just met her third brother, Jackie, who'd been born this July. Jackie was really named John, but, for some reason, no one called him that. It didn't make any sense to Ivy.

Still, he was sweet and quiet, and, unlike Caleb, Ivy didn't feel he looked funny. Besides, he let her hold him. If he weren't in the other carriage with his nanny, Ivy would be holding him now. However, apparently Caleb's constant babbling tended to wake Jackie up.

Even now, Caleb rested against Papa's shoulder, still making sounds that could hardly pass for words. Ned, who was now a little gentleman in his trousers and necktie, sat next to Papa. He looked darling. Ivy couldn't believe he was five already. He played quietly with a wooden duck, though Ivy didn't really understand the game, which was sliding it back and forth on Grandmother's skirt and making duck noises.

Ned was sweet, all things considered.

"Alice will be coming home this Christmas, permanently," Mummy said. "Did you know that, dear?"

Ivy blinked. "Really? Why?"

"Because she'll be fourteen," Papa said, "and your mother wants to pull her apart and reassemble the child herself." He gave a little huff.

Ivy had to smile, though she looked down so her mummy wouldn't see. She'd been hearing a lot lately about Alice's becoming a woman, and Ivy didn't really agree with all of it. Alice was so perfect already—why turn her into something she wasn't?

Papa had his moments of wisdom, truly.

"Philip, you know very well that Alice needs further training! That's why she's at Miss Selle's, but in a few years, we'll travel, and she can learn to dance ..." Mummy rambled on, but Ivy stopped listening. She adored hearing her mother talk, but sometimes the words weren't worth listening to. Yet the cadence of her dear voice still washed over Ivy.

At last they arrived at the Edinburgh station. It was a full place, busy as always, and Ivy stayed near to the people she loved, but she wasn't really afraid. She felt a jerk on her skirt and glanced down to see that Ned had grasped on to her, his eyes wide as the people jostled about them.

She took his hand and pulled him close to her. She could keep him safe.

Soon they were in their first-class compartment, and the train began chugging south, toward England and home.

A NOTE TO THE READER

H I THERE! THANKS SO much for reading my novel. This one was a challenging book to write on so many levels. It required a ton of research and even more delicacy.

Because of the era I'm writing in, I had to remain accurate to the feelings of the time, which were sadly quite prejudiced against anyone with even the minorest of mental illnesses.

It is true that people were put in "lunatic asylums" based on the smallest things. A bit of research will prove that things like "reading novels" were at one point considered a cause of insanity!

Though I was unable to find evidence of anything like McCale House existing, it would be feasible. If I've learned anything about the Victorian era during my research, it's that there was always an exception to the rule, and no one ever talked about them.

I'd also like to note that I'm not an expert on mental health issues. I did as much research as I could, but I know I've made some mistakes or logic leaps that someone with more experience would doubtless be able to identify.

That said, I also believe that no one's story is the same, and given the era, the way mental health issues were identified, referred to, and addressed is very different from the way they are now. I tried to balance all those factors when writing *Ivy Introspective*.

All that aside, I hope Ivy's story encouraged you! I meant it to be full of grace and hope.

Consider leaving a review of this book to let other readers know what your thoughts were! Also, if you caught any typos, shoot me an email at contact@kellynrothauthor.com to let me know.

This series continues in book 3 of The Chronicles of Alice and Ivy, *At Her Fingertips*. This novel will release in 2021. I hope you get a chance to try it out!

Of course, we're back to Alice, but in book 4, *Beyond Her Calling*, we'll return to Ivy (and Violet and Jordy!).

If you'd like to follow along with me on my authoring journeys, you can head over to:

kellynrothauthor.com/newsletter

My email list is full of lots of fun stuff for readers and writers alike (and yes, you can choose which types of emails you receive).

TTFN!

Kellyn Roth

A Free Novella for You

Interested in a free novella, available only for subscribers to my mailing list?

January 1944

June Halsted moved her son to Hearthstone Cottage to escape the memories of her failed marriage and estranged family. A struggling artist in the midst of one of the coldest winters in Yorkshire, she finds herself seeking solace at church ... only to meet Mark Hayes, a kindly farmer with a limp and a knack for cheering up her son.

Inspired by The Tenant of Wildfell Hall, *this novella is a sweet romance with Christian themes.*

Go to *kellynrothauthor.com/newsletter* and subscribe to my email list to receive your free story!

ALSO BY THE AUTHOR

The Chronicles of Alice & Ivy

The Dressmaker's Secret
Ivy Introspective
The Knights of Pearlbelle Park (novella)
Becoming Miss Knight (novella)
At Her Fingertips
Beyond Her Calling
A Prayer Unanswered
After Our Castle

The Hilton Legacy

Like a Ship on the Sea
Like the Air After Rain
Like a Storm Against the Cliffs

Kees & Colliers

Souls Astray
Goldfish Secrets (short story)

The Lady of the Vineyard
Flowers in Her Heart

Standalone Short Stories

Esther Ashton's New Dress
Kind: a Christmas short story of post-WWII Munich
Eddy & the Tidepools

Anthologies

Springtime in Surrey
Novelists in November
Fingerprints in Frost
Voices of the Future: Stories of Courage & Compassion

www.ingramcontent.com/pod-product-compliance
Lightning Source LLC
Chambersburg PA
CBHW031214260626
47169CB00007B/2050